Jan,2020

Algonquin Area Public Library

P9-DEZ-140

WITHD

Algonquin Area Public Library
Eastgate Branch
115 Eastgate Dr.
Algonquin, IL 60102

Affirm
press

Christian White is an Australian author and screenwriter whose projects include feature film *Relic*. His bestselling first book, *The Nowhere Child*, was sold into 16 territories and has been acquired in a major screen deal.

Christian lives in Melbourne with his wife, Summer DeRoche, and their adopted greyhound, Issy.

ALSO BY CHRISTIAN WHITE

The Nowhere Child

Praise for *The Nowhere Child*

'A nervy, soulful, genuinely surprising it-could-happen-to-you
thriller – a book to make you peer over your shoulder
for days afterwards.'
A.J. Finn

'[White] is a born storyteller, one who seems to instinctively
understand the weave of a proper yarn, and *The Nowhere Child* is
tight, gripping and impressive in all the right places.'
The Saturday Paper

'Hugely entertaining … a multifaceted, unsettling debut.'
The Age

'*The Nowhere Child* has everything that comprises an excellent crime
novel. It's taut, raw, emotional, intriguing. The tension becomes
unbearable, the story gets creepier as it goes on and the puzzle keeps
you reading beyond midnight. Possibilities lurk at the edge of the
plot like shadows. Christian White – take a bow.'
Better Reading

'[White's] control of the structure of the novel is impressive
throughout … He should be emboldened to undertake that
notoriously hard task: the second novel.'
The Australian

'*The Nowhere Child* is a page-turning labyrinth of twists and turns
that moves seamlessly between the past and the present, revealing
the story in parts and successfully keeping the reader guessing until
the final unexpected reveal … It's an exhilarating ride
and a thrilling debut.'
Books+Publishing magazine

'An exciting new voice in crime fiction.'
Sunday Life magazine, Fairfax

THE WIFE

AND THE

WIDOW

CHRISTIAN WHITE

MINOTAUR
BOOKS

NEW YORK

This is a work of fiction. All of the characters, organizations, and events portrayed in this novel are either products of the author's imagination or are used fictitiously.

First published in the United States by Minotaur Books, an imprint of St. Martin's Publishing Group

THE WIFE AND THE WIDOW. Copyright © 2019 by Christian White. All rights reserved. Printed in the United States of America. For information, address St. Martin's Publishing Group, 120 Broadway, New York, NY 10271.

www.minotaurbooks.com

Library of Congress Cataloging-in-Publication Data

Names: White, Christian, author.
Title: The wife and the widow / Christian White.
Description: First U.S. edition. | New York : Minotaur Books, 2020.
Identifiers: LCCN 2019044596 | ISBN 9781250194374 (hardcover) | ISBN 9781250194381 (ebook)
Subjects: GSAFD: Suspense fiction.
Classification: LCC PR9619.4.W478 W54 2020 | DDC 823/.92—dc23
LC record available at https://lccn.loc.gov/2019044596

Our books may be purchased in bulk for promotional, educational, or business use. Please contact your local bookseller or the Macmillan Corporate and Premium Sales Department at 1-800-221-7945, extension 5442, or by email at MacmillanSpecialMarkets@macmillan.com.

Originally published in Australia by Affirm Press

First U.S. Edition: January 2020

10 9 8 7 6 5 4 3 2 1

THE WIFE
AND THE
WIDOW

CHRISTIAN WHITE

Affirm
press

For Sum

PROLOGUE

John woke with a start and thought, *there's someone in the house*. He'd just heard a noise downstairs, something like the parting of dry, windblown lips. Then, the sound of creeping footfalls up the staircase.

He stared into the darkness above his bed and listened, but aside from the gentle whirr of the central heating, the house was silent again. He rolled over and looked at his wife, ghostly in the dull moonlight falling in through the window.

He'd probably had another nightmare, he thought.

Creak.

The sound came from the first-floor landing, a foot stepping down on the loose floorboard at the top of the stairs. He hadn't imagined it that time. He was sure of it.

He sat up and stared through the layers of darkness. As his eyes adjusted to the low light, the shapes of the bedroom appeared, like a picture shifting slowly into focus. He saw the towering wardrobe silhouetted against a field of black. The dresser cluttered with his wife's jewellery, glinting dully in the moonlight like dozens of tiny eyes. A pencil-thin sliver of light spilled beneath the closed door, flickering.

He slid out of bed, opened the door and stepped out. There was a Harry Potter night-light in the hallway. His daughter Mia kept it there, so she didn't get scared on her way to the bathroom at night. A fat brown moth fluttered blindly against it, over and over. John watched it for a moment, transfixed. Had that been what he'd heard?

Then, from out of the shadows at the far end of the hall, stepped a man.

John tried to speak but fear cramped his jaw.

The man took another step forward. He was tall, bulky, and his head was shaved. He wore white canvas tennis shoes and a heavy black coat that John recognised.

'Hello, John,' the man whispered. 'Do you remember me?'

'… Yes,' John managed to say, his voice barely audible.

'Do you know why I'm here?'

'Yes,' John said softly. 'I think I do.'

1

THE WIDOW

Kate Keddie stood in the airport bathroom, practising her smile in the mirror. She hated her mouth. It was several teeth too big for her head, so grinning usually made her look maniacal and deranged. She tried gently curling up the corners of her lips. She was going for confidently demure. She got Shelley Duvall on bath salts.

'What are you doing with your face?' Mia asked. Kate's ten-year-old daughter had skipped out from one of the bathroom stalls to wash her hands. She'd tied the string of a heart-shaped *Welcome Home* balloon to her wrist, and now it bobbed above her like a buoy.

'Nothing,' Kate said.

'How much longer until Dad gets here?'

'Ten minutes until he lands, then his plane has to taxi in, he has to collect his bags, clear customs … all up we're looking at about sixteen hours.'

'You're killing me, Mum!' Mia slapped her feet against

the polished concrete floor, buzzing with the sort of nervous excitement she usually reserved for Christmas morning. She'd never spent this long away from her father.

John had spent the past two weeks in London for a palliative care research colloquium. Kate had spent most of that time striking days from the calendar with a fat red texta, longing for his return. She hoped that old cliché about absence making the heart grow fonder was true of John, but a dark part of her feared it might work the other way too. She had read somewhere that it only took two weeks to break a habit, and what was marriage if not a habit?

Kate took her daughter's hand and led her out into the terminal. The arrivals lounge at Melbourne International Airport was surging with people. Families gathered beneath hand-painted banners, watching the big frosted-glass doors outside customs. Behind them, drivers in black suits scribbled names on little whiteboards. There was a collective energy to the crowd that made it seem like one big entity rather than a hundred small ones, all moving in gentle, nervous harmony, like the legs of a caterpillar.

Any second now, John would emerge through the doors dragging his little blue American Tourister behind him, eyes sunken and weary from the long flight. He would see them and beam. He wouldn't be expecting them. He had insisted on catching a taxi back home, and Kate had insisted that was totally fine by her, knowing full well that she and Mia would drive out to the airport to surprise him.

She was eager to see her husband, but more eager to hand him back the reins. She was a good mother, she thought, but a nervous one. She had never taken to the role as easily as other women seemed to – her mothers' group friends, or the capable, busy-looking mums at school pick-up. Kate felt much more comfortable with John's backup.

'Do you think Dad remembered my pounds?' Mia asked, staring over at the display screen outside a currency exchange kiosk. Lately she'd grown obsessed with collecting foreign money.

'You reminded him at least two thousand times,' Kate said. 'I doubt he'd have the nerve to come back without them.'

'How much longer *now*?' she groaned.

'Five minutes. Watch the flight board. See?'

Qantas Flight QF31 from Heathrow (via Singapore) landed on time and without incident. A silence hung over the waiting crowd that soon enough gave way to shouts, tears and laughter as the first passengers exited into the lounge. Some people poured into the arms of their loved ones, while others beat a path through the crowd to their waiting drivers or the taxi rank beyond.

A pretty woman with a corn-coloured ponytail collapsed into the arms of her waiting man. Then, temporarily forgetting where she was and who was watching, she kissed him passionately on the mouth. Nearby, an elderly Asian couple waved frantically as a man pushed a pram towards them, twin boys dozing inside. Kate watched them, waiting for her turn.

She was a little surprised John wasn't among the first passengers to arrive. He always flew business class, which gave him access to express lanes and priority service.

Mia went up on tiptoe to scan the crowd. 'Do you see him?' she asked.

'Not yet, monkey,' Kate said.

They watched the big glass doors keenly. They slid open again. This time, a smaller group of passengers paraded out.

'I see him, I see him!' Mia squealed, pulling her balloon down and facing its message towards the door. Then her shoulders sank. 'No. Wait. That's not him.'

The second wave of passengers dispersed. There was still no sign of John. The glass doors closed, opened. An elderly gentleman hobbled out, holding a cane in his left hand and a dusty old Samsonite in his right. The corridor behind him was empty.

Kate checked the flight board, double-checked they were in the right place at the right time, then triple-checked. Surprise gave way to concern.

'Mum?' Mia said.

'Keep watching, monkey. He probably just got caught up at baggage claim or he's being hassled by a fussy customs officer. He'll be here. Just you wait.'

They waited. Eventually, trying to keep the alarm from creeping over her face, Kate found her phone and dialled John's number. The call went straight to voicemail. She tried again. Again, voicemail. He had probably forgotten to switch his phone out of flight mode, she told herself. Either that or he had left his charger plugged into the wall of his hotel suite and arrived in Australia with a dead battery.

She began to chew her nails.

The glass doors opened. Kate drew in a tight breath. Three stragglers emerged: a middle-aged couple, who seemed to be in the middle of an argument, and a young backpacker with dirty skin and a tangle of dreadlocks falling across one shoulder. Nobody was waiting for them. The doors closed, opened. This time the flight crew wandered out, chatting casually to one another, happy to have reached the end of their shifts.

Where are you, John? Kate thought.

If he'd missed his flight, he would have called or texted or emailed, wouldn't he? He may not have known she'd be waiting at the airport, but he did know she'd be waiting. She tried calling him again. Nothing. She looked around the terminal. Most of the crowd had gone, aside from a few passengers at the car rental stalls and a man in a grey coverall vacuuming the strip of carpet by the front doors.

'Where is he, Mum?' Mia asked.

'I'm not sure, monkey. But he'll be here. It's fine. Everything's fine.'

With her eyes trained on the glass doors, Kate reached out and found Mia's hand. She held it tightly. They continued to wait. Five minutes passed, then fifteen more.

The last time they spoke was over Skype, the morning John's flight was due to leave London. Kate and Mia were sharing an armchair in the living room, leaning over the screen of the MacBook. Seventeen thousand kilometres away, John sat on the bed in his hotel room. It was a typical suite, wallpapered in soft greens with a minibar to his left and a room-service menu to his right. His passport, wallet and phone were stacked neatly on his suitcase by the door.

'Are you all set for the flight?' Kate asked.

'I've got the three things all seasoned travellers should carry,' he said. 'Earplugs, valium and Haruki Murakami.'

'Is valium drugs?' Mia asked.

'Yes, honey,' he said. 'But the good kind.' He laughed, but their connection was weak and time-delayed. The screen froze and skipped, making the laugh sound like something out of a fever dream.

John was three years older than Kate but looked five years younger. He had a youthful head of hair and neat, symmetrical features. He was naturally trim and athletic. On the screen, his face seemed to have a little more colour than usual. It was summertime in London, after all.

Mia slid forward onto her knees so her face was centimetres from the screen. 'When you get on the plane make sure you sit behind the wing,' she said. 'That's the safest place to sit if it crashes.'

'Business class is right up front,' he said.

'Uh oh. In most crashes the first eleven rows get *pulverised.*'

'Mia, your father doesn't need to hear about being pulverised,' Kate said. 'How do you even know what *pulverised* means?'

Mia shrugged. 'Internet.'

'She figured out how to switch off the parental lock again,' Kate said. 'Our daughter the hacker.'

John leaned back on his elbows and looked over to his left, beyond the screen of his laptop. Kate was struck with an odd and completely unfounded impression that he wasn't alone. She put it down to paranoia.

'Leave the safe search off,' John said, after a moment. His tone had turned flat. Kate couldn't tell if he was joking or not. 'Life doesn't have a filter, so why should the internet?'

'Wonderful,' Kate said. 'Well, tonight I can show her *The Exorcist* and tomorrow we'll watch all the *Rambo* movies.'

He didn't laugh.

'We try to protect the people we love from certain truths,' he said. 'But I'm not sure that's always right, or fair. If we don't talk about the monsters in this world, we won't be ready for them when they jump out from under the bed.'

Kate had wanted very badly to reach through the screen and touch his face. What kind of monsters?

'Are you alright, John?' she asked.

'I think so,' he said. 'I think I'm just ready to come home.'

'Kate?'

'Yes,' she said. 'Kate Keddie.'

'Oh, *Kate*. John's wife. Oh, jeez, it's been a while, how are you?'

Chatveer Sandhu was the administrative assistant at the Trinity Health Centre for Palliative Care, where John worked as a physician.

'I'm sorry to bother you,' Kate said. 'But I'm having a little trouble getting a hold of John and thought you'd be the best man to ask. I'm assuming his flight from London got changed or his schedule moved around and someone forgot to contact me?'

There was a pregnant pause, and Kate had to fight hard against the urge to fill it. She looked over at Mia, who was sitting in a plastic chair next to the information booth. Her eyes were desperate and sullen. Tears were welling in them.

'Are you still there, Chat?' Kate asked.

'Yes,' he said. 'Sorry. I'm just … I'm not exactly sure what you're asking.'

'I'm at the airport and my husband isn't.'

It seemed fairly straightforward to her, but after another brief moment of silence, Chatveer said, 'I'm going to transfer you over to Holly. Hold the line for me.'

'Transfer me? No, Chat, I just need—'

Too late. She was on hold. While she waited, she continued to bite her nails. She chewed too far, winced at the pain.

Classical music drifted down the line: Henryk Górecki's ominous Symphony No. 3. One of John's favourites. A neglected masterpiece, he called it. Before they were married, Kate had been happy to leave classical music to the pretentious intellectuals. She had felt far more comfortable in the company of Mariah Carey than of Claude Debussy. But after John spent a good part of their first date discussing Wolfgang Amadeus–this and

Ludwig van—that, she had gone out the next day and bought a best-of-classical deluxe double CD collection and forced herself to listen to it. She liked it now – at least, she thought she did.

'What can I do for you, Kate?' Holly Cutter asked suddenly in her ear, her tone sharp, already impatient.

Holly Cutter was frustratingly successful. Along with being Medical Director of the Trinity Health Centre, she was also a qualified nurse, spiritual counsellor, medical educator, clinical researcher, an honorary professor at the University of Melbourne and a board director of the International Association for Hospice and Palliative Care. A typical overachiever.

'Hi, Holly,' Kate said. 'I'm not sure why Chatveer transferred me, but I'm at the airport with Mia, and John's flight has landed but he's not on it. Is it possible he got caught up at the conference, or his trip was postponed or delayed or—'

'I don't know anything about that, Kate,' Holly said.

Kate felt like tossing her phone across the terminal.

'In that case, would you mind transferring me back to Chatveer?'

'Chatveer doesn't know anything about this either.'

Kate felt flushed and foolish, mad and sticky. And Mia was still crying.

'I'm not exactly sure what's going on here,' she said. 'But I think there's been some sort of a miscommunication.

John has been in London for the past two weeks, at the palliative care research colloquium. He's supposed to be coming home today and—'

'Listen,' Holly said. 'I don't know what you know or don't know, and I certainly have enough on my plate without getting in the middle of anything here, but if John attended the research colloquium this year, we wouldn't know about it.'

'I don't understand,' Kate said. 'Why not?'

'Because John hasn't worked here for three months.'

2

THE WIFE

'Motherfuckers,' Abby Gilpin said, loud enough to scare away the ravens. They were feasting on a week's worth of garbage that had been scattered into the middle of the street. The garbage bin her teenage son had dragged to the top of the driveway for pick-up this morning – after she had reminded him approximately fifty-seven times – had pitched forward in the wind and now lay on its side, lid flapped open like a gaping mouth.

A few of the garbage bags were intact, but the ravens had split most of them open, exposing a tangle of food scraps, plastic wrap, eggshells, coffee grounds and used tissues. Steeling herself against the smell, Abby stood the bin upright and started cleaning up the mess. Her hand landed on a wad that was soft and wet, which she immediately dropped, but not before spilling something foul and unidentifiable down the left side of her leggings.

Abby wasn't generally fussy about her appearance

– she mostly got around in black leggings and baggy jumpers – but picking up garbage in the street on her hands and knees still seemed beneath her. The road was wet. That morning, the island had been hit with the most violent thunderstorm of the season, and it had rained nearly non-stop since. The sky had temporarily cleared, but it was only a matter of time before it started up again.

Working fast, she managed to get all but one of the bags back into the bin. She was seconds away from slamming the lid shut when she noticed something. Through the semi-transparent skin of the bag was a pair of tan-coloured workboots. She made a hole in the side of the bag with an index finger and looked inside.

The boots belonged to her husband, Ray. Aside from a little mud in the tread and a few scuff marks, they looked brand-new. It was possible Ray had bought the wrong size, but it seemed strange for him to just toss them out instead of putting them aside for the Salvos. Bunched up along with the boots were a pair of Ray's cargo trousers and one of his grey work shirts, *Island Care* printed across the breast pocket. They still smelled of the lemon-scented laundry detergent that was always on special at the Buy & Bye.

A gust of frigid wind sent her hurrying up the driveway and into the garage, the clothes bundled under one arm.

She yanked the pull-string light switch in the dark, and, after a satisfying *click*, a bank of fluorescent lights blinked on overhead. The garage was a double and should have been big enough to fit two cars and then some, but like most garages theirs served as a miscellaneous overflow. There were tall, wavering stacks of packing boxes, plastic tubs, empty pots, resistance bands with little resistance left in them, a weightlifting station shrouded in cobwebs, a ride-on mower that Ray got cheap at a garage sale three years ago before finding – surprise, surprise – that it didn't run.

A narrow path had been carved through the junk, along with a wide rectangular space for Ray's work truck, a mud-splattered four-door utility. The only other space cut out of all this *stuff* was for Abby's workbench, a hulking, paint-stained thing they'd picked up from an antique store on the mainland. Somewhere beyond it was the box of old clothes they'd been meaning to drop at the Salvos for months.

Abby ran her fingers along the wooden benchtop on her way past. She'd have to make time to get out here again soon – maybe some quiet evening, or on the weekend, when the kids were out and Ray was watching the footy. It was on this workbench that, through trial and error and many a trip to Belport Library in search of how-to guides, Abby had become a halfway-confident amateur taxidermist. Arranged neatly on the bench or mounted on the pegboard behind it were a dark-green apron, scalpel blades, surgical gloves, insect pins, fishing line, rubber bands, playing cards (for 'carding' ears), borax laundry soap (for curing hides), critter clay, modelling tools, tongue depressors, pliers, super glue, a staple gun and two dozen sets of glass eyes in various sizes.

Underfoot was a humming bar fridge containing a few bottles of water, a six-pack of beer and Abby's next specimen: a possum that Susi Lenten had found dead beneath the powerlines outside her house. Alongside the fridge was a plastic tub packed with various chemicals including tanning solutions, pickling agents, luminol and bactericide.

So far, all she'd stuffed were mice, rats and birds. They lived on various shelves around the house, sagging and bulging in all the wrong places. But that just seemed to make them almost human-like in their imperfection. As a rule, she only used animals that died of natural causes, so it was not uncommon for people around the island to call her up any time they found a dead creature on the road, in their garden, or on the beach. They'd say things like, 'I've got a magpie up here on my balcony – poor little fella flew right into the screen door; hasn't been dead long but you might wanna hurry cause the flies won't be far off,' and 'You need to get this bush rat out of my freezer before Shivaun divorces me – she needs the space and I know better than to argue with a woman as pregnant as she is.'

Abby couldn't say why she enjoyed taxidermy, and didn't care to question it too much. It was as messy as it was meditative, and she didn't make any money out of it.

The few animals she didn't keep for herself she gave away as gifts, usually to people who accepted them through gritted teeth and with wide, terrified eyes. But there was something darkly wonderful about the craft that kept pulling her back. Death imitating life, she thought, and liked the way that sounded.

She finally found the Salvos box on a dusty shelf, sandwiched between a sandy old picnic blanket that smelled like wet dog (which was strange, because they didn't have a dog) and a milk crate full of old car parts. She dumped Ray's trousers, shirt and boots into the box, turned off the light, and went inside.

Home was a small weatherboard beach house full of things that didn't work: sticky windows, rattling pipes, and electrical outlets that buzzed dangerously whenever something was plugged in. They were saving up to make renovations but wouldn't have nearly enough until next season, or maybe the one after that.

Abby was in no hurry to fix it. She loved every crack and quirk: the groaning floorboards, the constant pop of settling wood, the loose screen door that banged endlessly in the middle of the night. She was not a complainer, not some woman living a quiet life of desperation, fearing middle age as it bore down on her. No, that wasn't Abby. She was content. She was happy.

She knew her fifteen-year-old was in the kitchen before she entered; the heavy scent of Lynx body spray gave him away. Eddie was standing at the counter wearing a blue apron and chopping garlic. He'd be a good-looking man one day, in the far-off, distant future, but right now he was passing awkwardly through the Ichabod Crane phase of puberty: gangly limbs and an archipelago of violent red acne across his forehead.

He didn't look up when Abby entered.

'What's for dinner?' she asked him.

'Vegetarian gourmet pizza,' he said in a dry tone, the same he might use to deliver a lecture on the history of the ladder.

'Sounds fancy.'

He shrugged and skilfully cleaned the blade of the knife on his apron. His eyes narrowed and he began furiously slicing mushrooms, as if he were punishing them for something.

'Take it easy,' Abby told him. 'It won't be vegetarian if you lose a finger in there, you know.'

He said nothing. He was in a mood, Abby guessed. She fetched a beer from the fridge as her husband wandered in from the bathroom, smelling fresh, his hair slick and wet from his after-work shower.

'Beer?' Abby offered.

'Water's fine.'

'Water instead of beer.' She screwed up her mouth at the words. 'I used to know you.'

Abby was a runner but balanced out her fitness with

an unhealthy amount of fat, sugar and booze. Ray, on the other hand, was on some kind of health kick. No, that was understating it. Ray was on a brutal fitness regime that bordered on self-harm.

He'd never been close to overweight. Beefy, maybe, but he carried it well. But lately, deep contours and ridges had formed on his chest. The skin around his neck clung tight to a jaw she'd never realised was square, and new muscles filled out the sleeves of his T-shirt. This steady hardening and tightening of his body reminded Abby of an archaeological dig site. She imagined brushing away the sand, dirt and fat until only a skeleton remained.

'Sounds like a midlife crisis to me,' Abby said. She filled a glass from the tap and handed it to him. 'Pretty soon you're going to start tucking your shirts in.'

He sighed, which made Abby think she might be riding him too hard. She slid her arms around her husband. She felt Ray, but at the same time she felt the anti-Ray. Ray with the crusts cut off.

It occurred to her that it had been a while since they last had sex, and longer still since she'd seen Ray fully naked. The last half-dozen times they'd made love was in the dark with the lights off, after a box of red wine.

She felt Ray's fingers lightly touch her love handles, then pulled away.

Other, less secure women might have felt nervous if their partners started systematically changing everything about themselves, but a wicked, guilty part of Abby knew this fitness stuff was just another phase. Last year, he started taking night classes on the mainland and declared himself an entrepreneur. The year before it was all about franchises. Next month he'd probably start writing that bestselling novel he'd been talking about since they'd met; maybe after some piano lessons.

All she had to do was wait it out. She hated thinking that, but that didn't stop it from being true. What Ray didn't realise – or refused to – was that it would take more than a few hours on the treadmill or a semester of business classes to get off this rock. Belport Island had a way of drawing you in, holding you down and whispering, *I'm never gonna let you go, baby.* Abby had learned a long time ago that it was easier to lean into it than to struggle against it.

'There's nothing wrong with trying to improve your life,' came a voice from the hall, in a tone like strawberry shortcake laced with rat poison. Lori entered, clomping loudly in Doc Martens, wearing an oversized Nirvana T-shirt and a face as long as a wet weekend.

'By the way, Eddie forgot to bring in the firewood and now it's soaked.'

'Are your arms painted on?' Eddie asked.

Lori rolled her eyes. She was a beautiful girl, with straight dark hair and features that seemed hand-picked by a team of experts to match the shape of her face.

Somewhere around her thirteenth birthday she had turned calculative and secretive. She was sixteen now and there was no sign of that changing. Still, Abby knew that puberty was like the rising and falling tide: first you drifted out, then you came back in. And if she didn't, Lori could at least make a very successful CEO someday. Either that or a prolific serial killer.

'I think it's good you aren't just happy to settle, Dad,' she said.

'Thanks, hun,' Ray said.

'She was looking at me when she said *settle*,' Abby said. 'I'm not the only one who saw that, right?'

Lori folded her arms across her chest and said, 'I just don't understand why you need to go out of your way to make him feel like an idiot.'

'I don't understand why you need to go out of your way to act like an arse,' Abby said.

'It's not that far out of her way,' Eddie offered.

'Ding, ding, ding,' Ray said. 'Round one over. Fighters return to your corners.'

Lori tugged a Post-it Note down from the fridge and handed it to Ray. 'Eileen Betchkie called for you. She didn't say why but she took a long time saying it. I couldn't get her off the phone.'

'Eileen?' Abby said. 'Weren't you working on her property today?'

Ray nodded. 'I probably missed a blade of grass and

22

she wants me to come back and fix it. I'll call her back tomorrow.'

Island Care was primarily a caretaking business, focused on maintaining unoccupied holiday houses across the island, but while Ray was always busy in the colder months, he still never earned enough to keep them going once the tourists returned. To help make ends meet, he took yard maintenance and lawn-mowing work where he could find it. He hated working for locals. Abby would have thought it easier to work for people you knew, but Ray found it quietly humiliating. Still, they weren't in a position to turn it down.

'She's probably just lonely,' Abby said.

'Or she has a crush on Dad,' Lori suggested.

'Sadly, I think you're both right,' Ray said.

He sat down at the table and stared at an intimidating stack of bills, as if looking hard enough might change the due dates. 'Any chance of you picking up an extra shift at the Buy & Bye?' he asked Abby.

'At this time of year, it's unlikely,' she said. Then, seeing the concern in Ray's eyes, added, 'But I can ask. But we'll be okay, right?'

'Always,' he said. 'If there's one thing this family knows, it's how to survive.'

3

THE WIDOW

'John Paul Getty the Third was the grandson of an American oil tycoon,' Fisher Keddie said, marching back and forth across the brightly lit interview room, somewhere on the second floor of the Brighton Police Station. 'He was abducted in 1973, and when his grandfather refused to pay the ransom, his kidnappers sent him John Paul's ear in the mail. His *ear.*'

John's father had insisted on meeting Kate at the police station. He was a short, bulky man, with receding hair and a pair of glasses that looked too small for his face. His eyes, usually deep and thoughtful, looked crazed.

'Then there's Walter Kwok,' he went on. 'Frank Sinatra Junior, the list goes on and on. All sons of wealthy men, taken in an effort to extort their family's wealth. That's what this is. It has to be.'

The officer taking their report waited patiently for Fisher to stop ranting. He was a big man who had apparently missed a small patch of black whiskers on his morning shave. They poked out from a tuft on his left cheek, and Kate found it hard not to stare. He'd given his name, but Kate hadn't caught it, and the nametag on his breast pocket was too faded to read.

'Does John have any identifiable scars or tattoos?' the officer asked, when there was room in the conversation to ask it.

'I feel like you're not listening to me,' Fisher said. 'This family is worth a lot of money. We should be, I don't know, tapping phones, preparing for the ransom call. And yes, he has a jagged scar on his left forearm from where he came off a swing when he was nine.'

'That's not right,' Kate said. 'He had a plastic surgeon fix it before our wedding. He hated that scar. I liked it, but he hated it. He said it looked like a baked bean.'

The officer two-finger-typed the answer into his computer, then read the next question off the monitor. 'Any medical conditions that may affect his vulnerability?'

'No,' said Kate.

'Does John take any prescription medication?'

'Can you imagine if it was a woman that had gone missing?' Fisher asked, joining them at the desk. 'You'd have helicopters out and sniffer dogs and you'd be going door to door.'

'Does he have a history of drug or alcohol dependency?

'No,' Kate said.

'Has your husband ever expressed suicidal ideations?' he asked, in a tone dryer than unbuttered toast.

'Jesus Christ,' Fisher said. 'No, of course not. John's a normal guy. He's happy.'

I wonder if that's true, Kate thought. It was starting to feel less like they were talking about her husband, and more about a stranger. Filing a missing person report, she was quickly learning, was not unlike applying for a loan or sitting for a job interview: there were dozens of questions and each one made her feel more ignorant and naive.

'What do you do, Mrs Keddie?' the officer asked.

Kate hated that question. 'I'm a stay-at-home mother.'

'You have kids?'

'A daughter. Mia. She's ten. It didn't feel right to send her to school so she's with her grandmother.'

The officer noticed a speck of muck on his space bar and gave it a polish with a well-licked finger. 'Does your husband enjoy being a doctor?'

'A *physician*,' Fisher corrected. 'And yes, he does. He enjoys it very much.'

'Still, working in palliative care must take a toll. My wife and I had to put my father-in-law in a place like that last year. We couldn't afford Trinity, but I imagine they're all pretty much the same. Death is everywhere, hanging over everything. Must be a pretty depressing place to spend your nine-to-five. Is that why John quit?'

'I don't know,' Kate admitted, trying to keep the sound of heavy resignation from her voice. 'He didn't tell me.'

'He didn't tell you why he left?'

'He didn't tell her he *had* left,' Fisher said. 'Any of us, I mean. We only found out yesterday.'

'He kept it from you both?' the officer asked. 'Why do you think he'd do that?'

'I have no idea,' Kate said. 'I wish I did.'

The officer leaned back in his chair. 'Tell me about this medical conference.'

'It's a ten-day palliative care research colloquium. Trinity sends someone every year. It moves around. Last year it was in San Francisco, the year before that was Sweden, I think. John didn't want to go but someone dropped out at the last minute and his hands were tied.'

'How last minute?'

'He found out a few days before he left.'

'But you have reason to believe he didn't attend the conference.'

'I called the hotel where the conference was held. John was supposed to have a room there, but there was no trace of him on their records. I contacted the airline. The flight details he gave me were correct, but he never got on a plane. So far as I can tell, he didn't even buy a ticket.'

'Do you have any idea where your husband might have been for the past two weeks?'

'No,' she said.

The bigger question was where had John been for the past three months? Nausea swept through her system. Her body felt off balance; some parts were numb, others were aching. Her chest was tight. She fluctuated wildly between feeling scared for her husband and feeling furious at him, between wondering where he was, and where he had been.

If he wasn't going off to work each day in the fresh shirts Kate had ironed and left out for him, where was he going? How was he spending his days? Who was he with?

'Have you had contact with your husband since he left?' the officer asked.

'We talked every other day over Skype.'

'And it seemed like he was calling from London?'

'It looked like he was calling from a hotel room. It wasn't as if Big Ben was in the background, but I had no reason *not* to believe it was London.'

'When you talked to him, did he give you any indication something was wrong?'

If we don't talk about the monsters in this world, John's voice whispered, *we won't be ready for them when they jump out from under the bed.*

'He looked homesick,' Kate said. 'He missed us. He said he was ready for his trip to be over.'

'Anything else?'

'Like what?'

The officer shrugged, far too casually. 'Did he seem strange? Off? Was there anything unusual about his behaviour? Stuff a wife would notice.'

Fisher scoffed and rose with an exaggerated sigh. He went to the window. He closed his eyes tightly against a dusty sunbeam, shaking his head.

The officer watched him for a moment. 'Is there something you want to add, Mr Keddie?'

'Kate isn't the type of ...' He trailed off, waved a dismissive hand. 'Forget it, it's nothing.'

'The type of what?' Kate asked.

He looked at her, then lowered his eyes to his feet. 'You're not the type of wife who *notices*, Kate. If he were being coerced or threatened in any way, he might have given you a, I don't know, a secret signal or something.'

'There was nothing like that.'

'Are you sure though? Because – and no offence, Kate – you can be pretty fucking vague. Passive to the point of invisible. Christ, I need a cigarette. I hate that you can't smoke in here.'

Kate drew her lips tightly together and tried to ignore him. He was worried about his son and projecting his anxiety onto her. But his words stuck. *Passive to the point of invisible.* Wasn't that how John liked her?

The officer cleared his throat impatiently and asked, 'Do you or your husband own a caravan, cabin, holiday home, unoccupied rental property, anything like that?'

'We have a holiday house on Belport Island,' she said, feeling Fisher's eyes on the back of her head. 'But John wouldn't go there. He doesn't like the island.'

'Strange place to buy if your husband doesn't like the island.'

'We didn't,' she said. 'The house was a wedding gift from John's parents.'

'We summered there when John was a kid,' Fisher said.

The officer leaned back in his squeaky office chair and whistled. 'Wow. All I got on my wedding day was a serving platter and a couple of toasters.'

Neither Kate nor Fisher found that particularly funny; that, at least, they could agree on.

'Do you have any suspicion that your husband may have been abducted or harmed by someone else?'

'Not exactly ...' she said.

'Can you think of anyone who might want to hurt him?' the officer asked. 'Does he have any enemies? Anyone he doesn't get along with?'

Fisher drew in a tight breath to begin a fresh rant, but the officer put up his hand to silence him.

'I'm asking Mrs Keddie,' he said, then turned to Kate to wait for an answer.

'No,' she told him. 'Everyone loves John. He's very warm, and charming. He's the dinner party guest everyone wants to be seated next to.'

'So, you believe it's more likely he left on his own?'

'He wouldn't leave without telling anyone,' Fisher said. 'He wouldn't do that to Mia.'

'He wouldn't do that to *me*,' Kate said.

Fisher said nothing. The officer's eyes shone blue in the glow of his monitor.

'How would you categorise your marriage?' he asked Kate.

'How would I *categorise* it?'

'Do you consider it successful?' he offered.

She opened her mouth to speak, but her throat was suddenly dry. When she thought of her marriage, she had once pictured a stunning home perched on a vast, cliff-side estate. Now she saw the same house, held up by hollow stumps, rotting and infested with termites, leaning closer to the cliff edge each day.

'Happy,' she said. 'I'd categorise our marriage as happy.'

There's that word again, she thought, reaching between her feet. She lifted the gym bag she'd brought onto the table and unzipped it.

The officer cocked an eyebrow. 'What's in the bag?'

'I read online that you'd want to seize John's electronic equipment and get a sample of his DNA. I brought his iPad, toothbrush, comb and a couple of old razor blades I found under the bathroom sink. I don't really know how DNA works, but hopefully you can get something off them. I used gloves when I put them in the bag.'

He tilted his head and drew his lips together as if to

31

say, *aw, how sweet.* 'Someone will be in touch if those items become necessary. Just hang on to them for now.'

Kate zipped up the bag, feeling foolish. She put her hands under the table and dug her nails into her knees.

'What happens now?' Fisher asked. 'Will you put out an amber alert?'

'We only use amber alerts for missing children,' he said. 'This report will be entered into our system, and circulated and checked against ambulance and hospital reports.'

'That's it?'

'From what you've told me, there's nothing to suggest foul play. Generally speaking, an absent spouse who hasn't committed a crime or an adult who simply hasn't been in touch for a while is usually categorised as low risk.'

'Low risk?' Fisher snapped. *'Low risk?* He's my son!'

'Fisher, please,' Kate said. 'Panicking isn't productive.'

'Neither is sitting around doing nothing.'

'Look,' the officer said. 'In most cases like this, the missing person turns up on their own within a day or two. In the meantime, reach out to his friends and family, check if anyone has heard from him, maybe ask around at any haunts he might have, like a gym or local pub. But if I were you, I'd start by figuring out why he quit his job.'

The Trinity Health Centre for Palliative Care was an expansive, glass-fronted building surrounded by lawns and native gardens, walled in by a tall, immaculately manicured hedge that kept out the sounds of the city. It was a peaceful place, John had often said, despite – or perhaps because of – all the people who came here to die. Kate didn't find it all that peaceful. At best, it gave her the creeps. At worst, like today, it felt haunted.

She hadn't told Fisher she was coming here. If she had, he would have insisted on coming, and Kate wasn't sure how much more time she could spend with him before blowing her top.

She parked her Lexus at the far end of the car park, alongside a small wooden yurt with *Prayer Room* printed neatly above the door. The yurt was connected to the main building via a glass tunnel. Kate followed it into a large reception area painted in calming shades of blue and green, decorated with inoffensive, introspective artwork.

Standing in the middle of the lobby was a bubbling Japanese-style water feature. It sometimes made her wonder where poor people went to die, because they sure as hell couldn't afford to come here.

A slim man in his twenties bobbed around behind the front counter, dressed in a tailored grey suit and black turban. He looked up with a gentle smile when Kate approached. When he saw who it was, the smile faded. 'Kate, hello, I'm surprised to see you.'

'Hi, Chatveer,' she said. 'Is Holly in?'

'Is she expecting you?'

'It'll only take a few minutes.'

He drummed his fingers lightly on the desk, looked down the brightly lit corridor that led into the centre, then turned back. 'Can I offer some advice, Kate, as a friend?'

Are we friends? she wondered.

'Holly told me about the ...' he paused, chose his words carefully, '... *miscommunication* between you and John, and she doesn't want to get involved. And honestly, *you* don't want to get her involved. Talk to John about this. Believe me, it'll be better for everyone that way.'

'I would if I could,' Kate said. 'But John's missing.'

The words were sharp, jagged things inside her mouth.

'Missing?'

'I haven't seen or talked to him in three days. There must be a reason he didn't tell me he resigned from this place, and there might be a connection between that and wherever the hell he is. Please.'

He nodded once. 'I'll get Holly.'

Holly Cutter sat Kate down at one of the tables in the cafeteria and offered her a green tea. When Kate declined, Holly made herself one at a station in the corner.

A skeleton crew of staff cleared tables, polished cutlery and tried to make themselves look busy. Two middle-aged women – Kate guessed they were sisters – sat close to the serving area, two black coffees and a half-eaten sandwich between them. One of the women was crying, the other was staring into the garden through a rain-streaked bank of windows that ran along the far wall.

Kate thought about what the duty sergeant had said: this really was a depressing place to spend your nine-to-five. John rarely talked about his work and Kate rarely asked. Working in palliative care wasn't like other jobs. When he got home at the end of the day, it didn't feel right to say cheerily, *Hi, honey, how was your day?* When friends and family asked John about his work, he usually changed the subject quickly. For those few who pressed the subject, he had half a dozen meaningless clichés cocked and loaded in the chamber: *It feels good to give something back; a lot of people don't have anyone else; being around so much death just reminds you how precious life is.*

Kate had figured he'd talk if he wanted to, but now she wondered if he had been protecting her from something. Was this one of the monsters they hadn't talked about?

Holly returned, sat across from Kate and immediately looked at her watch.

'I don't have a lot of time,' she said.

'I only have two questions,' Kate said. 'I need to know why John resigned, and why he kept it from me.'

Holly frowned. 'I'm not sure I can help you with the latter, but I might be able to explain the former. John's resignation was my idea.'

'You fired him?'

'No. I pointed out what was at stake if he stayed.' She steeped her teabag, twirled it on its string, then set it aside on the table. It landed with a wet thud. 'John was doing good work here, and it was a shame to lose him. He was great with patients, the staff loved him and his research was yielding some very positive results. I'm sure I don't need to tell you that.'

'No,' Kate lied. John hadn't mentioned anything to her about research.

'I was very sorry to see him go,' Holly said. 'But I would have been sorrier if he stayed.'

'What does that mean, exactly?'

'Has John ever talked to you about *spiritual distress*?' Holly asked.

Kate shook her head.

'That doesn't really surprise me. It's a difficult concept to explain if you're not in the business. John was as much a counsellor here as he was a physician. It's like that, working in palliative care. We don't *heal*. We *guide*. But it doesn't really matter how comfortable you make a terminal patient; the end result is always the same. The trick is to help them find peace before the end.

'In the West we have a pretty messed up relationship with death,' she continued. 'We spend our lives trying not to think about it, yet at the same time we hold out hope that when the time finally does come, we'll somehow be at peace with it. Our philosophy seems to be, *We'll deal with it when it happens*. But that's rarely the case. More often than not, when people are close to the end, they talk about a sort of … void.'

'A void?'

Holly nodded and looked down at her fingers, as if they were alien entities.

'There's a lot of sadness in this place, Kate, but there's a lot more anger, a lot more guilt. As Medical Director, I no longer get to do much practical medicine, but I still spend a lot of time talking to our patients. To the ones well enough to talk, anyway. Sometimes we talk about the weather or music they like or who's winning the cricket. Then sometimes they say things like, *God feels very far away from this place* or *What did I do to deserve this?* They talk about a lack of peace. That's spiritual distress.'

Kate remained silent and waited for her to continue.

'When you've been in the business long enough you get pretty good at diagnosing it. Sometimes you can see it just by looking in someone's face. Their eyes turn a couple of shades darker. Usually it's something you see in your patients, but every now and then, you see it in your staff.'

'Are you saying John was in *spiritual distress*?'

'I'm saying that seven months ago, I noticed his eyes turn a couple of shades darker.'

'What happened seven months ago?'

Holly offered a small robotic shrug and whispered, almost to herself, 'The dam swelled.'

'I don't understand.'

'Working in this sort of environment is emotionally taxing,' Holly said. 'So, we practise something here called *leaves on a stream*. It's a quick form of self-therapy designed to disentangle yourself from negative thoughts. The idea is to visualise a stream, take each negative thought and place it on a leaf, put the leaf in the stream and let it drift away. But there's only so many leaves you can place in that stream before it forms a dam.'

'And that's what happened with John? He was … stressed?'

'People who work in law firms and design agencies get *stressed*. People who work in palliative care get *distressed*.'

Kate shook her head, feeling frustrated. She had come here for answers, but all Holly was giving her were metaphors and euphemisms. Kate wanted to slap her, to tell her to just talk like a human being, but instead she took a breath and asked, 'What was the leaf that dammed the stream?'

Holly leaned back in her chair and sipped her green tea. 'Did John ever mention Annabel?'

Kate shook her head.

'Annabel was John's patient. Mid-sixties – far too young to be in here. Advanced stages of PF – pulmonary fibrosis. It's a chronic and degenerative disease where lung tissue becomes scarred and stiff, which makes it hard to breathe and get enough oxygen into the bloodstream. There's no cure and plenty of causes. She'd been undergoing radiation treatment for lung cancer. She was a smoker. The radiation killed the cancer, but it gave her PF. The universe can be cruel sometimes. Annabel and John were very fond of each other. You're not supposed to have favourites, but sometimes you find someone you just click with, and when that happens, it's impossible not to feel their passing.'

'And that's what happened?'

'When Annabel died, John took a dark turn,' Holly said, nodding. 'This sort of thing is accumulative, but if I had to trace it back, Annabel's death was the leaf that dammed the stream. After that, he became distant. Cold. He started eating lunch in his car, snapping at the nursing staff. A wall went up.'

'What happened next?' Kate asked.

'I reminded him I was here to talk, but if his work performance kept suffering, then we'd need to have a more serious conversation. He handed in his resignation letter the following day.'

Guilt drifted in like a bank of fog. Kate's husband had been in distress and, somehow, she hadn't noticed.

Passive to the point of invisible, Fisher had called her. The accuracy of it stung. It wasn't just with John either: she had been that woman at work, was maybe still that woman in her friendship groups and on the school council – working to realise other people's bold visions. She was the agreeable assistant, the easy-going supporter, the designated driver. It kept her safe. It meant that she had spent the better part of the past two decades living inside a cocoon. It was a comfortably appointed cocoon, warm and safe, and she would have been happy to stay there forever. But since the airport, since the police station, since hearing John mourned the loss of a woman she never knew existed, the walls of her cocoon had been weakening. What would emerge from within?

'Try to understand,' Holly said. 'People don't usually leave a job in palliative care because they get promoted or a better offer. They leave because if they stay, it will consume them. I didn't want John to leave, but I didn't want that for him, either.'

The middle-aged women by the window stood, hugged each other for a long moment, then started slowly back towards the wards.

'Where do you think he is, Holly?' Kate asked. 'Where do people with *spiritual distress* go?'

She offered another robotic shrug and glanced at her watch again. Kate had got all that she was going to find here, and it didn't feel like much.

She pictured the banks of a stream, swollen and flooded with dead leaves. Then she saw herself slipping under the water.

4

THE WIFE

Abby rolled onto her back and pulled the covers tight against the morning chill. Ray stirred bedside her. With a heavy yawn, he swung his feet out of bed and rubbed his face with his big hands. Ray kept his own hours and was often loose with the whole nine-to-five thing, so it was unusual for him to get up so early.

'Where do you think you're going?' Abby asked. 'I need my bedwarmer.'

'I did some work at Lance and Sally Thinner's place last week and I think I forgot to close the damn storm windows. That wind was pretty savage last night. I won't relax until I get over there to check for damage.'

'Is that the place with the outdoor sauna?'

'Sauna *and* steam room,' he said. 'Apparently those are different things.'

Ray's caretaking business serviced nearly half the properties on the island. Along with general yard maintenance and storm damage repair, he kept driveways and gutters free of dead leaves, yards clear of fallen branches or downed trees, alarm systems in working order, and watched for squatters and break-ins.

Secured in a lock-box on the floor of his truck were the keys and alarm codes for all the homes he managed. But as Ray was fond of reminding her, strolling around big empty houses wasn't as glamorous as Abby thought. He said most days he felt like Jack Nicholson roaming the halls of that eerie hotel, keeping an eye out for the ghosts of dead children.

'Let's hope you don't go crazy and kill your family with a roque mallet,' Abby once told him.

'I thought he used an axe,' he had said.

'It's a roque mallet in the book. They changed it for the movie.'

'I'll take your word for it.'

Abby smiled at the memory as Ray stood with a grunt and found the work shirt he'd laid out over the back of the wingback armchair in the corner the night before. He buttoned it quickly against the icy air. The fire downstairs kept the house warm during the evenings, but as well as Abby stoked it, the embers always went out overnight.

'Jesus,' he hissed. 'It's freezing. My bloody fingers aren't working.'

'I can see that.'

She gestured to his chest. He looked down. He'd

buttoned his shirt wrong. Muttering a curse, he started over. 'You're working tonight, right?'

'Graveyard shift, so don't wait up.'

'Like ships passing in the night then,' he said.

When he drifted out of the room, a little warmth went with him. She listened to his footfalls down the hallway and out the front door, heard his work truck rattle and moan to life, pull out onto Milt Street and fade into the distance. Then there were just the flame robins chirping outside the window.

Craving coffee, Abby dragged herself up, and half-heartedly made the bed before going downstairs to get the fire started. It took some effort because the only kindling she could find was damp. She fed it for a few minutes, then wandered restlessly around the room waiting for her coffee to brew, the dull rumble of the percolator filling the air.

Two cups later, morning alarms sounded and water pipes rattled as the kids got up, followed quickly by an argument about hot water and allotted bathroom times. Lori emerged first, clomping loudly into the kitchen in her scuffed and mud-stained Doc Martens.

'Can't you just put those things on at the front door?' Abby asked.

'Not if you don't want me to be late for the bus. They take like, an hour to lace up.'

Lori shook apple Pop-Tarts from the box, slid them into the toaster and watched them cook.

'I'd be careful if I were you,' Abby warned. 'I think it was Nietzsche who said: if you gaze long enough into a toaster, the toaster gazes back at you.'

'Ha ha,' Lori said. She fixed herself a cup of coffee and checked her reflection in the pot, taking a moment to brush down her fringe. Her piercing eyes were surrounded by a layer of heavy black eyeliner.

'You look nice,' Abby told her.

'I'm not going for *nice*,' she said.

'Well, not *nice,* but cool. Grungy.'

'*Grungy?*'

'Goth? I don't know. Whatever it is you're going for, you're nailing it.'

Lori sipped her coffee, as black as her wardrobe. 'Erk, Mum, you're such a dork. Can I go to Finly after school with Carry and Elise? Elise needs something to wear at her brother's wedding and she wants us to come help. Can I go?'

'How will you get home?'

'We'll be done before the last ferry.'

'You can go on one condition: you give me a hug.'

'Seriously?'

'Come on. It won't kill you.'

'Does it bother you that you have to bribe me for physical affection?'

'Just a pinch,' Abby said.

Lori sighed and grumbled, 'Fine.'

She gave her mother the briefest of hugs. For a fleeting moment the teenager was gone, and the child remained in Abby's arms. But then the Pop-Tarts were flung up from the toaster, and Lori squirmed away to fetch them.

Eddie shuffled into the kitchen next and began banging open cupboards, looking for cereal. He had dragged his trademark hoodie on over his school uniform, and had drawn the pull-strings so tight that his face peeked out from a small fabric mouth, like a forest nymph peeking nervously out from a cave.

'Morning, kid,' Abby said.

He grunted a reply and rubbed the sleep from his eyes.

'Jesus Christ,' Lori told him. 'You look like you just learned how to walk upright.'

Eddie flipped his sister the bird. She replied with her own middle finger, which seemed to settle things between them.

Abby ran the same route twice a week.

That morning, starting from home, she turned left up Harvill Hill Road, feeling the incline in her thighs. The saltbush that lined the road was dewy, dancing wildly in the breeze. Further down, the low intersection between Brown and Delahunt Streets was flooded. It happened around the same time each year and took most of the winter to drain. The council had dragged out two bright-orange sawhorses to stop frustrated drivers from trying their luck.

Fat rain lashed against her face, streamed down her cheeks, soaked her running sneakers. Her winter weight jiggled. Her left knee made a worrying clicking sound every few steps and something didn't feel right in her ankle, but she pushed through it. Abby loved to run during winter. The combination of endorphins and bitter coldness was exhilarating.

At the crest of the hill, a panoramic view of the island opened up to reveal large patches of dense bushland and a handful of freshwater lakes to the south. To the north, the town spread out like barnacles on the overturned belly of a whale. At least two thirds of the houses on the island were empty this time of year, bleak and functionless, like socks without feet.

When the weather was warm, Belport swelled with tourists, campers and holiday-makers. But when the sun went away, so did the people. Blinds were drawn on stale rooms, plastic protective sheets were thrown over furniture, and all the big cedar beach houses that dotted the island sat empty for the majority of the following nine months. The island should have felt bigger with fewer people in it, but it was somehow smaller, as if the coastline was slowly closing in. She had tried to explain this feeling to Ray once, but he'd come back at her with a load of facts about erosion.

Beyond the island, Abby could see the ferry coming in, cutting a foamy white line between Belport and the Bellarine Peninsula, connecting them like an umbilical cord.

From Harvill Hill, she turned right and jogged down to Bay Street, Belport's main drag. A single traffic light dangled across the intersection of Bay and Bramwell, blinking amber against the grey, storm-lit afternoon. On one side of the street stood the All-You-Need Gas & Petrol station. On the other was the Belport Inn, known colloquially as the Belly, a cosy, Irish-themed pub full of stained-glass lamps and nautical paintings.

The restaurants, gift shops and newsagency were all closed for the off-season. Huddled together at the bottom of Bay Street were the post office, the public library, and the Belport Police Station.

The boardwalk carnival rose on her right as she neared the coast, looming in silhouette beneath an overcast sky. The front gates were padlocked. The Sky Winder, a famously dull roller-coaster, stood still and silent, its scaffolding like a giant, jagged ribcage. The Ferris wheel, a twinkling ring of yellow lights in summer, was dark.

Abby kept running, down along the promenade, through the deserted foreshore campgrounds and down onto the beach, where the sand was wet and hard. The choppy blue waters of Bass Strait stretched on and on to her right. The air smelled like fish and salt.

A flock of nervous seagulls watched her from under the awnings of the shuttered bait shop, as if wondering why a human would be punishing herself like this.

A stitch had settled in Abby's left side that sent darts of pain through her abdomen, but she kept going. Her breathing was hot and arrhythmic, her legs like dry bamboo, shuddering with each stride. Her bowels felt like slippery eels trying to escape a bucket. The fear of shitting herself had never been more real. She *hurt*, but it was a wonderful hurt, one that reminded her she was alive.

She didn't stop to catch her breath until she reached the big stone seawall that stood at the far edge of the beach. The wall separated the beach from the boat ramps on the other side. Huge clumps of tangled seaweed clung to it like tentacles. A large metal warning sign was bolted to it: *Strong currents, submerged objects, slippery rocks, shallow water, unexpected waves. Alcohol prohibited, diving prohibited.* Across it, written in red spray paint, was *Fun prohibited.*

Hands on hips, Abby straightened up and looked out over the water while she caught her breath. Between May and October, it wasn't uncommon to see humpbacks, southern rights, blues, and even the occasional orca pass by the island on their annual pilgrimage from their feeding grounds in Antarctica to Australia's warmer waters, but today the water looked hostile and sullen. It was hard to imagine anything going on beneath it.

There's not a whole lot going on above it either, Abby thought.

Abby changed her normal run to go past the Buy & Bye, the supermarket where the owner, Henry Biller, gave her three shifts a week during the winter and six during the summer.

When she walked in, Henry, a solid man with ruddy cheeks and a gentle smile, was running a broom over an already spotless floor.'

'I don't think that floor's getting any cleaner,' she said.

'If you've got time for leaning you've got time for cleaning,' Biller said with a smile. 'You're three hours early for your shift, by the way.'

'I was on my way past and thought I'd pick up my pay so I can get to the bank before it closes. Anyway, would you let me work if I turned up looking like this?'

He took in her rain-drenched, sweat-soaked hair.

'Good point,' he said. 'Can you watch the store while I run to the safe?'

He dusted his hands off on his apron and slipped through the plastic flaps at the back of the store that led to the receiving bay. There was no need for her to watch the store while he was gone. Aside from her, it was empty.

The supermarket wasn't huge, but the shop floor was laid out to make the most of the space. There were twelve aisles, and in a fit of optimism Henry had installed seven check-outs, though they rarely needed more than two. There were three short lanes of shopping trolleys and a large liquor department in the top-right corner. The place was stocked to bursting point over summer, but Biller let the stock run down at this time of year.

A bitterly cold wind swept off the bay, howling up the rugged, rocky slopes of the island, strong enough to shake the glass-fronted wall of the store. Beyond the window – *Grocery/Liquor/Bait!* spelled out backwards on the glass – the bay was wild and dark.

'Could be another big one,' Biller said when he'd returned.

'Nah, we won't get another big storm for the rest of the season,' Abby said. 'This island can only handle so much excitement.'

Biller handed her a yellow envelope. He paid in cash to keep it off the books. 'It's a little light. It's that time of year. Mind if I fix the rest up next week?'

Abby hesitated a moment. She might have told him things were tight all over the island and that the Gilpin household was no exception, but instead she nodded and stuffed the money into her sports bra. 'Funny, I was going to ask if there were any extra shifts going.'

He wet his lips and pushed his hands into the pockets of his apron.

'I'm sorry, Ab.'

'No big deal,' she told him. 'It's the price for nine months of peace, right?'

'That's what we keep telling ourselves.'

She turned to watch thunderheads gather on the horizon. One lone powerboat chugged in towards Elk Harbour, trying to outrun them.

When Abby got home, there was a police cruiser parked outside her house. A woman in a crisp blue police uniform was bobbing around outside her front door, leaning to get a look through the windows.

'Do you have a warrant?' Abby called out, startling her.

Bobbi laughed. 'You bitch. You scared the shit out of me.'

They hugged. Abby and Bobbi used to work together at the Buy & Bye, where Bobbi would complain about having to wear shoes and a bra and would routinely remove both during the course of her shift. She'd left the supermarket years ago to join the police, but she and Abby had only become closer.

'I'm here to pick up your disgusting baby stuff,' Bobbi said. 'Maggie sent me.'

'It's not disgusting, I swear.'

'It's fifteen years old.'

Bobbi's partner, Maggie, was eight-and-a-half months pregnant. She had been asking about Eddie and Lori's old hand-me-downs since the foetus was the size of a peanut, but Abby had been slow to hand them over. She wasn't sure exactly why. It wasn't as if she and Ray were planning on pumping out a third kid, but the idea of giving away all those cute baby relics filled her with a mysterious sadness.

'Follow me,' Abby said.

She led Bobbi down the outdoor passage connecting the house to the garage. The rain had eased, but a clogged roof gutter was sending a torrent of water splashing down into the grass, turning dirt to mud. They had to step around it.

'It's like a fucking zoo in here,' Bobbi said.

On the shelving unit that ran along the rear wall of the garage, were some taxidermy animals she hadn't managed to give away. Small stuff, mostly: birds, mice, a marsupial rat and a fat grey toad that Abby had a hell of a time skinning.

'I think I'm getting better,' Abby said. 'I might even be ready for the rabbit Whitley Higgins's been keeping in his freezer for me. He found it on his back doorstep and thinks his cat dragged it over just for me. I'm still not entirely sure what I'll do about the ears.'

'Sometimes I don't know why we're friends,' Bobbi said.

While Abby pulled out the crate of baby clothes, Bobbi picked up the worn and well-dog-eared paperback sitting on the workbench. On the cover was a landscape of dead trees, at the feet of which was a chalk outline depicting two dead bodies, entwined. The title, printed in bright red font, read: *The Buck River Murders: A true story of family, revenge and betrayal.*

'I'm almost done with that if you want to borrow it,' Abby said.

Bobbi turned the cover over in her hands, nodding. 'Any good?'

'It's a meaty one, Bob. Back in 1986 they found two bodies near this river in Denver. One was a black guy in his sixties who'd been killed by a shotgun blast to the chest; the other was a teenage runaway, and *he* died from blunt force trauma to the head. The bodies were dumped within ten metres of one another, but the police couldn't find any other connection between them.'

Abby got through a lot of books during winter, and true crime was a particular favourite. It seemed darkly appropriate in a place like Belport, where the streets didn't just feel empty, but *emptied.*

Abby set the crate down on the workbench and flipped open the lid. It was filled with jackets, hats and teeny-tiny booties. She had even kept the bright-blue puffy beanie they got for a trip to the snow when Eddie was still in nappies. She held out a bodysuit with green and black stripes and inhaled all the memories that were trapped in its fibres. It filled her with a deep sense of nostalgia.

'We bought this from a market in Queensland,' Abby said. 'It's all hand-stitched.'

'God, who'd have thought your kids used to be cute enough to pull these off,' Bobbi said. She had just plucked out one of Lori's old sleeping gowns, and it seemed impossibly small.

'I know, right? What happened to them? I can't believe they used to actually fit into—'

'Oh no,' Bobbi said, fingering a jagged hole at the base of the gown, roughly the size of a fifty-cent piece. 'Ab, how long since you last checked these?'

Abby didn't answer. She'd just discovered a pair of red woollen booties, riddled with holes. She riffled through the crate, pulling out item after item. Everything was moth-eaten. It hurt her more than it should have.

When the weather cooled, moths appeared all over the island. Fat, brown and blind, they gathered in huge numbers by Abby's verandah light, thrumming in wild chaotic unison like hundreds of pieces of a greater whole. They clung to the air vents above Abby's check-out at the Buy & Bye, lay in wait whenever she went to split an old shard of firewood and danced wildly in the headlights over her car. *And*, they ate her kids' clothing.

'Damn,' she said softly.

'Don't beat yourself up. Those little fuckers get in everywhere. A couple of mornings ago I heard Maggie give this God-awful scream from the kitchen. She'd just poured herself a bowl of bran flakes and it was practically full of moth larvae. I asked her what the big deal was – it's not like she's a vegetarian. She didn't think that was funny.'

'I wonder why,' Abby said.

'Seriously though, are you okay?'

Abby neatly folded the clothing, set it back down in the crate and shut the lid. She shrugged. 'Yeah, this just feels a bit like a bad omen.'

Right on cue, the two-way radio on Bobbi's lapel shrieked. It spat radio static for a moment, and then a gruff male voice said, 'Bobbi, are you around? Over.'

Bobbi put her index finger to her lips. She was, after all, on duty. She gave the radio a squeeze and said, 'What's up, Sarg?'

'I need you over at Beech Tree Landing,' the voice on the other end of the radio squawked. 'This might be a big one, Bobbi. Over.'

Abby and Bobbi exchanged a curious glance.

'That's a worry,' Abby said. But neither of them could quite hide their excitement.

5

THE WIDOW

Kate's home was an elegant renovated Victorian house in the inner suburb of Caulfield. It was open and bright, with original leadlight windows and polished banisters. The extended living space was wrapped with floor-to-ceiling windows that, at sunset, reflected and refracted light like a prism. But it was long after sunset now. John was out there, someplace beyond the glass, someplace beyond the dark.

And somehow, beneath a four-metre-high ceiling, Kate felt claustrophobic. Her sneakers slapped loudly against the oak parquetry flooring as she looked for her daughter. Under other circumstances she would have insisted on enforcing her strict no-shoes-inside policy, but a few scuffs didn't seem like such a big deal anymore.

Mia was sitting on the leather sofa in the living room with her grandmother, Pam. She had hardly talked or eaten since returning from the airport without her father and was now staring dreamily out the window. With the front light switched off, the glass was a black mirror, reflecting a pale, ghostly version of Kate's daughter.

Pam didn't hear Kate approach – she was completely deaf in one ear and refused to use a hearing aid because it would make her look too much like her mother. She was in her seventies but had the taut smooth skin of someone much younger. Clutched in her hands was a Gucci handbag and an extravagant pair of Saint Laurent cat eyes – six-hundred-dollar sunglasses.

'Daddy loves you very much and I'm sure he misses you,' Pam told Mia. 'He just needs to stay away a little longer. For work, that's all. He'll be back soon.'

'How soon?' Mia asked.

'Just as soon as he can, darling.'

John's parents had descended on the house and set up base. Fisher was a chain-smoking wreck, while Pam was unnervingly calm. Kate wasn't sure which was worse.

Kate slipped onto the sofa, pulled Mia towards her and said, 'Actually, monkey, that's not quite right. The truth is, we're not entirely sure where your dad is right now, but we're looking for him. And wherever he is, I'm sure he's trying to get back to us too. Are you hungry?'

'I'll eat when Daddy gets home,' she said.

'We don't know how long that's going to be, monkey.'

'You don't know anything!'

'Fine,' Kate said. 'Eat or don't eat. I don't care.'

Mia slunk off the sofa and marched away, banging loudly up the staircase and slamming her bedroom door shut. Kate closed her eyes and hoped, prayed and begged that Pam could keep quiet for two damn—

'She's only ten,' Pam said. 'One of the many jobs a mother has is filtering.'

Life doesn't have a filter …

'I don't want to scare her, Pam. But I don't want to lie to her either.'

'Even false hope is better than no hope, dear. Especially for a child.' She smiled. 'Now, I know you're not Catholic, but my mother did always say that a little prayer can help us to feel better. Will you join me?'

Even with her son missing, Pam had taken the time to touch up her make-up before descending from the guestroom, wearing so much jewellery that she sounded like Christmas coming around the corner. She had either popped a valium or knew something Kate didn't.

Pam pulled a small missal from her bag and flicked through it thoughtfully for a while, then stopped and looked up with a satisfied smile. 'This is perfect.'

Fisher paced on the other side of the glass sliding door, back and forth across the entertainment deck, smoking cigarette after cigarette, phone stuck to his face. He glanced through the window at Kate, stubbed out his cigarette, collected the butt in his breast pocket then came back inside smelling like all her mother's old boyfriends.

Pam took hold of Kate's hand. 'I just thought it might help to say a prayer, love,' she told Fisher. 'We're all feeling a little overwhelmed. Will you join us?'

Fisher ran a hand through his receding hair, sat down next to his wife and sighed. Pam let go of Kate's hand long enough to make a cross, then took it again in her warm, stubby fingers.

'In the name of the Father and of the Son and of the Holy Spirit,' she said, squinting at the book in her lap. 'Oh, gentle and loving Saint Anthony, whose heart was ever full of human sympathy; our son, John, is lost and in need of guidance. Please whisper our petition into the ears of the sweet infant Jesus, and the—'

'Is there anyone we haven't called yet?' Fisher said. 'Any friends or colleagues?'

'Fisher,' Pam said in a loud throaty whisper.

'We should write a list,' he interrupted again. 'Write down everyone he's been in contact with over the past month, from people at his gym to whoever makes his morning coffee.'

'*Fisher*,' Pam snapped. She was still holding onto Kate's hand and now gave it a sharp squeeze. The polished rings pinched Kate's skin, but she kept quiet.

Without another word, Fisher went back onto the deck and lit a fresh cigarette. Kate hesitated a moment, then followed him.

The night was still and crisp. A plane cut through

the sky above them, blinking red and blue lights against a vast field of black. Below the plane and beyond their sprawling garden of weeping willows, the city glistened beneath a fat moon. The moonlight was sombre, the darkness outside it heavy and deep as an ocean.

Fisher stood by the safety railing, fiddling with a red packet of cigarettes. He took one out and lit up. Kate joined him. Neither spoke for a long time. Kate kept her eyes fixed ahead, listening to the sharp inhale of cigarette smoke and the long, wheezing exhale.

'What you said in the police station,' she started. 'About me being vague, passive to the point of being invisible.'

'Can we not do this now?' Fisher said. 'I'm just chewed up over this whole mess. I'm sorry for what I said, really, but—'

'You were right,' she said.

He dragged on his cigarette and said nothing. Kate watched him for a moment, then turned back to the moon.

'You see me as someone who needs protecting,' she said, the words burrowing up from somewhere deep and dark and well hidden. 'You think that because John does, and John believes it because I let him. I thought that's what he wanted. I thought that's how he wanted me to be. So, I fostered that. I nurtured it. But that's not who I am, Fisher.'

He turned to her and asked, 'Who are you?'

'I'm stronger than people think, so please, from here on in, don't talk to me like I'm a child, don't look at me like I'm a hysterical woman. Give me the respect of talking straight.'

He flinched.

'Alright,' he said.

'Alright.'

Fisher flicked his cigarette into the garden that stretched ahead of them like a bottomless void. The butt sailed for a while, exploded into red sparks, then faded. Kate let that mark the end of their conversation and went back inside the house.

Mia was in her bedroom, dressed in the Spider-Man onesie John had bought her. The room was bright, full of yellows and blues, but the little girl sitting cross-legged on the carpet was somehow colourless.

Her small hands were pressed into a steeple, and she was whispering.

'Can I come in?' Kate asked.

Mia shrugged, which Kate chose to take as an invitation. She sat down next to her daughter and asked, 'Were you praying?'

'I guess,' Mia said. 'I don't know. Gran said I could ask God to bring Dad home. Can God really read people's minds?'

'Your grandma believes he can.'

'If God can read my mind, I'm worried he might not bring Dad home.'

'What makes you say that, monkey?'

She shrugged. 'Sometimes I have bad thoughts.'

'We all do,' Kate said. 'We can't have good thoughts all the time. That's not how people work.'

She studied her fingernails. 'Sometimes I have bad thoughts about God.'

'Like what?'

'Well, for starters, how did Noah fit so many animals on the ark? And if rain filled up the planet then that would mean it was fresh water, so how did the saltwater fish survive? And where did all the water go and by the way why did God kill all those Egyptian babies? And what's with Abraham and—'

'TMI, monkey.'

'Oh,' she said. 'Sorry.'

TMI (too much information) was an expression used often in their house. If Mia was explaining what part of the pig bacon came from over breakfast, or describing the life cycle of maggots when driving past roadkill, or listing the different modes of execution used to carry out death sentences in America, or a million other disturbing things she somehow found online, *TMI* stopped her in her tracks.

'It's good to be questioning stuff,' Kate said. 'I still

haven't really decided where I land with the whole God thing, but you don't need to be thinking about all that right now.'

'But I can't help it, and if God is real and he can read my thoughts, then he knows I'm thinking all that, and if he knows I'm thinking all that, maybe he won't bring Dad home.'

'If God is real, he understands. And if he isn't, your dad is still coming home, Mia.'

'How do you know?'

Because I won't survive without him, Kate thought.

'Because he has you to come home to,' she said.

A hint of colour returned to Mia's face. She folded against Kate, who drew her close, feeling the warmth of Mia's small body against her own, and wanting badly to cry.

Around three am, Kate climbed into her big empty bed, pulled herself into a tight ball beneath the covers and told herself John was coming home. He would come home, and he would warm the cold side of the bed, and she would wake in his arms.

She cried for a long time that night. She wanted to sob, craved it, but she didn't want to be heard, so she let it out in dribbles, fits and starts. She was a champagne bottle whose cork was slowly edging out, but she couldn't allow herself to pop. After several painful hours, her mind began to quieten, and her body slipped into a sort of stand-by mode. It didn't feel like sleep, exactly. More like entering a state of suspended animation. *Wake me up when John gets home.* She must have slept though, because when the phone rang, it took her a few long moments to recognise the sound.

'John,' she whispered. Her voice sounded heavy and spooky in the darkness. She scrambled for her phone. She had gone to bed clutching it and now it was lost in the tangle of sheets. She could see its glowing screen beneath the top sheet, hear its muffled ring. She found it and hit the answer button without looking at the caller ID. In her heart, she knew who it was.

'John?'

There was a pause on the other end of the line, then a man with a Middle Eastern accent said, 'I'm sorry to call so late, ma'am, but this is Tom from Sanctuary Security. We have an alert registering in our system that says your home alarm has been triggered.'

Thinking of Mia, Kate swung her feet off the bed and switched on the bedside lamp. Her legs were hot and sweaty; she'd gone to bed in jeans.

'Are you sure?' she asked. 'I don't hear an alarm going off?'

'That's strange,' the man from the security company said. He had started chewing something. It sounded like an apple. 'Can you confirm you're at 118 Neef Street, Belport Island?'

'Belport Island? No. I'm at home, in Caulfield. You must be calling about our holiday house.'

'Are you saying you're not at that address, ma'am?'

'No, I'm not.'

'Well, someone is,' he said.

6

THE WIFE

The last couple of hours before close were always especially slow at the Buy & Bye. Abby alone in the store, with nothing but her thoughts and the sound of muzak to keep her company – an instrumental version of Cat Stevens's 'Father and Son'.

Bobbi had promised to drop in with all the juicy details about what her sergeant said *might be a big one*, but so far, she was a no-show. While she waited, Abby restocked the Schweppes fridge, topped up the liquor cabinet, updated the specials basket, swept the floors, mopped the cool room, scrubbed out the deli, rotated the fruit and vegetables, cleaned out the break-room refrigerator, oiled that damn shopping trolley with the damn squeaky wheel, then checked her watch.

Time was dragging offensively slow, like an Easter Sunday sermon. Every time a car rolled past the shop, Abby leaned over her counter to look for the white and blue of Bobbi's cruiser, desperate for a distraction. She was about to check all the use-by dates on the milk cartons when she saw an ancient green Saab roll up outside. All but one of the hubcaps were missing, and the rear side window had been smashed and covered with a collage of plastic shopping bags. They flapped in the breeze like gills.

The Saab door opened, and a seventy-something woman in high heels stepped out, swaying and stumbling awkwardly like a newborn foal. Eileen Betchkie.

Despite the chill, Eileen was wearing nothing more than a tight mini and a tighter tank top, pink bra strap dangling strategically off one shoulder; she had bleached yellow hair, midnight-blue eyeliner and a couple of healthy handfuls of false cleavage.

She'd make a hell of a drag queen, Abby thought, *if not for her walk.* She moved with a hunch, as if the ghosts of all of her past mistakes rode on her shoulders, and if the island grapevine was accurate, she'd made plenty. She'd burned through four marriages, gone bankrupt twice, had three convictions for drugs and one for prostitution.

They were just rumours, of course. If Belport had one thing in abundance, it was gossip.

The electronic bell above the door chimed as Eileen swept inside. There were goosebumps on her broad, bare shoulders. Her arms were muscular and toned, as if she'd spent a life chopping wood.

'Evening, darling,' she said when she reached Abby's check-out.

'How are you, Eileen?'

'Oh, I don't know. I think I'm depressed. Or lonely. Or both. Did you catch *60 Minutes* last night? There was this woman somewhere in the UK who dropped dead in front of her TV, and nobody noticed for seven years. *Seven years.*'

Eileen was one of the Buy & Bye's most regular regulars, and Abby had already started bagging up her items: two packs of Winfield Reds and a five-litre cask of Rawlings Pinot Noir, which had the honour of being both their cheapest and largest boxed wine.

Eileen pronounced it *Pee-not Norie*, and lived by the motto, *Don't ever reach for the top shelf unless you're not the one who's paying.*

'Can you imagine what was left of the poor woman when her family finally bothered to drop by for a visit? Mummified. Liquefied. Erk. Do me a favour, Abby: if a week goes by and you haven't seen me in here, come knock on my door.'

'Of course,' Abby said. 'It's all part of the service here at the Buy & Bye. We help you find what you're looking for, pack your shopping bags, and every once in a while check you're not a corpse.'

Eileen grinned. Her teeth were unnaturally straight and white. 'Speaking of abandonment, why is your husband ignoring my calls? I may not have as much money in the bank as the rest of his customers, but my old man had a saying: *Every client is the most important client.* He sold Holdens for forty-six years and loved every second of it. He would have died right there in the middle of his showroom if the gout hadn't hit him like it did.'

'You'd be better off asking Ray that, Eileen. Did he forget to do something at your place?'

'He never showed up,' she said. 'There's a row of paperbark trees outside the shed that are older than me, and after the winter we've had it won't take much more than a beefy fart to knock them over. Ray said he'd fell them, but I haven't heard a peep out of him. Now, I'd rather give my business to you, sweetheart, but little Wei who runs the bait shop said he'd do the same job for half. He's Chinese. They have a better work ethic than us; I've always said that.'

'That's weird,' Abby said.

'What?'

'Oh, it's nothing. I thought Ray said he was at your place. We probably just got our wires crossed, that's all.'

'Well, either way, tell him to get his arse onto my paperbark trees.' She opened her Winfields and left the plastic wrapper on the counter for Abby to collect. She put a cigarette to her lips and retrieved a blue lighter from between her breasts. Noticing Abby's expression, she said, 'Relax, darl, I'm not gonna light up indoors.'

The streetlights flickered on outside the shopfront as Eileen walked out into the darkening street.

Eileen was the last customer for the day. Bobbi still didn't show up. Abby spent the rest of her shift slowly closing up. As she drove home over the crest of a hill, she looked out over the island and saw lights on in all the big holiday houses. The lights were on timers, designed to discourage break-ins and squatters. All that endless emptiness spooked her, so she found a song on the radio she could sing along to and turned it up loud.

When she got home, Abby found Ray in the bedroom. He was laying out his clothing for the next day and was regarding the contents of their closet the way an explorer might regard a mysterious tablet etched with a forgotten language.

'You wear the same thing every day,' she said, startling him. 'How can it possibly take you this long?'

'Oh, you know, dress for the job you want and all that.'

She looked into the closet. It was nearly entirely grey, filled mostly with grey work shirts with *Island Care* printed on the pockets.

It made Abby sad that Ray spent his work days alone. It reminded her of the smell of a childhood lunchbox, made her picture an old man eating alone in a restaurant. He had tried to take on employees before, but they never stuck with the job long. Last season he hired Russ Graves, a man who was, to hear Ray describe it, a few peas short of a casserole; not smart enough to get bored and not imaginative enough to get lonely. But as it turned out, he was both. His resignation letter explained that if he didn't quit, he was likely to fill his pockets with stones and throw himself into Elk Harbour.

'How was work?' she asked.

'I spent the better part of my afternoon fishing a dead possum out of Dan and Louise Buckley's indoor swimming pool,' he said.

He peeled off his singlet.

'Did you bring it home for my taxidermy?' she asked.

'I thought about it, but it had been in there for a while from the look of it. And the smell. I don't think even you'd go near it without spewing. How about you? Work okay?'

'Same old,' she said.

'You're home late. Did you work back?'

'Delahunt Street is a lake,' she said, stepping out of her slacks and into her raggedy old pyjama bottoms. 'It took me an extra ten minutes to get home.

'It'll be at least twenty-four hours before it drains, and that's only if we don't see any more rain overnight, which seems unlikely.'

'God, when did we become the type of couple to talk about the weather?' She dropped her Buy & Bye tunic into the washing basket and climbed under the covers.

71

'Jesus, it's freezing in here. Hurry up and come keep me warm.'

Ray slunk into bed and she spooned him aggressively.

'Eileen Betchkie came in tonight,' she said.

The muscles in Ray's forearms tensed suddenly, then relaxed. It was a micro-movement, nearly imperceptible to the untrained eye, but a wife knows.

'Oh, yeah?'

'Yeah. She told me you didn't go by her place, but I thought you said you were there yesterday. Apparently there's a load of paperbark trees that will blow over if you fart on them. She worded it better than that, but you get the gist.'

'I swear to God that woman is losing it,' he said. 'I spent the whole day in her yard with the chainsaw and either she didn't notice or she forgot. I don't know which is scarier. To be honest, I'm not sure she should be living out at that place all alone.'

Abby inhaled slowly. 'So you did go to her place yesterday?'

He was silent for a moment. He then rolled over in bed to face her and asked, 'Where else would I have gone?'

'Stepping out on me with another woman, obviously.'

He laughed, then looked into her eyes sincerely. 'I would never cheat on you, Ab. You know why?'

'Because I'm a dreamboat?'

'No, because this island has a very limited pool of eligible women.'

'Shut up.'

'I love you.'

'I love you too,' she said.

He pecked her on the cheek, then rolled over to switch off the bedside lamp. Within minutes, he was snoring.

For reasons she wouldn't understand until much later, Abby tossed and turned for most of the night, slipping in and out of sleep like a boat through rough seas.

7

THE WIDOW

Kate didn't know how long she'd be staying in Belport. She had made up her mind that, for whatever reason, John was staying in their holiday house on the island. He had tripped the house alarm – again, for whatever reason – and all she had to do was go and bring him back. Simple. It didn't matter that the alarm company sent a security car to check the place out and found nothing. John would be there. She would drag him home and they would worry about the shattered remains of their marriage later.

Unfortunately, Kate wasn't an idiot. She knew it wouldn't be so easy. She might need to spend a night or two on the island, so she packed as if she were heading off to spend six months in Europe. Zipped up inside the suitcase she was now dragging out to the car were six bras (strapless, sports and push-up among them), two winter parkas, three pairs of jeans, one dress, three pairs of shoes (she had to remove a fourth pair to get the suitcase shut) and, most bizarrely, a swimsuit. It seemed she couldn't even pack a suitcase anymore.

Since John's disappearance, such simple things had become near impossible. Preparing meals, for example, now seemed like a bizarre foreign custom, needlessly complicated. She had attempted to cook noodles for Mia the previous night and quickly found herself lost in a sea of utensils. She had eventually folded to her knees on the kitchen floor, called for pizza and cried until it arrived.

Mia, who'd be spending the next few days at her grandparents' house, had packed far more sensibly. Everything she needed was slotted into her pink backpack. Mia hadn't insisted on coming to the island, to Kate's relief. No doubt her daughter wanted to come, but in a wise, old-soul sort of way, she'd known better than to ask.

They bundled into the Lexus and Kate started the engine.

'You sure you don't need to pee before we go?'

It was only a short drive to Pam and Fisher's place, but Mia had a habit of suddenly discovering she needed the bathroom seconds after the electronic gate clicked shut behind them.

Mia looked down at her bladder as if consulting it, then shook her head. 'I'm alright.'

Kate looped the car around the top of the driveway, then crept slowly towards the road. It was a gloomy morning, and traffic was sluggish. Kate inched through it, like wading slowly through deep water.

They arrived at Pam and Fisher's three-storey Brighton townhouse a little after nine am, and Kate turned to look at her daughter.

'Two sleeps,' Kate said in a reassuring tone, as much to herself as to Mia. 'Three at the most.'

Mia nodded stoically, unfastened her seatbelt and sighed. It was a heavy sigh. Too heavy for someone her age, and too loaded with pain and worry.

'Are you going to be alright?' Kate asked.

'I'll be fine, Mum. Are you?'

'Am I what?'

'Are you going to be alright?'

'… You don't need to worry about me, monkey. I'm okay. And in a couple of days, I'll come home.'

'Promise?'

'Promise.'

Fisher and Pam came out to meet them. Fisher, who had insisted on coming to Belport too, had an overnight bag over one shoulder. The thought of spending so much time with her father-in-law filled Kate with a very particular brand of anxiety, but if given the choice between that and going alone, she would have picked Fisher.

Mia climbed down from the passenger seat and Fisher lifted her into a hug and said, 'Do me a favour and look after your gran while I'm gone, okay?'

'Okay, Grandpa,' she said, mournfully.

Pam crossed the yard behind him in slippers, leaving deep footprints in the wet grass. She took Kate's hands in hers and kissed her softly on the cheek. 'I know you have to head off soon, but there's something I need to tell you before you go. It's important.'

'What is it?'

Pam pulled back but held tightly onto Kate's hands. 'John is fine,' she whispered.

'I know. I think he just needed some time out. We'll bring him home, Pam.'

'John is *fine*,' she said again, and Kate wondered if she'd heard a word Kate had said. 'I had a dream.'

'A dream?'

'You know those dreams I have now and then – I can always tell when they mean something real.' Pam gazed skyward. 'I was standing at the gates of heaven. I wasn't shown through them, of course, but I was allowed to look inside. I could see all the way to John's throne, and you know what?' She laughed; a short, maniacal snort. 'It was empty. John's throne was empty, because he doesn't need to sit in it yet. He's still alive, Kate. He's still alive, I'm sure of it. Just you wait and see I'm right. Just you wait.'

Kate and Fisher exchanged a concerned glance over the bonnet of the car. As if reading her mind, Fisher said, 'Pam's sister is on her way down from Beechworth to help out with Mia.'

Kate nodded, smiled nervously. She knelt to look Mia in the eyes and said, 'You don't need a reason to call me. Day or night, whenever you feel like it. I need you to be a big girl for me while I'm away, alright?'

She nodded. 'Two sleeps.'

'Three at the most.'

'And, Mum?'

'Yes, monkey?'

'You be a big girl too.'

Belport Island was accessible only by a thirty-minute ferry ride from a port on the Bellarine Peninsula, a little over a two-hour drive away. It took them a while to get out of the city, but then the traffic parted, and the highway turned clear and straight.

Kate stuck to the slow lane and kept the car a few kilometres under the limit. Her slow driving must have frustrated Fisher, but he didn't ask her to speed up. Unlike him, Kate was in no hurry to get there. For her, the island represented a cold exclamation mark at the end of a sentence: whatever drama John was caught up in would be revealed, and her life would be up-ended.

Out here on the road, rolling on with commas and semicolons, it was easy to believe that it was all a mistake, that John would have a simple explanation for everything. While the sentence was still open there was still room for hope. *Hope* was one word for it, anyway. *Denial* also worked.

The heavier the silence grew between Fisher and Kate, the deeper her mind slipped into fantasy. Embarking on the familiar route to Belport, she was lulled into thinking John had gone on ahead to set up the beach house for their arrival. The air in the house was always stale when they first got there, so John had gone in advance to sling open all the windows. He had removed the protective sheets from the furniture, put fresh covers on the beds, and was waiting for her and Mia to arrive.

She imagined the weight in the passenger side was her daughter instead of her father-in-law. It was easy if she kept her eyes fixed on the road ahead, just so, and didn't turn to look in his direction. Yes, Mia was in the car with her. She'd have fallen asleep by now, tired after spending the first leg of the trip discussing the shells she'd collect when they made it to the beach, and playing I-spy and punch buggy. When they finally arrived, it would somehow be summer again, and a warm breeze would be blowing. John would be sitting on the swing chair on the front deck. He'd watch them roll up the driveway, a warm smile on his face. With his free hand (the other would be holding a beer) he'd pat the space next to him, inviting Kate to join him. And she would.

'He's probably just taken himself off somewhere. He used to do it sometimes, when he was a teenager,' Fisher said. They were the first words either of them had said since leaving the city, and they broke through Kate's fantasy like the snap of a dry branch.

'What do you mean?'

'Once, he'd told us he was on a school camp, but when Pam washed his jeans a few days later she found a receipt from a McDonald's in the city. He'd just gone off for a night and stayed in a hostel. When we confronted him about it, all he said was that he needed a little time to himself.'

He took out a cigarette but knew better than to light it. Instead, he rolled it on the palm of his hand. 'I understand why he did what he did. Not fully, I suppose, but I know what it's like to have to be alone. What I don't understand is, why did he go to Belport? He's always hated it there.'

'Always?'

'You didn't know that?'

'He usually groans about going, but I thought he liked it there as a kid.'

Fisher sighed. It was a loaded sigh, spilling over with things unsaid. 'Once upon a time, maybe. But even as a kid he never quite relaxed while we were on the island. When we gave you the place I thought he might finally see Belport the way I used to – as an escape, somewhere to decompress. But he never did.'

She watched the road. Scrubland peeked out from beneath the steel safety barriers that lined the highway. One stretch had seen a bushfire roar through a summer or two earlier. The shoulder was still burned black, but the vegetation beyond was lush and green.

'Did John ever tell you he asked for my blessing before he proposed to you?' Fisher asked. 'He came to me looking for approval. I told him it doesn't usually work that way. Usually it's the father of the bride that a man needs to convince. But he just wanted to know if I thought it was a good idea, that you were a good match.'

'I didn't know that,' she said.

He glanced down at his wedding band, polished gold and half a size too small. It made Kate picture cooking twine wrapped around sausage casing.

'He spent his childhood seeking other people's approval. Pam thinks it's because I was too hard on him, and that I didn't give him enough praise as a kid. But I just think that's who he is. He's a thinker.'

'What did you tell him?'

'I told him you were a safe bet,' he said.

A safe bet. Had he intended that to be a compliment?

It had taken Kate a long time to understand why John chose to marry her. There were plenty of other women in his life who were much more attractive and interesting.

He could have had his pick. Kate had forgettable looks. She was quiet, like a duck slipping silently through a pond. Yet John had courted her, aggressively, like a man who knew exactly what he wanted.

Over the years of their marriage, Kate had peeled back the layers of her husband and caught a glimpse into his past, and she came to understand why he had chosen her. John had one other serious relationship before Kate. Her name was Audrey Finn – a movie star name. She was stunningly beautiful and a gifted artist. More than once, Kate had stalked her on Facebook after one or two glasses of white. Audrey Finn knew sign language because her sister was deaf. Her father was some sort of diplomat, and she had spent parts of her childhood in Japan and the United States. What John had told her implied that he simply couldn't hold Audrey's interest.

Enter: Kate. Two years out of university, working at a low-level accounting firm in the northern suburbs. She had never had a serious boyfriend and had never travelled. She'd be crazy to abandon someone like John, and he knew it.

'Kate, this should go without saying, but whatever happens, whatever we find out on that island, you and Mia will always be supported.'

'Whatever happens?'

'I've been trying to figure out why John would go to Belport, why he'd lie to you about leaving his job, why he'd lie to us. I've come up with a couple of theories, and, well … none of them are good.'

Kate wet her lips and stepped harder on the accelerator. The speedometer crept up towards the speed limit, then over it.

'All I'm saying is, we should prepare ourselves,' Fisher said. 'Mentally. We might be about to learn some things about John that we'd be better off not knowing.'

'Like what?'

Fisher looked out the window. 'We all have things that ought to stay buried, things a person should keep to themselves. Things that, if they were ever dragged into the light, would change the way people saw us. I suppose my point is, how well can you really ever know anyone?'

Kate wondered what dark things Fisher had buried.

'You think he's been having an affair, don't you?' She kept her eyes fixed on the road but felt his gaze on her. 'He could have met someone there in the summer. A local woman. They could have stayed in touch. It's easy enough nowadays.'

'John wouldn't do that,' Fisher said, but his words were like a backdrop in a Hollywood studio, held together by balsawood and coated in cheap paint. 'You're speeding, Kate.'

She slipped into the passing lane, cruised around a silver BMW and pulled hard back into the left lane.

'Straight talk, remember?'

'Straight talk,' he echoed. 'Yes, I did wonder if he was seeing someone else at first. When men do something out of character, there's usually a woman involved. Now, in a strange sort of way, I hope that's what this is.'

'You hope he's having an affair?'

'Compared to the alternative, frankly, yes.'

She eased off the pedal. 'What's the alternative?' she asked.

'I've been thinking about what his boss told you. *Spiritual distress.* I hadn't heard that term before, but it pretty much sums up a long period in John's teen years. For a while there he got … dark.'

She nodded. 'I remember the photos from his deb. It looked like Alice Cooper's wedding.'

'It wasn't just the black clothing and the heavy metal music,' Fisher said. 'He was obsessed with spirit boards and demonology and murder. He started reading horror novels by this mad American – Lovecroft? Something like that. And he was constantly researching a hundred-year-old poet called Aleister Crowley, who ran an occult religion. Pam pushed the Bible on him, which went about as well as you'd expect. That's when she started volunteering at every mass, like she thought she could make up for it.'

'That was a long time ago, Fisher. We all go through phases when we're young and trying to figure out who we are. You might be putting things together that don't really fit.'

'Yeah. I suppose I'm just trying to find *something* to explain all this.'

Kate was troubled by her father-in-law's words, but she was also relieved to see him so emotionally vulnerable when for so long he'd appeared cold and distant. It made him seem three-dimensionally human.

Fisher turned, looked out the window, and didn't talk for the rest of the trip.

The giant steel doors of the ferry opened like the jaws of a leviathan, and Kate drove inside. Ahead of them was a rusted out old campervan with a bumper sticker on the rear window that declared, *We're spending our kids' inheritance.*

The last time Kate had come to Belport was six months earlier, when the weather was so hot you couldn't sit out on the top deck without 50+ sunscreen. People were getting around in board shorts and bikinis, and there was a fifteen-minute wait at the kiosk. The undercarriage of the ferry had been jammed with traffic: cars filled with camping equipment and kayaks tied to roof racks. Now the ferry was practically empty.

Fisher went to the kiosk for coffee while Kate walked out onto the front deck and stood in the icy air. The ferry ride was only half an hour, so soon Belport rose ahead of her like a giant turtle shell spotted with moss. A bank of late-morning fog was rolling in across the water, shrouding parts of the island.

She thought about what Fisher had said, about being prepared for what they might find. If they didn't talk about the monsters in this world, then they wouldn't be ready for them when they jumped out from under the bed. What monsters were waiting for her in Belport?

8

THE WIFE

Lori stood on the front verandah, madly chewing the nail of her pinkie finger, wearing the face of someone who had just made a wrong turn in a bad neighbourhood. Eddie had gone ahead of her to catch the bus, but she was hovering. There was something on her mind.

Abby watched her from the kitchen window, skulking behind the succulent planter box that lived on the windowsill, like a documentarian waiting to see what her subject might do next. Lori, with no idea she was being spied on, took two steps off the verandah. She then turned, marched back to the front door, hesitated, then turned again.

Abby knocked on the glass. Lori flinched.

'Something on your mind?' she called. 'You look like your father on the night you were born.'

'It's nothing,' Lori called back, then started down the steps and into the front yard.

Abby stepped into her sneakers and caught up to her. She was still in her pyjamas, but there was nobody around to judge.

'What's going on, Lori?' Abby asked.

'It's nothing. Honestly.' She looked down at her boots, kicked them against the bottom verandah step. 'I was just going to ask, is everything okay between you and Dad?'

'Everything's fine,' Abby said. 'Why?'

She shrugged. 'I don't know. It's probably nothing. I'm gonna miss my bus.'

'Jesus, Lori, shit or get off the pot.'

She sighed. 'Fine. Dad was up super early again this morning, and I get up super early to pee, and I guess I thought you guys must be fighting or something because when I went to the bathroom door, I heard him …'

'What?'

'I don't want to say.'

'Ew, Lori.'

'God, yuck, no, nothing like that.'

'Then what?' Abby asked.

'Maybe I was just hearing things, but I'm pretty sure he was … crying'.

Ray didn't cry. Lori must have been hearing things, and if she wasn't, then there were a million logical explanations.

The trouble was, right now, as Abby drifted from room to room in her empty home, she couldn't think of one.

There was plenty to be done around the house: laundry to fold, firewood to chop, *The Buck River Murders* to read, a possum to skin and stuff, but the thought of spending the day inside filled Abby with a heavy, mysterious sadness, so instead she decided to head out for another run.

A few minutes into her usual route, her lungs grew hot and raspy, her breathing shallow. If she didn't take it down a notch she'd be hurting for a week, but she couldn't bring herself to stop. When she eased her stride or slowed down to avoid a clump of driftwood, dark thoughts of Ray caught up with her, clapped down around her shoulders like a wet jacket.

First, Ray had told her he was working on Eileen Betchkie's house, which Eileen disputed. Then he was crying in the bathroom. Something was up. Something bad, and Abby hoped to God it had nothing to do with another woman.

She arrived at the seawall, stood beneath the *Fun Prohibited* sign and wanted to retch. She doubled over, gasping for air. She looked out over the water. Fog formed a white wall just beyond the buoys. For a second it felt like the mainland didn't exist. She watched a pelican emerge from it like magic, drift by overhead, dropping a shit as it passed her.

As she stood, she heard voices. There was a set of old stone steps that led up and over the seawall. On the other side was Beech Tree Landing, a series of concrete boat-launching ramps. That's where the voices were coming from. She climbed the steps, peeked over the wall, and froze.

'Holy fucking shit,' she whispered. Her words caught on an arctic breeze and got carried away.

There were five police cruisers in the expansive bitumen car park. Beyond them, parked across two of the extra-long spaces usually used to fit boat trailers, was a large white van emblazoned with the words *Crime Scene Services*. Forensics people, dressed in white coveralls and blue paper caps, scurried around with plastic ziplock bags and evidence boxes. Abby scanned the faces of the police, looking out for Bobbi's, but all she saw were stern, unrecognisable officers.

A police boat cruised in a slow arc around the ramps, bobbing and listing on the water. Two constables stood outside the main entrance to the boat ramps, standing guard. Both wore enormous, formless jackets with reflective strips sewn onto the sleeves. Neither were looking in her direction, but she kept her head down anyway, kneeling on the top step of the wall. It felt as though someone had built a movie set on her island.

She watched a woman step down from the Crime Scene Services trailer, carrying a camera with a long lens and heavy-duty flash attached. She met a cluster of officers at the pier entrance.

At the end of the pier stood the old ferry terminal, a dilapidated weatherboard structure that had been abandoned and condemned a decade earlier when a state-of-the-art terminal was built around the corner in Elk Harbour. The waves and salty air had stained the walls of the building pale green, and its roof was Jackson Pollocked with bird shit.

The woman, along with the other officers, walked out to the terminal and disappeared inside.

This must have been why Bobbi was called here. *Nothing good.* Abby stared hard at the scene, actively storing each detail in her mind so she might compare notes with her later. There was a black museum in the dark stillness behind Abby's eyes – and one behind most people's eyes, she guessed – whose shelves were lined with Ann Rule and John Berendt, and whose walls were decorated with crime scene photos and portraits of serial killers.

'—shouldn't be here,' a stern voice said, cutting through her thoughts. Abby had been so engrossed that she hadn't noticed a police constable approach. He had one hand on his hip, the other on his holstered firearm. 'Did you hear what I said?'

'I …'

'You need to leave,' he said.

'What happened here?' she asked.

The constable's shaggy black eyebrows lifted into arches.

'Nothing good,' he said.

He stood his ground and glared at her. Abby nodded, climbed back down the stone steps and onto the beach, leaving the crime scene behind her. She turned and jogged inland. She forgot all about what Lori had told her, and left feeling quietly thrilled.

When she made it back to the top of Harvill Hill Road, she turned and looked over the water. The island ferry was coming in.

9

THE WIDOW

The Island Ferry docked at Elk Harbour in Belport at twenty-five minutes after midday. The doors opened, lowering into a ramp, and spat the Lexus out like a dislodged chunk of meat. Kate and Fisher followed the road up and over the promenade, towards the town proper.

'It's been a long time since I've been back here,' Fisher said, watching swatches of coastal woodland pass by the window. 'I don't know why anyone would live out here all year round. The isolation would drive me crazy.'

'I've thought about it before,' Kate admitted. 'Every summer, the last weekend of our holiday, it's all I can think about, actually. More for Mia than anything else. Kids grow up too fast nowadays. I always thought a childhood on the island would be simple, and humble, and ...'

'What?'

'I was going to say, *safe*.'

'Mm,' he said. 'I used to think that too.'

They reached Bay Street, which was usually packed with tourists. Today, like the rest of Belport, it was grey.

Most of the shops and restaurants they passed were shut until December: Island Gifts, where last year Mia bought a stuffed seal and about three dozen postcards she never sent; Pond & Beyond Seafood, who cooked a mean grilled blue grenadier and always threw in extra onion rings; and Belport Bike and Kayak Hire.

The hardware store, laundromat and Buy & Bye were still open, but there was little movement inside. Kate's car felt like the only thing in motion.

'Do you need to stop for anything first?' Kate asked.

'No,' Fisher said. 'Let's just get there.'

'Are you alright?'

He seemed surprised by the question. It probably wasn't something he was asked often. 'I think so. You?'

'I think so. For now. I keep wondering how to explain all this to Mia. Best case scenario, we get to the house and find John camped out there, working through some stuff. What do I tell her? *Daddy needed a holiday?* How much am I supposed to protect her from?'

'John was about her age when my mother passed away. He asked all sorts of strange questions. Would grandma get hungry underground? Would they poke holes in the top of the coffin so she could breathe? Stuff like that.

It's quite far from the same thing, but I think the most important thing is just to listen.'

At the top of Bay Street, she took a left onto Ewing Street, then a right onto Double Bluff Road, which took her higher on the island. She came to a T-junction, then turned left onto Neef Street. She'd driven down this road countless times but couldn't remember ever doing it without John or Mia. Driving along this street and looking at the neighbouring houses used to feel like coming home. Now it felt eerie and wrong. The slate-grey, cube-shaped mansion that she used to think was elegantly modern today looked like an invading alien spaceship. The sixteen-bedroom residence that once reminded her of Downton Abbey now looked haunted.

Finally, they arrived at the holiday house. It was a California-style beach house, set back from the road behind a tall wooden fence. It didn't seem real; it looked like a replica of what had been there the previous summer. It might have been that she wasn't used to seeing it in the off-season – the lawn was a little overgrown and the landscape gloomy – or it might now be coloured by all the dark things that had happened over the past few days.

Has the house changed, she wondered, *or have I?*

She pulled through the front gates and parked at the top of the driveway, behind a stand of white birch trees that looked much healthier than they had during their last hot summer. The driveway was empty, and she couldn't see any lights on in the house. When she killed the engine, a hush fell over the world: no sound of distant traffic, no construction.

There was a chill in the air. Kate had packed two winter parkas but she didn't have time to fetch her suitcase. She wanted to get inside. She broke away from Fisher and hurried through the cold, then paused at the front door. She had brought the house key, but as far as she remembered it was the only one they kept in Caulfield. On a hunch, she reached beneath the front steps and found the plastic hide-a-key rock they kept for emergencies and visiting relatives. The rusty gold key was inside.

She unlocked the front door, disarmed the alarm, and slipped inside. She hovered on the threshold a moment and performed a quick scan of the entrance. It took a few seconds for her eyes to adjust to the low light. All the blinds in the house were drawn, just as they'd left it on their last day of summer. She looked down. A business card had been flicked beneath the door – *Sanctuary Security: we'll keep you safe!*

'John,' she called.

There was no answer, so she went inside. Fisher followed her into the hall, then went upstairs to check the bedrooms.

'John,' he called. 'Mate, are you here?'

Kate went into the kitchen and, almost on instinct, checked the fridge. It was a hulking old thing, busy with magnets, and John had promised to replace it as soon as it gave up and died, but so far it had kept on trucking. Inside were some bottles of water, a few tubs of hummus and a litre of milk. She checked the use-by date: three days left. Beside the fridge, inside the microwave, was a tub of untouched mac'n'cheese.

There was a brown shopping bag on the counter. Printed across one side were two interlocking Bs. Inside, she found Valerian capsules, chamomile tea, three different types of antihistamines, a litre bottle of Wild Turkey, water crackers, a five-pack of Mi Goreng instant noodles and a box of Frosties cereal.

There was a yellow Post-it Note stuck to the counter by the phone. On it was written, *S. Hallston 2pm*. She had no idea who S Hallston was and no idea what to make of the note, but the handwriting was undoubtedly John's. There it was, irrefutable proof that John had been here. This confirmation made her want to throw up and put her fist through a wall, but not necessarily in that order.

She tiptoed through the downstairs hallway next, glancing through each door she passed, checking the rooms for any sign of a disturbance. Laundry, bathroom, toilet, guestroom. Each door had been slung wide open.

She scanned the living room but there was no sign of him. She turned to leave, then hesitated, looking back into the room. Something was different, but she couldn't pick it right away. A plasma screen and the spines of dozens of old DVDs and Blu-rays looked back at her from the large entertainment unit against one wall, opposite the fireplace. The three-piece sofa set was just as she remembered, as was the furry blue rug that Mia liked to stretch out on to watch TV. But something was different. She was sure of it.

Then, it struck her. The far right corner of the living room had always been marked with dozens of people's names and heights. They had inherited the wall with the house, and all the names along with it. It wasn't just John, but John's cousins and friends. As soon as Mia was old enough, John had marked her height each summer, and each summer Mia had marvelled at how much she'd grown. Two years ago, Mia had insisted Kate finally join the wall, and she had done so, proudly. But now, all the names and heights were gone. The wall was eggshell white, just like the rest of the room. It was as if she'd wandered into a parallel universe where everything was identical except for this one small, seemingly trivial detail.

Kate dabbed her finger on the new paintjob: it was still slightly damp.

'What have you been doing out here, John?' she whispered.

She left the room quickly, feeling spooked, and

climbed the stairs to check the master bedroom. They had stripped the bed at the end of their last holiday, but it had since been roughly made. There was an unnatural yellow tint to the room; dull afternoon sunlight fell in through the curtains. It made the scene feel like a memory she wanted to walk into. If this were a movie, a flashback might have shown her and John lying in bed, spooning, making love or reading the Sunday papers.

On the other side of the bed, below the window, she found John's suitcase. She knelt, unzipped it. All the clothing she had thought he packed for London was there, washed and neatly folded. Trousers, shirts, socks, underwear and toiletries case. There was a black leather notebook wedged in a transparent compartment in the lid of the case. She took it out and leafed through the pages.

It was full of drawings. Kate immediately recognised John's untrained, slightly childish drawing style: lots of uneven narrow lines, hatched shading and muddled perspectives. But up until that point she'd only ever seen his doodles in the margins of the Sunday newspaper, little houses and transparent cubes. She had never seen him draw anything like this.

He'd used coloured pencils – no doubt taken from Mia's room – and all of them dark shades: blacks, heavy browns and deep reds. There were fifteen sketches in total, each showing the same scene: a dark, featureless room and a man with his face to the corner. Page by page, as in a flip-art book, the figure grew in detail, from a shadow to a man with short hair, tennis sneakers and an oversized black jacket. On the final four pages, a long, jagged crack formed on the man's face. Small brown shapes were spilling out from inside.

'Moths,' she whispered, even though she wanted to scream. Then, from someplace deep in her mind, Holly Cutter said, *Spiritual distress.*

As Kate closed the notebook and slipped it into her pocket, she felt the touch of a finger rest lightly on top of her head. Startled, she gasped and spun around. When she saw that nobody was there, she ran her hands through her hair. A chunk of dust came loose. It must have fallen from above.

It drew her attention to the ceiling. There was a flat, rectangular manhole cover there that gave into a cavernous storage cavity in the roof. Mia called it *the door to the roof*, and when she was younger, believed the cavity was home to a hideous, child-eating gremlin. If the door was open, then the gremlin would slink down into the house at night and scramble down the hallway and into Mia's bed.

In the years of checking the ceiling door, it had only ever been open once – John had left it ajar after going up there to look for his old Sonic Youth CDs – until today. There was a pencil-thin space between the cover and the lip of the opening. There was no reason for John to go up there, but then again, there was also no reason for him to be in Belport.

Kate remembered an article she'd read a few weeks earlier on Facebook. It was a news report about a man who lived alone in an apartment in Kyoto, Japan. When the man noticed food disappearing from the kitchen, he installed security cameras in every room of the apartment. When he sat down to watch the footage, it showed a woman creeping out of his hallway closet in the dead of night, eating food from the kitchen and using the bathroom. After he called the police, the woman was arrested. She claimed to have been living there for months.

'Kate? Kate!' Fisher called from across the hall. 'Come here!'

She followed his voice into Mia's room, which was painted a bright blue. Fisher was standing in the corner, looking at something that was obscured from Kate's view by a towering wardrobe. On top of the wardrobe was a large plastic tub full of Mia's summer toys, and plastered on its big double doors were posters of yoga cats.

'What is it?' she asked.

'Does this look familiar?' Fisher asked.

She crossed the room, then stood, shocked. A single bed had been dragged towards the wall and dressed with crisp new white sheets. One area of the wall had been covered with soft green wallpaper. There was a bar fridge

– God knew where from – and on it stood a menu for room service. On the menu was printed, *High Holborn, London*. She was looking at a set.

'My God,' she said. 'It looks like a hotel room.'

'I think that's the point. Is this where he Skyped you and Mia from?'

She tried to answer but the words caught in her throat. She had started to come to terms with the fact John lied to her about his trip to London, but seeing their daughter's room set up like a TV set made the lie something more sinister. This was premeditated. Deliberate. Antagonistic. Like an animal sensing a predator, she had the sudden urge to run. In that moment, she wanted to sell the house and never go back. The buyer could keep the furniture, kitchenware, linen, swimsuits, toys and the fucking High Holborn hotel room – or they could burn it all.

'I'm not sure what scares me most,' she said. 'The fact John snuck off to this place, or the fact he's left in such a hurry. There are unpacked groceries in the kitchen and food in the microwave. Something bad has happened, Fisher.'

Fisher's phone rang. He whipped it out gunslinger-fast and slapped it against his ear.

'Yes, hello, this is Fisher Keddie … Hello?'

'Who is it?' Kate asked.

He strained to listen, then shook his head. 'I don't know. The reception's terrible in here.'

'It's better on the back deck.'

He nodded, then hurried out of the room. Kate moved to follow him, but paused at the small window that looked out over the front yard. There was a tall old beech tree just outside the glass that Mia had inexplicably named Simon. Usually all you could see was its canopy, but its leaves had dropped for winter, and now Kate could see through its skeletal branches all the way down the street.

There was a mud-splattered work truck parked near the corner of Milt Street. *Maintenance* was printed down one side. She couldn't make out the driver, but she had the feeling they were watching the house. Fisher was pacing loudly in the hallway, speaking in urgent tones. Kate glanced in his direction. When she turned back to the window, the work truck pulled off the shoulder, did a U-turn and disappeared over the crest of a hill.

When Fisher came back into the room, he had turned pale.

'What is it?' Kate asked.

'That was the Belport Police.'

'... Yes?'

'They ...'

'What is it, Fisher?'

'They want us to meet them at Belport Medical right away,' he said, wrestling against each word as it left his mouth.

'The hospital?' Kate cried. 'Why? Is it John? Is he hurt?'

Fisher looked down at his hands.

'Dammit, Fisher,' Kate said. 'What's happened?'

10

THE WIFE

'They found a dead body,' Henry Biller blurted, his tone wild and giddy. It was Biller's night off, but he had popped in on his way home from the Belly for some frozen pizza and gossip. He had strutted in through the big double doors with what Lori would call a shit-eating grin, his cheeks ruddy from the cold and one too many beers. He had come with a dozen theories about the increased police presence on the island, and he wasn't the only one.

It was another cold and windy night, and Abby had expected a dead shift, but business had been unusually busy. There had been a steady stream of local foot traffic through her check-out, and everyone wanted to talk about one thing: what had happened at Beech Tree Landing?

Caddy Larson, who worked in the kiosk on the island ferry, told Abby that the morning run had been practically full of cops. She'd had to put an extra tray of egg-and-bacon pies in the oven just to accommodate them. According to Paul and Liz Ryan, who picked up a jumbo-sized tub of ice-cream and a bottle of Jim Beam, police were going door to door and asking if anyone had seen or heard any suspicious activity. Chris De Luca, who lived in a caravan out by the lighthouse, swore he'd heard the word *floater* on his police scanner.

Abby had told each of them what she'd seen at Beech Tree Landing and had drawn a twisted sort of satisfaction from the respect her story commanded. Theories ranged from a drug lab being on the island to some sort of mafia-related crime or a serial killer on the run from the law, but the general consensus was—

'The cops found a body,' Biller said again, clapping his hands together.

'That's the rumour,' Abby said.

'It's no rumour.' He came over, leaned on her checkout, and lowered his voice to a whisper, as if that made the news more official. 'I'm telling you, they found a body on the island. Everyone at the pub is talking about it.'

'Everyone in *Belport* is talking about it,' Abby said. 'What have you heard and who did you hear it from?'

'A couple of coppers came to see me today,' Biller said, grinning.

'Came to see you? Today? In the store?'

'Mm hm. Out-of-towners too. I think they shipped a bunch of cops over from the mainland to help widen the investigation. One of them looked like a foetus with a badge. The other one thought he was Columbo. They asked me if I'd noticed any strangers coming into the store lately, anyone with a suspicious demeanour.'

'What did you tell them?'

'I asked them if they could be any more specific,' he said. 'So, they showed me a photo of a man they were, quote, *seeking information about*. Pulled from some guy's driver's licence by the look of it.'

'Did you recognise him?'

Biller hiked up his dusty jeans and stood with his hands on his hips. 'He was in here a few days ago.'

'What? When? Did you serve him?'

Biller nodded, smugly. 'There was nothing all that strange about him from what I could see. Looked pretty straight, and it wasn't like he was paranoid and checking if he was being followed or anything. If he was caught up in something dodgy he certainly didn't act like it, and that's what I told the cops.'

'That's so creepy, that he was in here,' Abby said. 'What do you think happened?'

'This many cops on the island, it has to be murder, right? So my guess is the guy in the photo is either dead, or the one who did the killing.' He looked at her with small, sinister eyes. 'What have you heard?'

She filled him in on what Caddy Larson had told her, and Paul and Liz Ryan, and Chris De Luca's police scanner. Then she told him about the crime scene at the boat ramps, saving the best for last. Biller listened to all of it with a wild, buzzing expression, peppering the conversation with the occasional nod, *wow* or *Jee-zus!*

'You actually saw the crime scene?' Biller asked.

'Uh huh,' Abby said. 'That whole area was crawling with police. They even had a boat on the water, and there were forensics people going in and out of the old ferry terminal.'

'The ferry terminal,' he echoed. 'Well that raises a whole list of new questions.'

'How do you mean?'

'Well, you know what they say about that place, right? What goes on in there?'

'No, what?'

The wrinkles on his forehead deepened. Abby had seen this look a number of times, on the faces of many of Belport's lifers. Biller was trying to determine her security clearance.

'Maybe I shouldn't say,' he said.

Abby had lived on the island for nearly eighteen years, and for all intents and purposes she was a bona fide *local*. But she wasn't a lifer. She wasn't born up the road at Belport Medical. All communities had layers of secrecy, she guessed: hidden truths and secret doors. Abby's years on the island had earned her access to a great many of those secret doors, but there were apparently still a few that remained locked.

'Come on, Biller,' Abby said. 'What about the ferry terminal?'

'Well, some people say the terminal is a, you know, a beat.'

'A *beat*?'

'A spot where gay men meet up for no-strings sex. So what I'm thinking is, maybe this was a hate crime or a blackmail attempt gone wrong or, I don't know, maybe it was a lover's quarrel.'

'I don't get it,' she said. 'Why would anyone want to have sex in that cruddy old building, gay or otherwise?'

Biller shook his head. 'Oh, Abby. Sweet, naive Abby.'

'Well whatever this turns out to be, it's the biggest thing to happen since Big Jenny beached herself.'

Big Jenny was the name locals gave a fifteen-metre southern right whale that beached itself on Belport Island back in '93. The corpse was too big to move, so the council had to carve it up and cart it away, one truck-load at a time.

'May she rest in peace,' Abby added.

'I think you mean *rest in pieces*, love,' Biller said with a wink.

Abby looked out through the glass of the shopfront. Full dark had fallen over Belport.

'I suppose it was only a matter of time,' Biller said.

'A matter of time?'

'Before the real world reached across the water and took hold of us.'

'A murder on the island,' Abby said. 'It's tragic, but also sort of …'

'Exciting?' Biller offered.

'Does thinking that make me a terrible person?'

'Love, thinking that makes you human.'

The end of her shift came around surprisingly fast. After locking up, Abby tallied the receipts and counted the night's takings, which, Biller would be happy, took a little longer than it had lately. She dropped the cash into a chute down to the safe, then ran her hands over the bank of light switches outside the staffroom door. The supermarket went dark.

Abby walked purposefully towards her rusty little Volvo, bracing herself against the chill. She scanned the shadows while she walked, half expecting the Belport Killer to lurch out at her from the darkness. Touching the pointy end of the car key in her pocket, she felt her senses becoming prickly and alert.

The quiet of wintertime in Belport had been a shock when she first moved here, but it didn't take long for Abby to accept it. In fact, after the madness of summer, she had come to crave that peace. But there were times – being startled awake by a creak on the roof, the snap of a twig in the woods, her brief walk between the supermarket and her car when the island was convinced there was a killer on the loose – when it still all-out rattled her.

Safely in her car, she was about to start the engine when a pair of car headlights flashed once in her rear-view mirror. She swivelled in her seat to look through the rear windshield and spotted the silhouette of a Jeep Cherokee parked across the street, in the shadow of the Uniting Church.

Abby cracked a window, craned her neck, and called out, 'Bobbi?'

'Yeah,' a familiar voice called back. 'It's me.'

When Abby hopped in beside Bobbi, the interior light flicked on, casting Bobbi in an unhealthy yellow light. She looked terrible. There were sagging dark pockets beneath her eyes and her ponytail had fallen loose, releasing a tangle of wild hair down one side of her face. There was an open bottle of tequila in her hands, the cheap brand with the little red sombrero-shaped lid. She was still wearing her unflattering pastel-blue police shirt, an empty holster at her hip.

'Shut the door,' she said.

Abby did as she was told. 'What's wrong? Has something happened? Is it Maggie? The baby?'

The car light faded out and Abby watched Bobbi's features shifting as she took a swig from the bottle, winced, then made a fist against the dashboard.

'Maggie and the baby are fine. They're great, actually,

which is why I can't take this shit home to them, which is why I'm here.'

'What's going on, Bobbi?' Abby asked. 'I've been waiting to hear from you since yesterday.'

Bobbi took another drink, and asked, 'What have you heard about what's going on in town?'

'Only rumours so far. Biller thinks you guys found a body.'

Bobbi gazed down Bay Street and grimaced. Her eyes crept slowly back to the bottle, and she drank. 'Biller's right.'

'He is?' A sinister but not altogether unpleasant chill ran up her spine.

'At the police academy, as part of your training, they show you a load of graphic photos,' Bobbi said. 'Gunshot victims, car crashes, suicides, you name it. It's all shades of fucked up, but it makes sense. It's designed to harden you up. They don't want you puking your guts up every time you arrive at a crime scene. But the difference between the photos and what I saw today is like the difference between seeing a bear in the zoo and one in the wild.'

Abby's heart began to thump. She felt woken up. She felt alive.

'You saw the body?' Abby asked.

Bobbi took a long drink, which was as good as a yes. Tears welled in her eyes. She dabbed at them with the sleeves of her police uniform. Abby's instinct told her to reach across the car and give her best friend a hug, but Bobbi hated hugs, even from Maggie. So instead, Abby tucked a loose strand of hair behind Bobbi's ear.

'Do you know who it was?' Abby asked. 'Biller seemed to think he wasn't a local.'

'He's a summer resident. He has a holiday place on the island, but God knows what he was doing here at this time of year.'

'Thank God,' Abby said.

'Thank God? *Thank* God? What exactly are you thanking God for?'

'I'm sorry, I didn't mean that. I just thought, thank God he wasn't a local. Obviously, it's tragic and horrible and fucked up either way, but it's bad enough there's been a murder on the island. If the victim was someone we knew …'

Bobbi traced the mouth of the bottle with her finger, then touched it to her lips.

'Can I see his picture?' Abby asked.

Bobbi turned with narrow, suspicious eyes. Abby had seen that look a handful of times. It usually came directly after she told someone about her taxidermy.

'A couple of cops came to see Biller today,' Abby said quickly. 'They showed him a photo of the guy. If Biller served him, there's a good chance I did too.'

It wasn't the whole truth, and if Bobbi was a halfway decent police officer – and Abby guessed she was – then she knew too. Abby wanted to see his face for one reason and one reason only: curiosity. The same curiosity that helped insert a scalpel blade into the belly of a dead animal.

Bobbi took one last swig of tequila, then screwed the little sombrero-shaped lid onto the bottle. She flicked on the light, reached into her breast pocket and handed a photo to Abby.

It showed a clean-shaven, good-looking man staring into the camera. He wasn't smiling, but there was humour in his face. The photo was cropped at the neck, but the collar of a charcoal-coloured business shirt was visible. It made him look corporate. A banker or a lawyer, maybe.

'Do you recognise him?' Bobbi asked.

'No,' she said, feeling disappointed. 'What do you think happened to him? Do the police have a theory?'

'It's too early to tell, but you know Belport. There aren't too many secrets here, and the ones there are never stay that way for long. Someone knows something.'

She took the photo back. 'I should get back. Maggie will be getting worried.'

'Are you okay to drive?' Abby asked.

Bobbi nodded and whispered, 'Thank you for letting me grief vomit all over you.'

Abby gave her hand a squeeze. 'That's what friends are for.'

11

THE WIDOW

The car park at Belport Medical Centre was vast and empty, aside from a lone police cruiser parked near the entrance. Kate parked and looked over at Fisher. He stared over at an ambulance pulled up outside the emergency entrance. There were two paramedics leaning against it, sharing a cigarette.

'Are you ready?' she asked.

'Straight talk?'

'Yes.'

'I'm not sure I can do this, Kate.'

'You don't have to, Fisher,' she said. 'They only need one of us.'

'I couldn't do that to you.'

'Fisher, it's fine. Stay here.'

'The crazy thing is, if Pam were here, she'd be able to do it,' he said, his voice soft. 'I know you probably think she's crazy, and I guess she is sort of crazy, but that woman's faith is strong enough to get her through anything. It would be strong enough to get her out of this car; strong enough to get her inside.' He turned to her and asked, 'Are you sure?'

Kate nodded, closed the car door and walked towards the hospital. A heavy-set, plain-clothes detective was waiting for her in the reception area. She was slumped in a plastic chair, deep in thought, picking at her nails. She stood when she saw Kate approach.

'Mrs Keddie, hello, I'm Detective Barbara Eckman. I spoke to your father-in-law on the phone.' They shook hands.

'Pleasure to meet you,' Kate told them, even though it seemed an absurd thing to say. She smiled on reflex, then, remembering where she was, frowned.

Eckman cocked her head at a curious angle and stared briefly into the middle distance, as if trying to remember something she'd rehearsed. Then she said softly, 'Are you ready?'

Was she? Her heart was pounding. Her body was trembling and cold. She sensed a primal darkness standing over them, following her like a shadow, and when she went downstairs and saw that body, it would clap around her shoulders, drag her down and stay with her forever.

'Yes,' she said. 'I'm ready.'

Eckman led her to a bank of elevators and pressed the button. Stepping through the doors, Kate felt claustrophobic and tight. She pictured a fat cow being led down a pathway flanked by steel fencing, unaware of what lay ahead in the slaughterhouse.

'When was the last time you spoke with your husband?' Eckman asked. Her tone was much more serious than the duty sergeant's had been back in Melbourne. He had been talking to a paranoid woman with an overactive imagination. Eckman was talking to her as if she was a widow, even though she hoped desperately that she wasn't. She clung to the dream Pam had described – John's empty throne in the kingdom of heaven – and hoped it really was prophetic.

'Two days before he was meant to arrive home,' Kate said.

'Do you have any idea why he might have come to the island?'

'No,' she said. 'I didn't even know he was here until the alarm company notified me. He told me he was in—'

'London, yes,' Eckman finished her sentence. 'I read the missing person report you filed.'

She caught something like an accusation in the woman's tone, and wondered dimly if her clammy, nervous small-town cop routine might be an act. After all, wasn't the spouse usually the prime suspect? If

Eckman were gauging her responses, what did she think of them? Kate didn't know how someone was supposed to act in this situation. Maybe she should have been sobbing or screaming or inconsolable.

They reached the basement and walked down a short corridor.

'This is it,' Eckman said. She paused outside a door and turned to Kate. 'Mrs Keddie, if you need more time …'

'No, thank you. I'm fine.'

Eckman considered her a moment, then opened the door and led her into a small viewing room. It didn't smell like formaldehyde as Kate had expected. It smelled like artificial pine and cherry. The ceiling was low. If John were here, he'd have to hunch, Kate thought. Then the darkness that had followed her whispered: *Ah, but you see, John* is *here, just on the other side of that glass.*

She looked at a window that ran the full length of one wall, which presumably gave a view into the room where the body was kept. For now, the other room was concealed by a crumpled, lilac-coloured curtain. Kate closed her eyes and for one final time allowed herself to picture John on the front deck of the house, beer in hand, patting the place next to him.

Eckman crossed the room and drew the curtain from left to right, revealing a large white room on the other side of the glass – something between an operating theatre and an industrial freezer. A strip of fluorescent lights buzzed above a bank of heavy steel mortuary drawers. In the middle of the room was a steel gurney. Beneath it, against the stark tiled floor, was a drainage hole. On top of the gurney lay a body, wrapped head to toe in a plastic sheet. The sheet was pink.

Why pink? Kate wondered, as if it mattered.

An unusually tall medical technician was standing next to the body. He wore powdery pink latex gloves and a matching paper cap. It was cold enough to see the man's breath. He reached across the body and folded the sheet down twice, first to the neck, then the pelvis.

Kate had half expected the body to look as though it was sleeping. It didn't. It just looked dead. Upon seeing it, a wave of heat swept over her. The skin was ghostly, wrinkled and waterlogged. The eyes were closed, but the mouth was open. There was a long narrow slit across the neck – a second mouth, lips lightly parted.

She wondered if fish might have eaten some of John while he was in the water, mostly because she couldn't stop herself wondering. She had heard that could happen. It made her think about a trip the family took to Bali years ago. John had dangled his feet inside a tank of Garra rufa fish. They swarmed to him, and he giggled as they chewed on his dead skin, tickling his feet.

'I want to go in there,' she said.

'I'm afraid that's not possible,' Eckman told her.

'This'll sound a bit morbid, but technically the body is still considered police evidence and we need to avoid any chance of contamination.'

'It doesn't sound morbid. It sounds ridiculous.'

'I'm sorry.'

'Who did this?'

'We're looking into it, Mrs Keddie. We have several leads at various stages of development.'

'Who did this to him?' She wasn't asking Eckman now, but the universe, which suddenly seemed like some vicious schoolyard bully, throwing rocks at passing cars without thought of consequences.

'Is it him?' Eckman asked. 'Is it your husband?'

The word formed in her mouth, round and full and total, but she couldn't manage to get it out.

'Mrs Keddie?'

'… Yes.'

'I'm very sorry,' Eckman said. 'But for it to count as a formal identification you'll need to state the deceased's name.'

'I can't … I …'

It hit her harder than she had anticipated. She had been holding out hope. Actual hope. This might have been a mistake, a misidentification, a misunderstanding, but it was none of those things. This was real. This was happening.

'Do you need a moment?' Eckman asked.

Her knees stiffened under her and for a moment

she saw herself pitching forward, cracking her skull on the glass. Then she felt a hand take hers. For a startled, intimate moment, she thought it was Eckman. But when she turned, she saw Fisher standing beside her, staring through the glass.

'His name is John Morgan Keddie,' Fisher said. 'That's him. That's my son.'

They didn't talk on the way to the motel. Their home for the night would be the Blue Whale Motor Inn. Eckman told them they wouldn't be able to stay at their holiday house for a few days because it was being searched, scanned and dusted. When Fisher called the motel to check if they had any vacancies, the man on the other end of the line said, 'Mate, this time of year all we've got is vacancies.'

It wasn't hard to see why. The motel was marked by a giant fibreglass whale on the front lawn. It wasn't a blue, as you'd expect, but an orca, positioned in a permanent breach, speckled with a decade's worth of bird shit. It must have been ugly when it was first erected, but now, after weathering years of wild storms, baking heat and salty air, it had become an eyesore. The black and white paint had chipped and flaked away, revealing a faded red underbelly that looked like old blood. One eye was rotting, the other completely gone.

Kate felt a twang of guilt staying there without Mia.

Her daughter was obsessed with the fibreglass whale and was convinced that staying in one of the rooms would be like sleeping under water. The walls would be made of glass, behind which fish and eels would swim. John had explained to her that it was just an ordinary motel, likely full of stale sheets, bad reception and mysterious stains on the mattresses. The most she could hope for would be an alarm clock shaped like a seashell or an aquatic-themed shower curtain. Mia held out hope.

It hurt to think about Mia. She couldn't even think about having *that* conversation with her daughter, about the avalanche it would cause. Pam probably would have told her. Fisher had called his wife from the hospital car park, Kate watching him from inside the Lexus as light rain covered up the windows. He had climbed back into the car and said, 'It's done.'

She could almost hear Pam saying: *Your daddy is up in heaven now, with Jesus and Mary and Charlie* (Charlie was Mia's pet rabbit, who met a sudden end when he hopped through their front gate and into heavy morning traffic). Maybe it was better for Mia to hear it that way. Pam would certainly be gentler with her. Still, as Kate thought about it, John's words crept in.

'If we don't talk about the monsters in this world ...' she said aloud.

'What's that, love?' Fisher asked.

'Nothing.'

When they reached the motel, Kate parked in the shadow of the orca. They collected their keys from reception and, without a word, separated. There were no fish swimming inside the walls of her room, Kate could now confirm. The walls were made of cheap plasterboard, the bed was too soft, and the air smelled damp. Still, it was a warm place away from the thumping wind coming off the ocean.

She put the *DO NOT DISTURB* sign on the door, sat down on the end of the bed and tried to cry. She had been carrying around a live emotional hand grenade all day, and if she didn't pull the pin out and toss it soon, it might just go off in her hands. Nothing came out. She might have been in shock, or she might have been broken.

Her phone rang a couple of minutes later. Mia was calling. Feeling like the world's worst mother, Kate didn't pick up.

12

THE WIFE

'Just because the victim was from out of town, doesn't mean that the killer is,' Lori declared loudly. She was uncharacteristically chipper, waving her fork at Abby as if it was a magic wand.

For better or worse – usually worse – the Gilpins were a sit-down-for-dinner type of family. Abby would have been happy eating all her meals in front of the TV. That's how she spent her childhood and she turned out okay. But *family time* was important to Ray. He envisioned a half-hour each night where those closest to him passed the salt around the table like a conch shell, talking about their hopes and dreams and fears. It rarely worked out that way. When the kids were small, dinner had often stretched to an hour as Ray got caught up telling a story while Abby fetched everyone an extra scoop of neapolitan. But when Eddie and Lori hit puberty, *family time* became *dinner with strangers*.

Nowadays, the way it usually worked was that Abby and Ray would make stilted conversation, painfully drawing information out of their children. It was like taking water from a well with a bendy-straw. Eddie moved food around on his plate. Lori cast brooding gazes across the table and Abby speed-ate her way to the finish.

Tonight was different. The body had Lori talking. She was perched forward on her chair, commanding the attention of the room.

'The killer could be someone we know,' she said. 'This might not even be their first victim. They might do this all the time. They might have lured hundreds of people to the island then fed their bodies to the sharks in Elk Harbour, but this time the cops beat the sharks to the body, and—'

'Take a breath, honey,' Abby said.

'All I'm saying is, that makes a lot of sense in my mind,' Lori said. 'What do you think, Dad?'

Ray sat across from her, furiously covering his meal with salt. It was Abby's turn to cook and a chef she was not. She'd put some packet fettuccine in carbonara sauce on the stove and scooped whatever hadn't stuck to the pot into four bowls. Each was a messy and unappetising tangle of limp, creamy noodles.

'I think there has to be something lighter to discuss at the dinner table,' he said, and shifted gears. 'How was school today, Eddie?'

Eddie was deep in thought, staring vaguely into the mouth of a Coca-Cola can, hood pulled up so high and tight that his peripheral vision must have been cut off. He didn't reply to his father.

'Earth to Eddie,' Ray said, clicking his fingers.

Eddie flinched, looked up blinking and muttered, 'Huh?'

Lori made a show of rolling her eyes. 'One of Mum's true crime books is happening right here on the island and my brother is sleeping through it.' She plugged her mouth with a forkful of pasta, swallowed hard to get it down, then said, 'You know who the killer could be? Denny Chow. You know him, Eddie, he's in your year at school.'

'Oh yeah that guy's weird,' Eddie said. 'He's schizoid or something. He came to class last week with a big stain on his butt. It looked like he'd shat himself and was just walking around with it in his pants.'

'Well that rules Denny Chow out, then,' Abby said. 'Whenever they interview the neighbour of a serial killer they always say, *He seemed like such a normal guy.* It's never: *Yeah, I knew he was a deranged killer because he had shit in his pants.*'

Lori laughed. It sounded unfamiliar, like an exotic bird call. Abby hadn't heard it in far too long.

'I'm serious,' Abby said. 'Whoever did this will *seem* normal.'

'I guess that rules you out,' Lori said.

'Ditto.'

'Maybe it has something to do with the Melbourne mafia,' Lori said. 'The victim might have owed them a gambling debt and when he wouldn't pay it off, they, you know, made him sleep with the fishes.'

Abby rose to fetch herself a beer. Her legs spasmed with pain as she pulled herself upright. She'd overdone it on her run. On her way to the fridge, she turned to Ray. 'Biller told me something sort of weird about the ferry terminal out near where the body was found. He said it was a gay beat. Have you heard about that?'

'That was the rumour when I a kid' he said with a shrug. 'But people also said there's a crocodile in Blue Lake, a drug ring operating out of the lighthouse, and a family of dwarves with giant heads that live in tunnels under the saltmarsh and come out at night to eat children.'

'The Melonheads,' Lori said, nodding. 'I've heard that one too.'

'My point is, around here, rumours are like holey buckets. They don't hold water.'

'I don't know,' Abby said. 'I've been thinking about all this gay beat stuff. If you have something to hide you have something to protect, and if you have something to protect, you have something to kill for.'

'A person died,' Ray snapped.

There was a subtle shift in energy in the room; suddenly there seemed to be a little less air. Abby, Eddie and Lori all turned to Ray in unison, like schoolchildren who'd just been caught smoking. He looked at each one of them in turn but held Abby's gaze the longest.

'A person died on our island,' he said, slowly. 'That isn't fun or exciting or silly. It's tragic and sad and scary. We should be showing some respect. Feel free to step in at any time, Ab.'

Abby felt a twang of resentment, shook it off, then did her best impression of a functional adult parent. 'Your dad's right.'

'Are you serious?' Lori said. 'You get off on all this stuff, Mum. Have you looked at our bookshelf lately? It's full of serial killers and mass murders and child kidnappings and—'

'That's different,' Abby said.

'How?'

She glanced across the table at Ray. 'Because those things didn't happen in Belport.'

'Yeah but they happened somewhere. Your argument makes no sense.'

'That's because I'm an adult. We don't have to make sense. So change the subject and eat your pasta.'

Lori looked at her bowl. 'Oh, so that's what this is.'

After dinner, the family dispersed. Eddie took care of the dishes, Lori disappeared into her bedroom to pretend to finish her homework, and Ray went upstairs to take a shower. Abby switched from beer to red wine and took a glass with her out into the garage.

She turned on the light and switched on the old three-bar heater she kept beneath her workbench. It glowed to life, filling the room with the smell of burning dust.

Abby pulled a knitted throw rug over her shoulders, set her wineglass down on the bench and swung open the bar fridge. Inside, wrapped in a plastic shopping bag with the Buy & Bye's double-B logo printed on the front, was the possum Susi Lenten had found dead beneath the powerlines outside her house.

Abby looked at the shape beneath the shopping bag for a moment. She had never worked on anything so large before. Critters like birds, mice and rats were harder to taxidermy than larger mammals because everything was smaller – at least that's what it said in *The Big Book of Taxidermy* she'd checked out from the Belport Library. But the bigger they got, the more *real* they seemed.

The wool throw rug she'd pulled over herself caught on an exposed nail and slipped from her shoulders. It was deathly cold without it. Despite the three-bar heater running at full steam, the badly insulated garage was impossible to heat. She might have performed her taxidermy at the kitchen table, where it was warm, but she was pretty sure Ray would divorce her if she suggested it.

Three fat brown moths scuttled out from below the bar fridge and flapped briefly against Abby's chin. Abby swiped at them but missed. They rose in a loose formation to the fluorescent tube overhead and whacked against it, over and over.

Abby watched them, thinking of the crate of ruined baby clothes. If she had a can of flyspray handy, she might have cut them down with it then and there. Of course, that would have violated Ray's strict catch-and-release policy. Whenever a spider or insect came into the house, Ray insisted on capturing it – usually in the plastic *Batman Forever* tumbler they kept under the sink – and letting it free in the coastal woodland that lined the rear of their yard. It didn't matter how hairy or creepy the creature was; 106 Milt Street was a no-kill zone.

After an animal was dead, however, it was free rein. Abby thought about this as she plucked the bag from the fridge and set it down gently on the workbench. She took a long sip of wine, hooked herself into a dark-green apron and snapped on a pair of surgical gloves.

She unwrapped the corpse. It was an adult ringtail with grey and white fur. Judging by its expression, it had no idea what hit it. One second it was crossing between wires, the next, *bam*, Kentucky Fried Possum.

'Hello there,' she said. 'What's your name?'

The possum stared back, mouth open, eyes bulging and glassy.

'You look like a Trevor,' Abby decided. 'I'm Abby and I'll be your stylist today.'

She pulled up her stool, switched on the radio – a TLC song was playing – and took up her shiny silver X-Acto knife. She fixed it with a No. 11 classic fine-point scalpel blade and got to work. Upon the first insertion of the knife, all her apprehension about tackling a larger animal slipped away.

Step one in taxidermy was to remove and preserve the skin. Starting at the belly, Abby cut a slow and steady seam, taking extra care not to puncture the bowels. She'd made that mistake a few specimens ago: she'd nicked the bowel of a bush rat, and the smell that seeped out had almost been strong enough to send her running from the room – almost strong enough, in fact, to make her hang up her apron, put away the borax and say *never again*.

She worked the knife along the inside of the skin, making small, measured swipes. With her left hand, she peeled the skin back. The manual described this part of the process as like removing the animal's jacket and trousers, but she thought it was more like peeling an orange.

TLC faded into Mariah Carey's 'Dreamlover', and Abby wondered who the hell had set the radio to this station. She would have got up to change it if she hadn't had her hands full. Still, she soon caught herself humming along as she entered a state of something like hypnosis. For the first time in twenty-four hours, she wasn't thinking about the body – not the human one, anyway. There was just the thump of the moths against the light, Trevor the ringtail, and Mariah—

'Fuck!'

In one small, fast motion, she'd just dragged the X-Acto knife over the thumbnail on her left hand. A rush of heat flushed the wound, and hot blood seeped quickly from beneath a fresh slice in the surgical glove.

She dropped the blade, wrapped her right fist around her left thumb and squeezed. She didn't want to look at it, didn't want to know how deep she'd cut. It didn't feel like it would need stitches, but she knew from experience that the real pain wouldn't come until later.

She slid back from the stool and went over to Ray's tool bench, to where she was sure he kept a first-aid kit for work. A drumbeat of pain began in her thumb. Keeping pressure on it, she navigated around the plastic tubs and empty pots, past the cobwebby weightlifting station and rusted-out old ride-on.

She reached the bench that ran along the far wall. This was Ray's domain. Aside from his work truck, it was the closest thing Ray had to an office. It was cluttered with various power tools. A mud-stained Stihl chainsaw sat on a plastic tub full of receipts with *TAX STUFF* printed down one side in thick black texta. A grass-covered

Buffalo Turbine leaf blower leaned against a stack of *For Dummies* books.

It took her nearly a full minute of panicked searching before she finally found the first-aid kit. She was seconds from running into the house, blood spurting from the jagged hole she'd cut into the surgical glove, when she spotted it, stood on its side, wedged between the bench and the back wall. It must have fallen back there. She slipped to her knees, reached in with her good hand, then paused. The lid of the kit was ajar and inside she saw what looked like—

Is that an arse?

She pulled the kit out into the light and took it back over to her workbench. She unclipped the latch, flipped open the lid, and froze.

Abby's first thought was that this kit didn't have what she needed. Instead of bandages, gauze swabs and stop-itch cream, there was a stack of magazines, facedown. The splash of pink skin on the top back cover gave Abby her second thought: *I've found Ray's stash of porn.*

She knew most men got off on pornography and couldn't fault Ray his urges, but it was a terrible place to keep his magazines: one of the kids could easily have found them.

She flipped the top magazine over to get a better look at what her husband might be into. Was it cheerleaders, girl-on-girl action, *mature* women, or—

'*Mountain Stud*?'

On the cover, a shirtless blond man stared lustfully back at her. His chest was toned and hairless, his lips pouting. He had one hand behind his head, while the other was unzipping the fly of his jeans.

Confused, Abby turned each magazine over and spread them out on the bench, a jarring clarity taking hold. *Y-Mag*, *Boyz*, *Truck Stop*, *Man O Man*. Her mouth opened slowly like a wound, the real wound on her left thumb forgotten and gathering blood. Panic drifted in like smoke as her eyes danced wildly over naked men. Some were flexing for the camera, others were locked in each other's arms, kissing passionately. On another, four black men with their faces cropped out stood over a young white man, whose hands were pressed together, as if he was begging or praying.

Later, as she revisited the moment over and over in her mind, she'd think there was something almost laughable about it. She'd picture herself frozen in a strange tableau: a woman in a dark-green apron, a blood-soaked surgical glove wrapped around one hand, the half-skinned corpse of a possum on the work bench, and a copy of *Stud-Fucker* open before her, a perfect thumbprint of blood in the bottom left-hand corner of the centrefold.

But now, she wanted to undo the past five minutes of her life. She shoved the magazines back into the first-aid kit, taking no care to put them in the same order as she'd found them. That didn't matter. She just wanted them gone. She slammed the lid shut, returned the kit to the space between Ray's bench and the wall, and went inside to find a bandaid.

13

THE WIDOW

'This is what we know,' Detective Eckman said. 'This morning we got a call from Ben Norbo, who owns the bait stall down on the promenade. He told us he'd found what he thought was an abandoned car at Beech Tree Landing.'

Kate and Fisher sat across from her, on the other side of a coffee-ringed desk in a back room of the Belport Police Station. There was a small window that gave an obstructed view into a damp concrete lane running between the station and the house next door. It was raining again. It had hardly stopped since they arrived in Belport.

'The car was submerged at the bottom of one of the boat ramps, as if someone parked it at the top, slipped it into neutral and watched it roll in,' Eckman continued. 'Ben was launching his Riva Aquarama and nearly tore up the hull before he noticed the car in the water.'

'Riva Aquarama?' Kate asked.

'A kind of boat,' she said. 'At first Ben assumed, as we did, that the car had been dumped by some kids after stealing it and taking it for a joy ride. It happens more than you might think. They hot-wire a car from the mainland, scrape enough money together to bring it over on the ferry and then cut lose. Sometimes they dump it, sometimes they burn it out. We thought that's what this was.'

'But it wasn't,' Fisher said. He had brought a small notepad with him and was taking notes.

'I'm afraid not. A constable was despatched to check it out, and a tow truck was called to get the car out of the water.' She grimaced. 'Your husband was discovered in the front seat.'

Kate felt hot and itchy all of a sudden. She felt alone and unreal. She was, in that moment, an old boat clinging to the side of a pier. The urge to let go and allow herself to drift out to sea was strong. If not for Mia, she just might have.

'The car was a rental, hired in your husband's name,' Eckman said. 'We're not sure how long it was there before it was discovered, but based on the decomposition, we think at least forty-eight hours.'

'Are you sure?' Kate asked. 'The alarm company called me last night. Someone tripped the security system. If John was already …'

Eckman didn't make her finish that sentence. 'It's possible the alarm malfunctioned or was triggered by some curious wildlife, but there's also a chance that someone else went into the house last night. Crime Scene Services are on their way there now to take a look around. You'll both need to provide us with your fingerprints before you leave the station today,' Eckman said.

Fisher looked up from his notepad. 'Why? Are we suspects?'

'We just need to compare them to any we might find at the house, that's all.'

Fisher scribbled something down in his notepad.

'How did it happen?' Kate asked. 'How was John … how was he killed?'

Fisher glanced at Kate, then waited for Eckman to answer.

'Spending a couple of days under water destroyed a lot of forensic evidence,' she said flatly. 'But we know his carotid artery was severed.'

'What does that mean, exactly?' Kate asked.

'His throat was slit,' Fisher said. The words sounded sharp and snake-like.

'Yes,' Eckman agreed. 'So far we've been unable to locate the murder weapon.'

'It wasn't in the car, with John?' Fisher asked.

'No.'

'And you searched the surrounding area?'

'We're in the middle of all that now, but so far we've had no luck.'

Fisher seemed relieved. 'If the weapon wasn't with John, there's no way he could have …'

'Could have what?'

'There's no way John could have done this to himself.'

Kate flinched, as if someone had just clapped a pair of meaty hands over her shoulders and screamed, *boo!*

'Of course not,' Kate said. 'Why would you even say that?'

Fisher said nothing. He just jotted something down in his notepad.

'There were very few signs of a struggle,' Eckman said. 'He didn't even have time to unfasten his seatbelt. So, we believe John knew the person who attacked him. He might have even been lured out there. We're going through his phone records and emails now. Is there anyone John knew in Belport? Anyone he might have talked to or visited?'

'Not that we know about,' Kate said. 'We didn't even know he had come here.'

'Speaking of that.' Eckman unzipped a black leather document folder and removed three photos. 'John arrived on the island two weeks ago, on the day he told you he left for London.' She placed the first photo on the desk and slid it across for them to see. 'We pulled this from the ferry's CCTV. That old boat is in desperate need of a security upgrade, but I think you'll agree that this is him.'

The photo was grainy, low quality and showed a high-angle view of the island ferry's front deck. There was a lot of negative space in the photo – the clean white deck, the steel railing, the ocean beyond – but there was a lone man in the corner of the shot. He was looking out over the water, hands stuffed into the pockets of a heavy parka, overnight bag wedged firmly between his feet. His face was angled slightly towards the camera, as if something to the ferry's right had caught his attention. A barge ship, maybe, or a pod of dolphins. The man was tall, lean and unmistakably, indisputably, John.

Kate had never imagined that her husband had been dragged to Belport against his will – locked in the boot of some crazed kidnapper's car, or at gunpoint in a dingy, crossing the wild waters. But seeing him now, freely making his way to the island, hurt.

'I've got a couple of constables trawling through the ferry's security footage from every day since then, but so far he's not been spotted. We assume this was his first and only trip to the island. He paid with cash, and purchased a return ticket for the day after his murder, which tells me he likely intended to come home when he told you he would.'

The news was comforting, in its own way. It suggested that in another reality, one in which John wasn't killed, he would have returned home and kept his secret trip hidden from her, maybe forever. She wouldn't have known, and it wouldn't have mattered. She would have lived the rest of her life in blissful ignorance. It also confirmed, at least in Kate's mind, that John hadn't gone to Belport to kill himself, as Fisher had suspected. Why would anyone buy a return ticket from someplace they knew they wouldn't be returning from?

Eckman showed them the second photo.

'This was taken from a camera mounted above the entrance of the Uniting Church on Bay Street,' she said. 'They had it installed to catch whoever was letting their dog take its evening dump on their entranceway. It's mounted on a weird angle but gives a clear view across the street to the car park outside the Buy & Bye.'

'That supermarket's still there?' Fisher asked.

'Yeah, it is.' Kate said. Kate knew the Buy & Bye well. It was quaint and overpriced, with a small toy section that Mia loved to browse. The pair of them would do all the family shopping there during the summer, a good excuse to get out of the house so John could enjoy some quiet reading.

She leaned forward to look at the picture. It showed an unsealed car park and the brick wall of the church. Beyond that, John could once again be seen. This time he was leaving the supermarket, two stuffed shopping bags in his hands. In this photo, John's face was directly in line with the camera. His brow didn't look heavy with worry or etched with concern. His face was blank, his expression unreadable.

'There are no cameras inside the store, but we're almost certain he only went there twice. The first was the day he arrived, to purchase …' She paused, reached into the document folder, and produced a photocopied receipt. Reading from it, she continued, 'Bread, milk, some canned meats and vegetables, some bottled water, extension cord, two power boards, batteries, a wind-up torch and some chocolate.'

'Sounds like he was stocking up,' Kate said.

Nodding, Eckman continued. 'He visited the store again on what we believe is the day he died, where he bought the groceries you found at the house.'

Fisher, who had helped himself to the third photo Eckman had left on the desk, asked, 'Who is this man?'

He passed the picture to Kate. It was of two men standing on a dilapidated old verandah, taken from what must have been a home security camera. The first man in the photo was John. In this one he was smiling, which filled Kate with hot rage. Even in the midst of all his deception, he had the nerve to smile. *Smile.* His face was suddenly unfamiliar, she realised. Fisher could just as easily have been talking about John when he asked, *Who is this man?*

The other man in the picture – the one Fisher was jamming a finger at – was barrel-chested with short, meaty arms. His back was partially to the camera, revealing a prominent bald spot in a nest of thick hair. The men stood on an unkempt lawn scattered with old car parts, a rusted-out barbecue and a couple of overturned oil drums.

'That's Russ Graves,' Eckman said. 'He's lived on the island all his life and is a bit of a local eccentric. He gets by working odd jobs, buying and selling used goods, stuff like that. When we were looking through John's emails we found a reply to an ad Russ Graves had run on Gumtree.'

Fisher scribbled the name *Russ Graves* into his notepad.

'What was the ad for?' Kate asked.

'Bug zappers,' Eckman said.

'At this time of year? Why on earth would John need a bug zapper?'

'Bug zapper*s*,' Eckman said.

'How's that?'

'Russ Graves had eleven bug zappers for sale. John bought them all.'

'That doesn't make any sense,' Fisher said. 'And when something doesn't make sense it probably isn't true.'

Eckman visibly struggled to hide her frustration. 'I understand, Mr Keddie but please just let's stay on track here. I wanted to ask you about the mock hotel room John had set up.'

'He set it up to make it look like he was Skyping from London,' Kate said.

'That's a lot of trouble to go to, to maintain a lie,'

Eckman said. 'Why wouldn't he tell you he was coming to Belport?'

Kate shook her head. She was getting tired of people asking her that question. Every time she heard it, it felt like she knew John less and less. She reached into her pocket and gripped the notebook with John's drawings. Eckman would probably need to see it. 'I don't know. There's something else. A couple of things, actually. There was a fresh coat of paint on the living room wall. I don't know what that means, or if it means anything, but—'

'Yes, I know about the painted wall,' Eckman said 'but that's not really our concern right now, Mrs Keddie. I need to understand this hotel room.'

Kate paused, then let go of the notebook and placed her hands back in her lap.

'Can we get back to this Graves guy?' Fisher said. 'Does he have a record? He has a security camera mounted on his verandah; that's a red flag right there.'

Eckman took a deep breath. 'Mr Graves is still being checked and vetted, but he has an alibi and, so far, it looks pretty solid.'

'Do you have any other suspects?' Fisher hissed. 'Any actual evidence? Do you have anything tangible?'

Eckman hesitated. Her tongue slipped in and out of her mouth twice, like a tortoise peeking nervously from its shell. 'We're working on it, Mr Keddie. For what it's worth. I can promise you that.'

'Right now,' Fisher said. 'It's not worth fucking much.'

'Fisher, please,' Kate said.

He shook his head and flipped through his notepad. Kate turned back to Eckman and asked, 'What's next?'

'We still have a number of leads to follow up on,' she said. 'The advantage of this happening in such a small community is that people tend to notice if anything is unusual. If you'll excuse the French, we have a saying on the island: *you can't take a shit today without someone smelling it tomorrow.*'

14

THE WIFE

The Belly pub, nestled at the corner of Bay and Bramwell streets, glowed warm and orange against the drizzly night. Wrapped in floral green wallpaper, its main lounge was lined with rows of wooden bench seats. The walls were cluttered with framed black-and-white photos of Belport in the 1930s and '40s. A fire crackled in a large stone fireplace set below a mantelpiece carved from driftwood.

When Abby got good enough with her taxidermy, the Belly's owner, Sheila Gosnell, promised to mount her prize piece above that mantelpiece. Sheila had likely envisioned a proud buck with wide, twisting antlers. Abby wondered what she might say if she presented her with Trevor the ringtail.

Abby and Bobbi sat in a booth by the fire; Abby was on red, Bobbi on white. It was Bobbi's idea to go out for a drink, but it was Abby who really needed one. She wondered if her best friend had picked up some sort of psychic SOS signal she'd put out after finding what was inside the first-aid kit.

'It's been too long since we did this,' Abby said, clinking glasses. 'I thought you were off drinking – in public, anyway – until Maggie popped that baby out and could join you.'

'I thought I owed you after unloading on you in the car the other night,' Bobbi said with a shrug. 'But there's something I need to talk to you about. What happened to your thumb?'

Abby looked down at the fresh bandaid she'd wrapped around the neat slice made by the X-Acto knife. After washing off the blood, she'd found only a nick barely wider than a paper cut, but like a paper cut, it hurt like a motherfucker.

'Taxidermy mishap,' she said. 'Speaking of, there's something I need to talk to you about too.'

Bobbi leaned back in the booth and rested a hand behind her head. She tipped her glass and said, 'Ladies first.'

Abby took a gulp of wine, then started to talk. She told Bobbi about *Mountain Stud* and the blond man unzipping his jeans. Bobbi listened with her lips tightly drawn, her expression giving nothing away. The only time she spoke was to send away Jim Biggins, a Belly regular who'd wandered drunkenly over to ask Bobbi about the murder. Although, after a few too many Woodstock and Cokes, it came out *murra*.

When Jim got the hint and left, and Abby finished her story, Bobbi hunched forward on her elbows and drank. There was something in her eyes that made Abby nervous; it looked as if she was making some sort of complicated calculation. She was silent for a long time, and then said, 'Shit.'

'Yeah, shit,' Abby agreed.

'Have you asked him about it?'

'I don't think I'd know how,' Abby said.

'Okay, well, first up, just because he's looking at those kinds of magazines doesn't mean he's gay. As someone who can speak with authority on this subject, sexuality is not black and white. Why do you think they have all those colours on the rainbow flag?'

'Logically, I know that. Emotionally, I can't help wondering if he pictures Brad Pitt while he fucks me.'

Bobbi cracked a smile and sipped her chardonnay. 'Nah, I reckon Ray's more of a Richard Gere type.'

'You're not helping.'

'But you said it yourself, it's not like you and Ray don't have sex. Eddie and Lori prove you've done it at least twice, and don't think I've forgotten all those late-night sex talks we had at the Buy & Bye. He's hot for your lady parts, is my point. So if I had to guess, I'd say he might just be a little … curious.'

A flash of something dark sprang into Abby's mind like a jump scare in a midnight horror movie. The old ferry terminal was a gay beat. That was the rumour, anyway. Just how curious was Ray? Was he curious enough to—

Stop, she commanded herself, slamming a lid over the thought and pushing it away, the way she had slammed the lid of the first-aid kit shut. The truth was, she had no real way of knowing what Ray was doing with those magazines. He might have found them stashed in one of the houses he looked after – there were plenty of rich pervs on Neef Street. That didn't explain why he hid them behind his workbench, but it was something to hold on to.

'I have to talk to him about this, don't I?' Abby said.

'I'm afraid so,' Bobbi told her.

Abby finished her wine and shook her head. She went to the bar to fetch fresh drinks. When she came back to the booth and sat down, she said, 'Your turn.'

'Huh?'

'You said you needed to talk to me about something,' Abby said. 'What is it?'

Bobbi shifted nervously in her seat and gulped her wine. Apparently, whatever she needed to say required a gutful of booze. That wasn't a good sign.

'Jesus, Bobbi, what is it? You're freaking me out.'

'I thought about coming by your house to tell you this,' Bobbi started. 'But then I thought it might be easier without the kids around, and Ray. But the real reason I wanted to do it here was that I kept thinking about my parents. Whenever Mum and Dad had a big decision to make, they'd take a long drive, no matter what the decision was – figuring out what sort of car to buy, deciding if it was time to put Nan in a home, anything. They'd drive and drive with no direction in mind, and they wouldn't come back without a clear plan.' Bobbi smiled. 'Ironically, the final drive they took was to decide if their marriage was worth saving or not. It wasn't, FYI.'

She drank. Abby waited for her to go on.

'I asked my dad about the long drives one day,' Bobbi said. 'I thought there might be something about movement and momentum that, I don't know, made it easier to think. He told me I was overthinking it. He said what it boiled down to was: *you don't shit where you sleep.* There are some things better left outside the home.'

'So you're shitting where we drink instead?' Abby asked.

Bobbi chuckled. 'Yeah. I suppose I am.' She leaned back in her chair and shoved her small hands into the pockets of her windbreaker. It was warm in the bar, but she hadn't taken it off.

'It's about the murder, isn't it?' Abby said. 'You know I'll always be here for you, Bob, and I get why you can't open up to Maggie, but surely the police force offers some sort of counselling service or—'

'This isn't about that,' she said. 'It's about the murder, but it isn't about *that*.' Bobbi sipped, nodded and resigned herself. 'We've been looking into the victim's phone records,' she started. 'And by *we*, I mean the detective running the case. There was a printout on the front desk and I wasn't supposed to see it, but I thought I'd sneak a look. I was curious, and I thought I might recognise some of the numbers. He didn't make many calls. A total of six in the two weeks before he was killed. Of those six, I recognised two. The first was Speedy Pizza. He called them four days before it happened. The second …'

A Paul Simon song came on over the jukebox, and for a moment Bobbi seemed lost in it.

'… Yeah?' Abby prompted her.

'The second call was made on the day he died, at eleven-sixteen am, and lasted four minutes and forty seconds,' she said. 'And, look, I didn't come here to scare you, or to accuse anyone of anything. I just wanted to give you a heads-up. There are a dozen explanations and all they'll need is one good one.'

'What are you trying to say, Bobbi?'

'On the day he died, the victim made one call,' she said. 'That call was to your house.'

'*Our* house?' Ray asked. 'That can't be right. It must be a mistake.'

She had found him stretched out on the sofa watching TV when she came home, but now he sat up to make room for her. He fished the remote from behind the sofa cushion and switched off the TV, his face knotted with confusion. Or was it concern?

Abby sat down beside him, tangled her fingers together, then untangled them and stood up again. 'Bobbi says there's no reason to panic. She was just giving us a heads-up. A detective will probably be coming to ask us about it and—'

'Ab, slow down, a *detective*? This is crazy. For all they know it was a wrong number.'

'The call lasted four minutes and forty seconds,' she said. 'That's too long for a wrong number.'

Ray frowned. 'Could it be one of the kids?'

'It was the middle of a school day. The kids weren't home. I'll ask them, to make sure.'

Ray fell quiet.

The nostalgic smell of burning wood filled the room. Wind swept down the chimney of the wood heater, aggravating the flames and creating an eerie, strangely ominous howl. Come to think of it, maybe it wasn't ominous at all. Maybe 'Jingle Bells' would have sounded the same way to Abby right now. Bobbi had placed a knot in her thoughts, and so far, all Ray had done was make it tighter.

'It was the day of the big storm, Ray,' she said quietly.

He flinched at that. He must have known what she was about to say, but he let her say it anyway.

'The kids were at school, I was at the Buy & Bye, and you ...'

'I took the morning off,' he admitted. 'It was too wet to work.'

'So, you were home?'

For a moment, in the flickering orange glow of the wood heater, he looked sinister. She pictured the blond man on the cover of *Mountain Stud*. Then his face calmed. He clicked his tongue. 'Come to think of it, I do remember getting a call that day.'

'You do?'

'Yeah. Some guy called about Island Care. A potential new client, that's all. See, a lot of these summer residents think hiring a caretaker for the winter is a waste of money until they arrive at their house and find a wasp's nest under their verandah or a family of fruit bats in their guestroom.'

'So he was calling to ... hire you?'

'Yeah.'

'What did he say?'

'He wanted to know what I did and how much it would cost him.' He tugged at his earlobe a second, then shook his head. 'I laid it all out for him and he said he'd have a think about it and call me back. When he didn't, I assumed it was because he'd changed his mind. Now

I know the real reason. Pretty spooky, when you think about it. I'll swing by the cop shop on my way to work in the morning and straighten it all out – won't mention that Bobbi gave us that heads up, of course,' Ray said. 'Belport is a small place. I'm probably one of a dozen locals he came into contact with.'

Nodding, Abby said, 'He ordered something from Speedy Pizza.'

'There you go,' he said, and tugged at his earlobe again.

If Ray had told her this before she opened the first-aid kit, Abby might have believed him. There would have been no reason not to. But if he could keep a secret like *that*, how was she supposed to separate the fiction from the nonfiction? Then again, she had to believe him, didn't she? What was the alternative?

She wanted to ask him about the magazines then but wasn't sure she wanted to know why he had them. All she could manage to say was, 'Ray, do I have anything to be worried about?'

He looked at her a moment, then grinned, bound his wrists with invisible handcuffs and offered them to Abby.

'You got me, copper,' he said.

Abby didn't think that was very funny.

15

THE WIDOW

Clank … Clank … CLANK!

The noise was coming from outside. It was the middle of the night, but the noise hadn't woken Kate. As far as she could remember, she hadn't slept at all since turning off the bedside lamp.

She listened.

Clank … CLANK!

She climbed quietly out of bed, thudding her knee against a chair in the dark. She reached the window and drew back the curtain, half expecting to see a deranged killer trying to break into the room. Instead, she saw Fisher. He was dressed in a tattered motel robe, empty steel bucket in hand, swaying drunkenly and harassing the ice machine.

He yanked at the machine's lid. It caught. He set the steel bucket down on the ground, kneeled and tried again. He was apparently too shit-faced to notice the sign, taped not half a metre from his face, declaring in bright red letters: *Out of order, sorry 4 inconveniens.*

'Goddamn fucking thing,' he muttered, giving up. As he climbed to his feet, he knocked the steel bucket and sent it rolling. He watched it roll, then shrugged. Abandoning the bucket, he ambled back to his room, swaying left and right as he walked. Kate watched him struggle with the lock, then finally fall inside.

She thought about going back to bed but knew she wouldn't sleep. Instead, she fetched the little rubber ice-cube tray from the minibar and walked outside into the cold night. It was freezing. She hurried to Fisher's door and knocked. There was no answer, so she knocked again. Finally, his face appeared in the window beside the door. His bloodshot eyes wandered down to Kate's feet and back to her face again. He looked drunk, and baleful.

He disappeared from the window and, after fifteen seconds of shuffling and rustling around in his room, answered the door. 'Kate, what is it? Has something happened? Is everything alright?'

'I have ice,' she said.

'Excuse me?'

'I saw you struggling with the machine and thought you might need some.'

She handed him the rubber ice tray.

'Oh, uh, thanks,' he said. 'I'm just having a little nightcap. Helps me sleep.'

'Mind if I join you?' she asked.

'Oh,' He furrowed his brow and glanced back into his room. 'Sure. Come in.'

Fisher's room was a mirrored version of her own. There was an empty bottle of Chivas Regal on the desk and a freshly opened one beside it. He fixed them both a glass, adding a few blocks of Kate's ice to each.

'I hope straight is okay,' he said, handing her a glass. 'I don't have any mixers.'

'That's fine.'

She sat down on the bed and sipped the Scotch. It stung on the way down but instantly warmed her belly. She usually couldn't handle spirits, but sipping her Chivas was like slipping into a warm bath – a little too hot at first, but soon it felt just right. For a long time, they didn't talk. Kate worried that Fisher might prefer to be alone, but when they finished their drinks, he quickly made two more.

'It didn't look like him,' Fisher said softly, letting the ice clink in his glass. 'I mean, it looked *like* him, but not quite right'.

'Like seeing him through a camera lens,' she offered.

He nodded. He took a cigarette from the pack, placed it between his lips and asked, 'Do you mind?'

'I think the rooms have smoke detectors.'

'I found a workaround.' He stood, swayed forward, caught his balance, then went and opened the window.

If Fisher was cold, he didn't show it. He dragged a chair to the window, sat down and smoked.

'You never met my father, did you?' he asked.

'No.'

John's grandfather was five years dead when they met. Emphysema, if memory served.

'He was a tough old bastard,' Fisher said. 'An arsehole, really. You're not meant to speak ill of the dead. You're supposed to say he called it as he saw it, he was a straight shooter, he wouldn't tolerate fools. But what all that boils down to is being an arsehole.'

He dragged on his cigarette and looked down at his drink, slumping forward slightly in his chair. 'He couldn't stand to watch another man cry. Far as I can remember, I only ever cried in front of him once. I was ten. I'd had a run-in with some older kids. I'd been riding home from school and had taken a shortcut through the Dustbowl – that's what we called this big, pie-wedge-shaped patch of dead land near where I grew up. I was waved down by three boys. They were tooling around at the big storm drain. One of them was Jim Haskin. A few sandwiches short of a picnic and mad as a cut snake, we used to call him. Not to his face, of course. I can't remember the names of the other two, but I can still picture their dirty faces.'

Kate said nothing.

'It was those other two kids who dragged me off the

bike,' Fisher said. 'But it was Haskin who wheeled it into the mouth of the storm drain, gave it a steady push right down into the dark and told me to *fetch*. They gathered around and watched me go in after it. Two steps in, my heart was pounding. Three steps, I was just about ready to scream.'

He smiled, but it was a tragic, distant smile, and made her feel cold.

'The darkness in that storm drain was total and complete, like death,' he said. He hiccuped and nearly lost his cigarette. Kate was all the way across the room, but she could see the tears in his eyes. 'My bike had been gobbled up by that darkness and it wanted to gobble me up too. So, I ran. Christ, I loved that fucking bike. For all I know it's still there, rusted out and waiting for me in the dark.'

'Fisher, you were ten. Anyone would have cried in that situation. I'd cry if it happened to me now.'

'Dad saw things differently,' he said, long-buried scorn in his voice. 'I came in the front door, crying like a puppy; he looked down at me like I was nothing. Like I was less than nothing. It wasn't just that he saw crying as a weakness. It disgusted him. I disgusted him. Made him sick to his stomach. You know what he told me, Kate?'

'What?'

'Be a man.' He finished his cigarette, stubbed it out on the windowsill and flicked it into the night. '*Be a man*. It seemed like such a strange thing to say to a child. I swore then that if I ever had a son, things would be different. But what does the Bible say about the sins of the father? That they shall be visited upon the sons to the third and fourth generation? Pam would know.'

'You're a good father, Fisher,' Kate said. 'Take it from someone who had a rubbish one. Whatever sins your dad committed ended with him.'

'If that were true, I would have stopped John from coming out here. There must have been signs something was wrong.'

'If there were, I missed them too.' She drank. 'Why do you think he came to Belport, Fisher? If he was lured here by the same person that lured him to Beech Tree Landing, why did he lie about where he was going?'

There was a stained-glass lamp in the corner of the room casting long, jagged shadows up the wall and over the ceiling. Fisher gazed at them and sipped his Scotch. 'Did John ever talk to you about his night terrors?'

'No.'

'When he was a teenager, fifteen or sixteen, he started having nightmares. *Terrible* nightmares. He'd wake up in the middle of the night, screaming and crying and shouting. It developed into a full-blown sleeping disorder. He became an insomniac, his grades suffered, he started falling asleep in strange places. He started to see things.'

'See things?'

'Sleep is a funny thing. When you don't get enough, it can do crazy things to the mind. After a month or two of barely any sleep, John started having hallucinations.'

'What kind of hallucinations?'

'He'd hear whispers that weren't really there, see dark shapes and shadows out of the corners of his eyes. Then he started to see the Visitor. That's what John called it.' Fisher swallowed an invisible obstruction in his throat before he continued. 'The Visitor would come mostly at night. He would stand in the corner of John's bedroom, watching him. I asked John to draw him for me once. He drew a man in a long black coat. There was a big crack in his face, and falling out of the crack were dozens of—'

'Moths,' Kate offered.

'What?' Fisher said.

'I found a notebook in the house. I'm sorry, I should have shown you, I just … Anyway, it's in my room. All these drawings of a man with moths coming out of his head. It's the same.'

'No,' Fisher said. 'Back then, they were caterpillars.'

A sudden chill crept up her spine.

'It was a long time ago. He took a whole lot of drugs – clomi— clomipra-something, then a year on Ambien. Eventually the nightmares stopped.' He stood and topped up their drinks. 'We never found out what caused them. It felt a little like putting a bandaid over a scab you just knew was set to fester. Pam was worried he'd been abused or molested or suffered some sort of trauma.'

'Is that possible?'

Fisher shrugged. 'If it happened, John either didn't remember it or didn't talk about it.'

'Do you think that has something to do with why he came to the island?' she asked.

'John had valerian capsules, chamomile tea and three different types of antihistamines from the grocery store. Those are all sleeping aids. Come to think of it, the litre bottle of Wild Turkey could probably be considered a sleeping aid too.'

'John didn't need sleeping aids. I would have noticed. I slept next to the man.'

'Would you, though? Would *he* know if it was the other way around?'

How well can you really ever know anyone? Kate thought.

'So, what are you saying?' Kate asked. 'You think he was having nightmares again?'

He nodded, drank, and said, 'I think that's why he bought those aids, and I think that's why he bought the bug zappers.'

'I don't understand.'

'I think that, for whatever reason, the Visitor came back.'

Kate shivered. She was suddenly cold. It might have been that the open window had let all the warm air out, or it might have been that Fisher's words had sobered her up. 'Even if that were true, what's that got to do with Belport?'

He stood up, using the wall for balance, and shut the window. He necked the last of his Scotch and placed the empty glass on the bedside table.

'It's late,' he said. 'Mind if we call it a night?'

'Fisher …'

'I'm tired, Kate. Just tired, that's all.'

16

THE WIFE

Ray was gone by the time Abby got up. There was a vague husband-shaped indent on his side of the bed. She pulled on a pair of day-old leggings, then tiptoed downstairs to make coffee and get the fire started.

The phone started to ring the moment she set foot in the kitchen, as if it had been waiting for its cue.

'Hello?'

'Morning, love. I didn't wake you, did I?'

It was Henry Biller, no doubt calling from his cramped, windowless office outside the Buy & Bye receiving area.

'No,' she said, flicking on the percolator. 'What's up?'

'I need an extra pair of hands at the shop today, and since you're looking for more shifts, I thought of you first. The cops are setting up something called an *information caravan* outside the community centre for people to come forward with information about the murder, which means two things: they're scraping the bottom of the barrel, and Bay Street's gonna be a carnival.'

The percolator gurgled and filled the kitchen with the smell of fresh coffee. There were noises in the hall. The kids were waking up and getting ready for school.

'I know I asked for the extra work, Biller, but I've got a lot going on right now. Is there anyone else who could cover?'

'Danny's staying at his girlfriend's place on the mainland, Enza is about as useful as tits on a bull, and Marge doesn't wear her hearing aid in the mornings, so she won't hear the phone.'

'So, when you said I was your *first* thought …'

'I meant my *only* one,' Biller said. 'How fast can you get here?'

'Give me an hour.'

'You're a lifesaver,' he said. 'If I ever get around to starting that employee of the month award, you're my number one pick.'

'Uh huh,' she said, and hung up.

She went upstairs and took a shower, then dug her dirty brown B&B tunic out of the laundry basket. It smelled like the deli counter that she'd wiped down on her last shift, so she added an extra layer of deodorant.

She ran into Eddie on her way back downstairs. He was putting his shoes on by the front door.

'Morning, kid,' she said, tapping him on the backside

as she passed. 'Have fun at school. Learn stuff.'

'Hi, Mum, bye, Mum.'

He opened the front door and had one foot halfway out when Abby called to him. 'Hey, Eddie, hold up a sec.'

'That's all I've got if I want to make the bus.'

She joined him at the front door and looked over his shoulder. It was a clear day, but the lawn was covered in a thick layer of white frost.

'Have you noticed anything strange about your father lately?' she asked.

'Strange? How do you mean?'

It was a good question. She didn't tell Eddie about the victim calling the house. She didn't want to creep him out, and she knew that if she did, it would get back to Lori, who was excited enough about the murder already.

'Nothing specific,' she said. 'I just wondered if he'd seemed, I don't know, *off* to you.'

'I don't know,' Eddie said. 'No. I don't think so. Why?'

'It's nothing,' Abby said. 'Forget it. Go catch your bus.'

Eddie slung his schoolbag over one shoulder and stuffed his hands into the front pouch of his hoodie. He gave a brief, monk-like bow, then hurried down the front steps and across the lawn, his sneakers crunching on the frost.

Abby drove, her mind feeling a little like chewed meat. She thought about the magazines, the call to the house that lasted four minutes and forty seconds, Ray's midnight teary in the kids' bathroom so Abby wouldn't hear. They were pieces of a larger picture, like dinosaur bones covered with dirt. She was on her knees, shifting sand from the bones with a toothbrush, exposing parts of a beast with no real idea what that beast was, or what it looked like.

Did she want to know?

Her thoughts dead-ended as she came over the crest of Neef Street and spotted Ray's work truck parked outside an enormous Georgian Revival.

Abby had to get to work, so she considered driving on, but something Bobbi had said in the Belly the night before suddenly seemed strangely significant: *you don't shit where you sleep.*

The things she needed to talk to Ray about were stacking up, and she'd much rather discuss them at home but this seemed like the island's way of telling her, *it's time.*

She eased the Volvo between two colossal stone pillars, then followed a long, straight driveway up to the house. It stood on a vast estate, looming like a haunted castle. There was a crack in the exterior wall just above the third-storey window. The crack cut a jagged line that stopped just below the roof, like the House of Usher.

She parked alongside Ray's truck, at the top of a large, horseshoe-shaped entranceway. The toolbox lay open on the rear tray. The front door was also wide open. Ray must have been airing the place out. She hurried to the top step and paused at the threshold.

'Ray?' she called. There was no answer other than her own voice echoing around the giant entranceway. She went inside, marching through the house, calling her husband's name.

'Ray? RAY?'

There were grand rooms in all directions, filled with open fireplaces and sophisticated furnishings wrapped in protective plastic, and each window on the west wall gave unobstructed views of the water.

'Hello, Ray?'

A prickle of fear crept up her spine when Ray didn't answer. What if—

Crack!

The sound startled her. It had come from outside. She moved through the house, out the back door and into a sprawling native garden: a sea of colour below a colourless sky. Stringybark trees and towering myrtle beeches foamed along the rear fence line. The estate backed onto the Belport Nature Reserve, a deep, dark and wild stretch of bushland.

Aside from a small population of brown snakes, all the animals that could kill you in Belport lived in the water. One was free to hike Belport's trails or wander silent roads without fear of being mauled, dragged off and consumed, but Abby couldn't help picturing giant shadow beasts lurking in those woods.

If the past two days had taught her anything, it was that there was plenty to be afraid of on this island.

Chop!

She followed the sound down a winding stone path, then onto a freshly mown lawn. She found Ray, axe in hand, clearing a gum tree that had fallen on a toppled birdbath by Ray's feet. He was knee-deep in a mess of shattered wood and narrow, twisted limbs.

Judging from the size of the woodpile he'd made, he'd been at it for quite a while. There were chunks of kindling scattered across the lawn. It was a bone-chilling afternoon, but sweat was pouring down his forehead. She approached quietly, not wanting to startle him into chopping off a toe. He looked strong and handsome, shifting the weight of the axe from his left hand to his right, lifting it high and swinging with precision. It cleaved through a branch with a sharp, dry *crack*. She noticed an almost tangible release of tension in the air.

'Hi, babe,' she said.

He looked up and grimaced. 'Abby?'

'I came through the house. The front door was open. I hope that's okay.'

'Are you following me?'

The accusation took her by surprise.

'Following you? No. I was driving past on my way to

'Why are you being so defensive about this?' Abby asked.

In lieu of a response, he lifted the axe and swung it. It cracked through a damp dead branch with a jarring *shaak!* 'What are you doing out here, Abby?'

'I told you. I was driving past and—'

'Why are you *really* here?'

'I didn't want to shit where we sleep,' she said.

He worked the axe handle between the palms of his hands and glared at her, waiting for her to continue. So, she did.

'You know how I got this?' she held up the bandaged thumb on her left hand. 'I was in the garage, skinning that possum Susi saved for me, and I nicked myself. I thought I'd find a bandaid in the first-aid kit behind your bench. Instead, I found your magazines.'

'I don't know what you're talking about, Ab.'

'*Boyz. Truck Stop. Man O Man. Stud-Fucker* ...'

'Jesus.' His lips closed tightly. His muscles tensed. He fingered the axe handle, looking into the forest of paperbark trees that lined the edge of the estate.

'Did you know him, Ray?' she asked. 'The guy who was killed, the guy who called the house, did you know him?'

'Of course not. He called the house. He asked me how much it would cost to hire me as his caretaker. That's it. Honestly, Abby, I don't know what the hell has got into you?'

'Into me? Ray, what am I expected to think? Why are you looking at magazines like that?'

'It's not …' He trailed off and rested the axe over one shoulder. The blade was sticky with tree sap that reminded Abby of blood. 'It's not what you're thinking.'

'Lori heard you crying the other night,' Abby said.

'Did she?' he said. His tone was suddenly cold. 'In that case, I wish Lori would crawl out of my arsehole and I wish you would too.'

Abby took an instinctive step backwards, nearly stumbling on a chunk of concrete from the birdbath. Ray, who had been staring down at the fallen tree, looked up. His face had contorted into a twisted version of itself. His skin looked waxy in the morning light, like a Madame Tussauds model. His eyes had been replaced with those of a stranger. She didn't know those eyes, and for a moment, she didn't know the man.

'Back off, babe,' he said.

'What?'

'Forget about those magazines, forget about that phone call, and *back off*. I said I'd take care of it, and I will.'

'I don't know if I can do that, Ray.'

For one jarring, terrifying moment, Abby pictured her husband lurching forward, raising the axe high over his shoulders and … Suddenly their jokes about Jack Torrance and the roque mallet didn't seem the least bit funny.

'Not even for the kids?' he asked.

'What are you telling me, Ray?'

'To tread lightly, Abby, and to back the fuck off.'

He hoisted the axe into the air and buried the blade in the trunk of the tree. Then he marched up the stone path towards the house. Abby gazed west, to the deep blue waters of Bass Strait, and wondered how it might feel to wade into them.

17

THE WIDOW

For a few blissful moments, Kate woke with her mind empty – then the phone rang. It was just after dawn, and she'd finally started drifting off.

'Yes?' she said groggily.

A small voice on the other end of the line whispered, 'Did I wake you?'

'Mia?'

'I know it's really early,' she said. 'But you said I didn't need a reason to call.' She sounded unsteady. Kate could tell she'd been crying.

'You don't, monkey,' Kate said, trying to keep her own voice under control. It took an effort not to burst into tears, but at the same time, she was surprised to find herself smiling in the early light. It was good to hear her daughter's voice. 'Are you okay?'

There was a beat of silence, then Mia said, 'I don't

174

know. I think so. Are you coming home soon?'

'Really soon,' she said.

'Grandma said they were talking about Dad on TV, but she wouldn't let me watch it and didn't tell me what they said.'

Kate sat up and wrapped an arm around her knees. She squeezed her eyes shut to stop herself weeping. 'How is your Grandma?'

'Weird. She's okay, but sort of crazy. I was watching YouTube this morning and she asked me what I was watching, so I showed her a video of a monkey riding a pig and she laughed *so* hard, like, hard enough that her whole body was shaking, like when I pretend to be electrocuted, but then, all of a sudden, she started crying.'

'People do weird things when they're sad,' Kate said. 'I'm sorry, monkey. I should be there, and I should have been there to tell you about your dad. These past few days, I … I'm not sure I've been the best mother.'

'It's okay,' Mia said eventually. 'People do weird things when they're sad, right?'

In the brief silence that followed, she imagined Mia perched on the floor beside the bed in the guestroom, smelling fresh and floral, like Pam's expensive old-lady soaps. Mia was only two hours away, but she seemed much further than that.

'What did he look like?' Mia asked.

'Who?'

'Dad.'

The question cut through her. She took a breath, then lied. 'He looked like he was sleeping.'

'Sometimes at funerals they leave the coffin open so you can see. Will Dad's be like that?'

'I don't know, monkey.'

'He'll have to be *embalmed*,' Mia said, sounding out each syllable. 'That's when they take out all your blood and put chemicals in and make it so your meat doesn't rot and you don't smell.'

'Did Grandma tell you about that?' Kate asked.

'I looked it up on wikiHow,' she said. Kate could picture her eyes, alive with morbid curiosity. 'After all that they clip your fingernails and put gel in your hair and put make-up on. It doesn't even matter if you're a boy or not. They still put the make-up on. Sometimes the eyes won't stay shut so they have to use superglue. Oh, and sometimes, if the body is, you know, leaky, they have to use plastic undies. Sorry, is this TMI?'

Kate thought about leaving monsters under beds and said, 'No, monkey. It's not TMI. What happens next?'

After hanging up with Mia, Kate couldn't get back to sleep. A series of practical questions kept her mind buzzing. When should she begin planning the funeral?

Who did she need to inform about John's death? What was she going to do with the holiday house?

Feeling overwhelmed and light-headed, she got out of bed and took a shower. She sat down on the tiles and closed her eyes. She imagined her pain was sand and tried to visualise the hot water washing it all away. It didn't work. She got out, dried herself and dressed. She brewed a cup of instant coffee – there was no milk in the minibar, so she had to take it black – and sat down on the spongy motel mattress.

She flicked through the channels on the TV for a while, then lay back on the bed and stared at the ceiling. As morning light filled the room, she thought of the manhole cover at the holiday house. She pictured the pencil-width opening and wondered what – if anything – lay beyond it.

Two coffees later she couldn't stand being in the room a minute longer, grabbed her car keys and decided to take a drive. On her way to the Lexus, she paused outside Fisher's room and looked through the window, half expecting to see a light on. The room beyond was dark. The night before, he'd had a bottle of Chivas even before she got to him, so she guessed he'd be sleeping it off for a few more hours. She knocked on the door gently, just in case.

Fisher emerged, faster than expected. Had he been sitting in the dark?

'Did I wake you?' she asked.

He shook his head and ran a hand through his hair. 'I don't think I slept.'

'I'm heading out. Need me to pick anything up for you?'

He held up an index finger as if to say, *one moment please*. He ducked back into the room and reappeared a second later. 'I'm all out of cigarettes. Would you mind?'

'Of course not.'

She climbed into the car and drove to Bay Street, easing to a crawl outside the Buy & Bye, where John had stopped for groceries, wearing a parka and an unreadable expression. The supermarket wasn't open yet, so she headed to Neef Street.

She pulled onto the shoulder opposite the holiday house and scanned the property for police cars. She half expected to find the property teeming with police, crime scene photographers and forensic investigators, but it was quiet and still. Someone had been there though. There were multiple muddy tyre marks leading in and out of the driveway, and strapped across the front gate was yellow tape that said, over and over, *DO NOT ENTER*.

Kate hoisted herself up and over the front gate – had she opened it, the police tape might have snapped – and started up the driveway on foot.

She supposed that technically what she was doing was trespassing on a crime scene, but this was her house, and she couldn't shake the image of that manhole cover, slightly ajar. It beckoned her.

She weaved through the police tape and into the house. All the lights had been left on. There were heavy indentations in the carpet – boot prints from the police, she guessed. The banisters at the bottom of the staircase were flecked with white powder, as were all the doorhandles.

She fetched a torch from under the kitchen sink and a fold-out stepladder from the laundry. She took both upstairs to the master bedroom and set them down below the manhole cover. It was still open, just a sliver. She took care climbing the rickety ladder to the fourth rung. The lip of the manhole was thick with cobwebs and muck, but there were clean marks in the dust. Someone had been here recently. She wondered if the police were so thorough that they'd check the storage space in the roof, but it didn't seem likely.

She slid the cover open. A layer of black hovered beyond. She trained the beam of her torch into the space, but all she saw were more cobwebs clinging to exposed ceiling rafters. She moved up to the top rung of the stepladder so that her head was inside the hole. If she really wanted to get a look inside, she was going to have to climb in. The ladder shook as she stepped off it, but thankfully it didn't topple.

She found her feet, then shone the torch wildly around

her immediate space, checking for spiders, before arcing it around the room to check for monsters and killers. The ceiling was low, its sloped walls packed with pink insulation. There was an old boogie board stored to the left of the manhole and a crate of old newspapers.

She shifted the torch beam down and gasped. There were bare footprints against the dusty floor, trailing deep into the storage space.

'Hello?' she called.

If anyone had answered her, she might have leaped back through the manhole fast enough to break her neck. But the storage space was silent. The back of her head tore through a thick cobweb. She frantically pulled white silk strips from her hair, then told herself to calm down. The torch beam trembled. She trained it on the footprints and followed them. One after another, they led her deeper into the dark.

It was cramped and hot. Her heart sped up. Sweat pooled on the collar of her T-shirt. The ceiling was too low. The space was somehow both claustrophobic and a vast, endless void at the same time. She clipped her foot against something hard and winced in pain. She shone the torch at her feet and saw a paint-stained old dumbbell. John had brought a set to the island once, years ago, with the intention of working out every morning, but she couldn't remember ever seeing him use them.

She scanned the space left to right and spotted the light switch. She hit the switch with the heel of her hand, but nothing happened.

She was about to walk away from the light switch when she noticed the electrical outlet below it, switched off. A power board was plugged in, and stuffed with double adaptors and extension cords that slithered out into the dark like snakes. She switched it on.

First there came a deep humming noise, rumbling out at her from different layers of space. Then, one after another, there were sparks of light. Stunning blues, bright greens and harsh whites. Bug zappers. Kate counted eleven – Russ Graves's entire stock. They were clustered at various points around the room, forming a loose perimeter from corner to corner of the attic.

With real terror, she pictured John's Visitor, its black eyes and featureless face, its thin mouth opening and moths fluttering out, filling the room. With the cavity now brightly lit, she had no need for the torch. She could clearly see the trail of footprints weaving around several stacks of clutter – a crate of pots and pans, a dusty stack of paperbacks, and a cardboard box marked, *Mia's Little Girl Toys* – and then gathered at a small object. A black metal lock-box.

Two perfect round circles in the dust told Kate someone had kneeled before the box. She reached for it but recoiled when one of the bug zappers cracked loudly behind her. She turned, half expecting to see Mia's child-eating gremlin scrambling towards her. An unlucky insect had met its end in the bug zapper, that was all.

Turning her attention back to the lock-box, she noticed it gleamed in the light and was clear of dust. She reached for the lid, but it was locked. She looked for a key but there was none. She shook the box, and a bead of sweat rolled down her cheek. It was too hot in here, too tight, too strange. She felt like she was suffocating and hurried back to switch off the power board. In the fading glow of the bug zappers, she dropped down the manhole, birthing through it, feet first.

In the minutes it took her to replace the manhole cover and pack away the stepladder, she convinced herself that all the answers she had come here for were locked inside the metal box. She set it down on the kitchen table and fetched the toolbox out from under the sink. Inside were a few loose bolts, an IKEA screwdriver set, a dried-up old tube of superglue and a claw hammer.

She tried the screwdrivers first, experimenting with different sizes and head shapes. She jammed, stabbed and wiggled each into the locking mechanism, but it didn't give. Next, she tried the hammer. She took it in her right hand, held the box steady in her left, then brought the hammer down. Her first attempt was weak; pathetic. She was being too cautious. Her second swing was hard. It came down on the lid with a crying *clink*. A shockwave reverberated all the way up her arm. Her blow left a shallow dent in the lid of the box, but it remained locked.

'Damn it,' she said, swinging the hammer a third time, more out of frustration now. The tip of the head caught the index finger on her right hand, and a dart of pain shot through her system. She yelped, dropped the hammer and threw the box across the room in anger. It shot out of the kitchen and into the hallway, struck the wall and fell to the floor in a shower of plaster dust. A triangular chunk was now missing from the wall, but the damn box was still locked.

Feeling hot rage, crushing sadness and actual physical pain, she began to sob, quietly at first, then madly. She folded to her knees, collapsed against the linoleum floor and let everything inside her spill out. Then, through wrenching, gasping tears, Kate screamed.

When she got back to the car, Kate was surprised to see a man standing beside it, cupping his hands to look through the tinted windows. The man had parked his own vehicle – a work truck – directly behind hers. *Maintenance* was printed down one side. Kate had seen the same truck the day before, idling outside the house. She hadn't been able to make out the driver, but now she saw it was a man in his late thirties or early forties.

'Can I help you?' Kate asked nervously.

The man spun around, his boots crunching against gravel. Now that he was facing her, Kate saw that he was quite handsome: a heavy brow and deep, sad eyes made him look thoughtful. There were flecks of white in his hair and he wore a pale grey work shirt with *Island Care* embroidered on the breast pocket.

'Shit, sorry,' he said. 'I was driving past and saw your car parked out front. Do you know the man who lived here?'

He pointed up at the house, yellow police tape zig-zagging across the front door.

She nodded. 'I'm his wife.'

Although she supposed that wasn't officially true anymore. She was his widow. *Widow*. That word was too sharp to swallow, too hot to hold in her hands.

'I was sorry to hear about what happened to him. The whole island's in a state of shock about it.' He noticed the lock-box under her arm. 'What do you have there?'

'Nothing,' she said, turning the box over in her hands. 'I misplaced the key.'

'I can help you open it, if you like?'

'I don't want to trouble you.'

'It's no trouble,' he said, and held out his hand. 'Can I take a look?'

She hesitated, then handed it to him. He studied it a second, then carried it over to his truck and set it down on the tray. He opened a red toolbox, took out a hammer and a flat-head screwdriver. She looked up the street. All the big houses were empty at this time of year. She was alone out here with this man.

'I tried that already,' Kate said.

Ignoring her, he wedged the screwdriver against the locking mechanism, then tapped the handle with the head of the hammer. After three or four well-placed strikes, the lock snapped inwards. He set his tools down and tried the lid of the box. With a little heavy-handed encouragement, it popped open. He looked inside for a long, cold moment, then closed the lid and handed back the box.

'Thank you,' she said.

'No worries.'

He reloaded his tools into the back of his truck, got in and drove away. Kate waited until the man was out of sight. She then climbed behind the wheel of her car, locked the doors and opened up the box.

18

THE WIFE

Biller was right. Bay Street was a circus. A bank of parked cars was clustered around the community centre, a budget-deprived brick building that shared a strip of land with the Belport Library.

The police had set up their information caravan on the wide front lawn, a sweep of lush green grass that turned yellow in the summer. It was less an actual caravan than a long white trailer with a marquee attached. Under the marquee was a small table with coffee and biscuits. Someone had placed a smooth rock on the top of the napkins to keep them from blowing away.

Several officers milled about, chatting to locals. A baby-faced constable stood with Mario Brumniach, who ran fishing tours in the on-season. They were standing over a map of the island. Mario was jabbing his finger against the map over and over. Nearby, old Nancy Malerman, who by now must have been pushing ninety, leaned against her walking frame, talking the ear off a heavy-set sergeant.

Abby watched all this as she drove past at a snail's pace. She had to drive slowly, partly because the streets were full of locals who were apparently too excited to look both ways, and partly because she was curious.

No, it wasn't curiosity anymore. It had started off that way – a murder in Belport had been a break in the monotony of island life. It had scratched the same itch taxidermy did, and true crime, and easing off the pedal when passing a car crash on the highway. But she was discovering that true crime was best experienced at a distance, in a safe, warm place, by an open fire or poolside at a resort.

Now everything seemed too close, too real, like going to a zoo without any cages. This – and she still wasn't entirely sure what *this* was – had come into her house. Ray had brought it inside.

Back the fuck off, he'd said. Right now, that didn't seem like terrible advice.

All the spaces in the Buy & Bye were taken, and in the end, she had to park in the Uniting Church lot across the street.

The Buy & Bye was bustling. It wasn't quite summer business, but it was close. There was only one open check-out and it had a line of people snaking all the way back to the meat counter.

Biller stood at the check-out, scanning, sweating and smiling in equal measure. If he were a cartoon, there would have been dollar signs over his eyes.

'There's my girl,' he bellowed when he saw Abby. 'Check-out three is loaded and ready when you are.'

She slipped behind her register, peeled off her coat and rolled up her sleeves. Half the line rushed up to meet her. The next hour was spent endlessly serving. It was mostly small purchases: snacks, drinks and cigarettes. Nobody was there for their weekly grocery shop. If The Sweet Drop Chocolate Shop was open this time of year – or Love Bite's Bakery or Muffins 'n Stuff or, hell, even The Dreamy Ice-Creamery – Abby guessed most of her customers would have gone there.

Everyone wanted to talk about murder, but Abby chose not to engage. It would only make her feel anxious – or worse, lead her to reveal her worries. Instead, she focused on scanning and bagging, on *next please* and *have a nice day*. If she lost focus, even for a second, Bobbi's words were waiting for her like a pile of dirty dishes.

Someone knows something. Was she that someone?

Eventually the line thinned, the happy shoppers of the Buy & Bye drifted back out into the cold, and Abby and Biller had a moment to think. Biller didn't waste any time.

'What do you know, Abby?' he asked, mopping his slick brow with the front of his polo shirt, exposing the soft white belly beneath it.

'What do I know about what?' she asked, but she knew exactly what he was asking. Biller waited. 'A lot of gossip and not much else,' she said.

Biller hoisted both garbage bags from each of their registers – neither had been emptied for over a week – and twisted the tops. He started hauling them towards the doors, moving with a spring in his step. 'Do us a favour, Ab, and restock the Coke fridge, and, oh, check aisle three for vomit. Rose Furleo had her little Bernie in here and she lets that little brat run riot. Who names their child *Bernie*, by the way?'

'I don't think I've ever seen you buzzing like this,' Abby said.

He stopped halfway to the door, then plopped the bags down on the floor. They landed with a wet smacking sound. 'Well, it just so happens I have a juicy little nugget of murder gossip, if you're interested.'

'Actually, Biller, I'm not so sure we should be sharing nuggets of gossip anymore, juicy or otherwise. Don't you think it's sort of disrespectful?'

Biller fixed her with a look she read as either vaguely suspicious or vaguely constipated. 'How's the view from up there, Abby?'

'Huh?'

'From up there on your high horse.'

She rolled her eyes and said, 'Fine, what's your juicy nugget?'

He grinned. 'Okay, so have you ever met my ex-wife, Helen?'

'Not officially, but I've heard so many stories about her I feel like I have.'

Going by what she'd pieced together from Biller's accounts, Helen Biller née Watts was a demon-headed monster ripped from folklore: a creature who collected the hearts of brave and gallant men to feast on in the three-bedroom Barwon Heads townhouse that she bought with her share of the settlement money.

'Now, I have a, well, I suppose you'd call it a habit,' Biller said. 'Of calling her up on the phone anytime I get shit-faced. Sometimes I tell her I'm still in love with her, occasionally I tell her I wish she was dead, but mostly we just talk.'

'Lucky lady,' Abby said.

'*Anyway*, last night was one of those nights. I made it two-thirds through the bottle of Glenfiddich I bought myself for an early birthday present, and before I knew it I had dialled her number. Helen would never admit this to me or anybody, but her heart's still in Belport. She likes to keep abreast of what's happening on the island, and we got to talking about the one thing around here worth talking about. As it turns out, she has a friend of a friend who works as one of those *forensics*. The ones who dust for prints and collect DNA. The way she tells it, there was blood all over the inside of that ferry terminal.'

Abby said nothing.

'Splattered all the way up the rafters, apparently,' he said, with a short, impressed nod. 'What do you think about that?'

'I think I should go and see about Bernie's vomit,' Abby said.

'Ah, you're no fun today.'

'It's like you always say: *if you've got time for leaning you've got time for cleaning.*'

With a shake of the head, he picked up the garbage bags and dragged them outside towards the hopper. On his way out the door, he passed a tall brunette who was on her way in. She was dressed in shades of grey, with hair that fell straight to the shoulders. Her hands dangled slackly by her side like a gunslinger's.

She was naturally pretty. She wore no make-up but her skin was clear and smooth. Her eyes were deep and thoughtful, but there was something sad about them. Abby was strangely captivated by her.

It might have been that she was a stranger, which was unusual for this time of year. She didn't look like a cop, but then again, neither did Bobbi. Her clothes looked too expensive to belong to a journalist, but of the two, that's what Abby would have put her money on.

'Can I help you find something?' Abby asked.

The woman flinched, looked up as if snapping out of a trance, and frowned.

'Cigarettes,' she said.

'No worries,' Abby slid open the cigarette cupboard below her register. 'What's your brand? We have hand-rolled, menthols, cigars – we might even have some cloves in the back of the display if you're feeling Gothy.'

The woman didn't smile. She seemed unaware that Abby had even attempted a joke. It made her think of Lori.

'I'll just take a pack of Starling Blues.'

'Excellent choice,' Abby said wryly. 'I could never afford this brand back when I smoked, but I always aspired to. I quit when I got pregnant. Not that it would have made much difference. I still couldn't afford them.'

She was rambling. The woman curled her lips – an imitation of a smile. 'How old's your child?'

'She's sixteen, going on thirty-seven,' Abby said. 'And I have a fifteen-year-old son right behind her. Do you have kids?'

She nodded but chose not to elaborate. She flashed her impression of a smile again, paid for her cigarettes, and said, 'Thanks, Abby.'

'... How did you know my name?'

She made a gun with her index finger and pointed it at the badge on Abby's chest that declared in bright red letters, *Hello, I'm ... ABBY*!

'Oh,' Abby said. 'Right.'

As the woman walked away, Abby thought her clothes

looked too expensive, too pristine, too untouched to stink up with cigarette smoke. Abby used to love the smell of a lit smoke, but ever since she had kids it made her want to throw up harder than Bernie Furleo.

A new thought popped into her head then, as if it had been circling in a holding pattern, waiting for the air traffic controllers to wave it in. It might have been that she was thinking of old clothes at the exact moment she heard the clatter of Biller's garbage bags against the floor of the dumpster, but she was suddenly transported back to the day of the big rain storm.

She'd come home and found a week's worth of garbage on the road. The bin had toppled over in the wind. She remembered the ravens that had gathered to feast on their garbage, and she remembered the one last plastic bag that had rolled into the middle of Milt Street.

After her shift, Abby drove home along the esplanade. The scraps of coastal woodland that lined the road swayed and danced in the ocean breeze, alive and shadowy. To her left, a steep, grassy embankment climbed sharply up to the nature reserve. To her right, ten metres below, waves crashed onto jagged rocks.

As she drove, she thought: *do this one thing and let that be the end of it.*

When she got home, she marched to the side door

of the garage and went inside. She found the pull-string light switch in the dark and tugged it. The harsh lights blinked on overhead. Squinting against them, she stood on the empty strip of oil-stained concrete where Ray's truck was usually parked and looked over at his workbench, behind which the first-aid kit was stashed. She then shifted her gaze to the bank of shelves that ran the length of the rear wall.

She took the Salvos box out and opened it. Inside, just where she'd left them, were Ray's work shirt, cargo trousers and tan-coloured boots.

Abby snapped on a pair of latex surgical gloves, carefully removed Ray's boots, cargo trousers and work shirt from the box, and thought, *What the hell am I doing?*

She made a space for the clothing on her workbench, between the scalpel blades, insect pins, tongue depressors, pliers, rubber mallet and staple gun. The fluorescent light hummed overhead, and an incessant leak dripped somewhere in the dark corner of the garage.

She kneeled to search through her taxidermy supplies. Tucked neatly beside the bar fridge was a large plastic tub. She slid it out, popped the lid and riffled through plastic bottles, glass vials and jars, searching for the luminol. As well as playing a small part in the taxidermy clean-up process, luminol was used by forensic investigators to detect trace amounts of blood at crime scenes. When it came into contact with the iron in blood, it emitted a blue glow that could be seen in a darkened room.

Being careful to distribute the chemical evenly and thoroughly, Abby sprayed the trousers, shirt and boots, praying the garage door wouldn't swing open to admit Ray's truck. When she was sure she'd used enough luminol, all she needed to do was turn out the lights. If the luminol found blood, she'd know right away. She took hold of the pull-string light switch in the middle of the garage, and took three deep breaths.

19

THE WIDOW

Inside the black metal lock-box was a one-paragraph obituary, cut neatly from a newspaper. Age had turned the paper yellow and water damage had blurred the ink in places, but it was still readable:

STEMPLE, David E.
Taken from this world on the 7th of August 1996. Wait for
us on the other side, Dave. Survived by two loving sisters, a
cherished son, and beloved wife, Annabel.

'Who's David Stemple?' Fisher asked when Kate handed him the death notice to read. They were in his room at the Blue Whale Motor Inn. Fisher was sitting at the desk, ready for a shower, a soft blue towel draped around his shoulders like a pet snake.

'I have no idea,' Kate said. 'But I found this locked inside a box in the attic of the holiday house.'

'The house? You went back there? Kate, that's a crime scene.'

'I know, I know.'

'Detective Eckman specifically told us not to—'

'I know, Fisher. I just … I was sick of feeling so powerless.'

'Do me a favour and stand still,' Fisher said. 'You're moving so fast it's making me feel nauseous.'

She had been pacing the length of the small motel room since she'd arrived, but now she sat down on the bed and stuffed her hands beneath her legs. Fisher really did look nauseous, but Kate thought it might have more to do with the Chivas.

He read the obit again through bloodshot, squinted eyes, then rubbed the bridge of his nose. 'This obituary is from 1996. How do you know it didn't spend the last twenty-three years in the attic? Although I suppose Pam and I still had the place back then, and I can't imagine why either of us would save something like this.'

'The lock-box was pretty much the only clean thing in a very dusty attic,' Kate explained. 'Even if it was up there all that time, someone has looked at it very recently.'

'Then it's evidence.'

'Evidence the cops missed,' she said.

'We shouldn't even be touching this,' he said, placing the obituary carefully down on the desk. 'There might be fingerprints or DNA on it. This might belong to whoever killed him, Kate.'

'It was John's,' she said firmly. 'He either brought it with him to the island or dug it out when he got here.'

'How can you be sure?'

'Remember the bug zappers Eckman told us about? They were up there too, in a circle around the lock-box. It was like he'd set them up to … I don't know … protect him from whatever it was that was inside the box.'

'The ghost of David Stemple?' Fisher asked, dryly. He popped two Disprin into a glass of water and watched them fizz, twirling the glass in a circular motion, trying to speed up their dissolving.

'He was scared of something, Fisher,' she said.

He nodded. 'I know. I don't mean to be flippant. This is just … a lot.'

He picked up his glass of Disprin even though it wasn't quite ready – big clumps of medication floated inside – and drank it in one gulp, wincing at the taste. 'Have you tried looking online?'

'Google gave me three hundred thousand results. It's a pretty common name.'

'*Stemple*,' he said, moving the word around his mouth, as if tasting wine. 'Maybe it does sound familiar now. I'll give Pam a call. She might know something … You okay, love?'

Kate had slumped forward on the bed, elbows to

knees and face to hands. She had spent her marriage looking at her husband through a keyhole. Now, she was catching a glimpse of what lay beyond the door, and what didn't confuse her, was terrifying.

'I just don't know why he didn't come to me with whatever the hell he was going through?'

This is what happens when we don't talk about the monsters.

There was a flash of something that might have been guilt in Fisher's expression, then he shook it off. 'None of this is on you, Kate. John had a support network. There were plenty of people he could have come to.'

'But I'm his wife, Fisher. I'm his … I'm his … *beloved wife.*' She trailed off a moment, then went over to the desk and picked up the obit. Reading aloud, she said, '*Beloved wife, Annabel.*'

'What is it?' Fisher asked, reading her face.

Annabel's death was the leaf that dammed the stream, Holly Cutter had told her back in the empty cafeteria at Trinity Health Centre.

'I have to make a call,' Kate said.

'It's good to hear your voice,' Chatveer Sandhu said. Kate imagined him sitting behind the reception desk, surrounded by those relaxing shades of blue and quiet, forgettable artwork, listening to the gurgle of the extravagant water feature. 'Everyone at Trinity was just sick when they heard the news. Did you get the flowers we sent?'

'No,' Kate said. 'But I haven't been home. I'm staying in Belport for a while.'

She'd gone back to her room to make the call and was now sitting on the bed looking out at the fibreglass orca. A wet seagull swooped down and landed in the dry spot beneath its breaching tail.

'Do you know yet when his service will be?' Chatveer asked.

'Not for a few weeks. There's still a lot to figure out.'

The truth was, she'd hardly stopped to think about things like funeral arrangements and flowers and eulogies, and, frankly, she understood now that there were two versions of John: the husband and the stranger. She would have to find a way to reconcile those two versions before anyone put shovel to dirt.

'You're probably looking for Holly,' Chatveer said. 'She's in a meeting right now, but I can give her a message or patch you through to her voicemail.'

She was pretty sure there was no meeting. After Kate's unannounced visit to Trinity, Holly likely instigated a strict no-Kate phone-screening policy. Either that, or she was standing over Chatveer's shoulder right now, waving her hands and whispering, 'I'm not here!'

'Actually, I was hoping to talk to you,' she said. 'I

wanted to ask you about one of John's patients: Annabel. Do you remember her?'

'Annabel,' Chatveer said. 'Of course. Advanced PF. She was a cantankerous old thing, but I liked her. We all did.'

'Holly told me John took her death pretty hard.'

What she'd really said was that when Annabel died, John *took a dark turn*.

'When you work in a place like Trinity, it's impossible not to connect with certain patients,' Chatveer said soothingly, clearly pleased to be comforting the poor widow. 'I'm just a glorified secretary, and I still spend half my week crying and the other looking at job ads. But, you know, John and Annabel really had something *special*. He'd sit with her for hours after the end of his shift. They'd just talk or watch *Modern Family*. They'd tease each other, like old friends. He was so good that way, Kate, but not everyone could appreciate their connection.'

'What do you mean?'

'Annabel's son was …' he paused to choose his words, then lowered his voice. 'He was a piece of work. Nobody leaves Trinity, at least not in the corporeal sense, and by the time Annabel came to us it was clear she was on her way out. But apparently her son found hospice care too depressing. The whole time she was in our care, he must have visited twice. Three times at the most. Now, I try to be guided through life by truth, love and empathy, but sometimes you just need to grow some balls. He had no problem visiting after she was dead.'

'What do you mean?'

'He …' Chatveer trailed off, then fell silent.

'What is it?'

'It's just, I'm not sure how much we should be talking about.'

'Holly doesn't need to know.'

'It's not just Holly,' he said. 'John didn't tell you about all this, did he?'

Kate didn't respond.

'I'm sorry, Kate, but he must have had his reasons.'

She considered this a moment. 'The second-last thing John ever said to me was, *If we don't talk about the monsters in this world, we won't be ready for them when they jump out from under the bed.* He kept a lot of things from me, to protect me, but he realised too late that it was a mistake.'

There was a long beat of silence, then Chatveer took a deep, steady breath. 'Annabel wrote John into her will, Kate.'

She leaned forward on the bed, pressed the phone closer to her ear. 'Really?'

'It was a small amount, I'm not exactly sure how much, but when her son got wind of it, he threatened the hospital with legal action, accused the staff of manipulating vulnerable people out of their money. It was all unfounded, of course, but he was furious.'

'How furious?'

'Not furious enough to do what you're thinking, I'm sure,' Chatveer said. 'To be honest with you, he had a point. This kind of thing isn't unheard of in palliative care, especially with the lonelier patients. They have money and want it to mean something, to go somewhere. But it's unethical. If John had known anything about it while Annabel was alive he would have put a stop to it.'

'Does this have something to do with why John quit?'

'Officially, John resigned.' He was almost whispering now. '*Un*officially, Holly didn't give him much of a choice. If Annabel's son carried through with his legal threat, and it seemed like there was a good chance he might, there would be all sorts of trouble heading their way. Don't get me wrong, Holly puts the needs of Trinity staff ahead of everything else, but you know she's a cut-and-run type of person. John became a liability, so she cut him loose.'

The rain outside eased enough for the seagull to creep out from under the orca's tail and take flight.

'What was Annabel's surname?' Kate asked.

'I can't remember off the top of my head.'

'Can you check?'

'I don't know, Kate,' he said. 'There's doctor–patient confidentiality to consider.'

'I wouldn't ask if it wasn't important,' she said. 'Please.'

Chatveer said nothing, but Kate could hear the tapping of fingers on a computer keyboard. 'Stemple. Annabel Stemple.'

'Did she ever talk about her husband, was his name David?'

Chatveer scoffed. 'Only all the time,' he said. 'From what I remember, he died a long time ago.'

The 7th of August 1996.

'Do you know how he died?' Kate asked.

'No, but I got the impression it was unexpected. Sudden, even.'

'What makes you say that?'

'The way she reminisced about him. It was more about the times they didn't get to share, rather than the ones they did.'

In a painful, sudden flash, Kate thought about the years that stretched out ahead of her. John wasn't coming back for them.

'I just need one more thing from you,' she said. 'Do you have access to Annabel's son's contact details?'

Another contemplative click of the tongue down the line. 'What was the last thing?'

'What?'

'You said the second-last thing John said to you was about monsters. What was the last?'

'... He told me he was ready to come home.'

Chatveer exhaled, then she heard him typing on his keyboard. A moment later he came back on the line and said, 'Here's the address, do you have a pen?'

Kate fetched some motel stationery from the desk. 'Go ahead.'

'Oh,' he said.

'*Oh* what, Chat?'

'Annabel's son. He lives in Belport.'

20

THE WIFE

As Abby stood poised to turn out the light in the garage, a terrifying question occurred to her: *What next?* What would she do if the luminol revealed blood on Ray's clothing? Would she run to the police and turn over the evidence, or carry her husband's secret with her wherever she went like a tumour? What was a wife supposed to do? How far was she expected to go for love? Another thought shot to the surface like a cork. Was her husband a killer? Even with the mysterious phone call, the secret stash of gay porn, his recent defensive behaviour, she couldn't imagine him ending another man's life.

But that isn't quite true, a dark voice whispered. *You can imagine it, because you've seen the Switch.*

'Do all men have a switch?' she asked aloud, as if this wasn't a conversation taking place in her head. Her voice, echoing off the walls of the garage, sounded like a stranger's.

And do all men act like Ray when that switch is thrown?

Abby and Ray argued occasionally, like any couple, but rarely loud enough to bring neighbours to fences. He had never hit her. Never come close. But he did have a temper, and she had seen it boil over into something mean and sharp-toothed.

She called it the Switch. The last time she'd seen it thrown was on a hot summer night a long time ago, while she was eight-and-a-half months pregnant with Lori. The memory slapped over her. It became a trapdoor, and Abby tumbled through it, falling backwards in time, until suddenly it was

seventeen years earlier, Abby and Ray were on their way home from Belport Medical. They had rushed to emergency because Abby had been convinced she was in labour. As it turned out, she'd been having false contractions, or 'a belly full of farts' as the doctor had described it.

It was a stifling night. The aircon in their old Datsun was broken – the car would be scrapped six months later when Abby slid off the loose gravel shoulder of Old Harbour Road and right into Les and Kathleen Bale's brick letterbox – so all the windows were down. Warm air filled the car, carrying the smell of bonfire parties.

It was the middle of January. Bay Street was jammed with traffic. Sandwiched between a yellow BMW and a silver Benz, they stop-started towards home, barely six inches at a time. The footpath was full of sunburned tourists. A gang of teenage girls in bikinis attacked each other with water balloons. The line outside The Dreamy Ice-Creamery snaked into the street. The sound of David Bowie spilled out of the Belly. Inside, as usual, middle-aged men and women would be tearing up the dance floor.

Ray watched all of this from behind the wheel of the Datsun and grumbled.

'This whole island used to be a hunting ground,' he said, keeping as little distance as possible between them and the car in front. 'Aborigines would paddle over from the mainland to collect shellfish and swan eggs. Now look at the state of it.'

'No offence, Ray, but I really can't talk about shellfish and swan eggs right now.' Her belly full of farts had settled into a state of nausea.

'All I'm saying is, with the amount of money these people piss away each year, you could practically cure world hunger.'

The fact that Abby and Ray (along with the rest of the town) depended on tourist money to survive seemed to have temporarily escaped him.

Finally, the traffic eased enough for them to get a run. 'Look at this,' Ray said, gesturing to the cars lining the street. 'Sports car, sports car, Benz, sports car. That's a

Blackhawk, for Christ's sake. Do you have any idea how much a Blackhawk—'

The car shook madly for a moment, then filled with a sudden metallic crunch. Ray, who had gently pressed the brake to let a kid with a BMX over the zebra crossing, clenched his fingers around the wheel and clenched his teeth even tighter.

Abby – who wasn't wearing a seatbelt because it felt like a boa constrictor around her pregnant belly – lurched forward. She let out a noise, something like a desperate, frightened whimper, and then wrapped her hands around her stomach.

They'd just been rear-ended.

'Jesus fucking Christ,' Ray muttered, breathing heavily through a burst of adrenalin. His hands were trembling. 'Are you alright?'

'I'm fine,' Abby said.

'He could have hurt you. He could have hurt the baby.'

He turned to look at her. His eyes were distant, set behind a fog of quickly growing rage. He glanced into the rear-view mirror, then shifted around in his seat to look through the rear windscreen.

'Fucking tourists,' he spat.

The car behind was a Benz. There was superficial damage to the front of the car, but nothing a little trust-fund money wouldn't fix. The driver appeared to be in his early twenties, a sprinkling of peach fuzz on his chin. He leaned forward over the wheel, surveyed the damage, then turned to his girlfriend in the passenger seat and mouthed the word, oops.

'He could have hurt you,' Ray said again.

'I'm okay, Ray.'

'He would have hurt the baby.'

'Ray, take a breath, don't do anything—'

But it was too late. He had already stepped out of the Datsun, hands balled into fists, red-faced, head thrown forward. He left the driver's-side door wide open and marched over to the Benz. The driver stepped out, a half-smile on his face, and Abby felt a wave of unease. With growing tension, she swivelled in her seat to watch.

Abby couldn't make out what the driver was saying over the noise of the street, but she could hear Ray, because he was screaming.

'You fucking idiot,' he shouted. 'If you're going to just come to my island and drive around like a fucking lunatic …'

Abby swung open the passenger door and waddled out, one hand on the top of the Datsun, the other under her belly. She got out just in time to see the driver roll his eyes.

'Dude,' he said. 'Relax. We were going about two k's an hour. I'll pay for the—'

'I don't give a shit how fast we were going or what

you'll pay for. My wife is pregnant, you rich fucking prick.'

The kid on the BMX, who Ray had stopped to let across the street, was sitting on his bike watching, wide-eyed and excited. A horde of beer-swilling young people stopped to watch the commotion, as did a young couple pushing their baby in a pram. People started to honk from the line of cars that had backed up behind them.

'Look,' said the driver of the Benz, throwing his girlfriend a nervous glance. She was still in the car, and when Abby looked at her, she locked the door. 'I don't know what to tell you, mate, it was an accident. Let's just exchange details and get out of everyone's way. There's no reason this has to ruin our night.'

'Ray,' Abby called. 'Come on. Let's go.'

'Get back in the car, Ab.'

'But—'

'I said get back in the fucking car,' he craned his neck to snap the words off at her, then turned back to the driver. Ray wasn't there anymore. The Switch had been thrown.

'Jesus, man,' the driver said. 'Take it easy on your girl. It's not her fault her husband is a psycho.'

Oh no, Abby thought.

'What did you call me?'

There were more honks from the line of cars behind

them; more people gathered to watch the chaos that was building in the middle of Bay Street.

'Take it easy, Ray,' Abby said. 'Please, just get back in the car.'

'Do you want me to pay for the damages or not?' the young driver said.

'You think you can just pay your way out of anything, don't you?'

'Whatever, dude. You're upsetting your girl and scaring mine, so I'm just going to leave.'

'You're not going anywhere until I let you.'

The driver took his hands from his pockets. He looked nervous now, shifting from one foot to the other.

'People like you don't learn,' Ray said. 'Your parents pay your way out of trouble until you're old enough to do it yourself. But you need to learn. You could have hurt my wife.'

'I know,' the man said, taking a step backwards, palms up. 'I'm really sorry.'

'Don't apologise to me. Apologise to my wife.'

Before the man could speak again, Ray grabbed his arm and dragged him over to Abby. His girlfriend screamed hysterically from inside the car.

Shouts of protest erupted around them.

'Take it easy, he's just a kid!'

'Let him go, someone call the cops!'

'Are you fucking crazy, mate? He's half your size!'

Ray couldn't seem to hear any of them. He was somewhere beyond them, beyond reason. The driver of the Benz flailed beside him. He wasn't fighting back, thank God.

The driver turned to Abby. He was sobbing. Fear, deep and resonating and traumatic, was etched on his face.

'I'm sorry,' he moaned. 'I'm … I'm sorry.'

The shouts around them grew louder. She grabbed hold of Ray's free hand, squeezed it hard, dug her fingernails into his skin, and said, 'Think about what you're doing.'

Ray swung his head around to face her. His face was twisted with the same maniacal grimace she'd see again seventeen years later, as he stood over a fallen gum tree and told her to back the fuck off.

'Babe,' she said, as calmly as she could. 'You need to stop.'

Somehow, amid the shouts from the crowd and the honking of built-up traffic, Ray heard her. Slowly, his jaw relaxed, focus returned to his eyes and the Switch was reset. He came back to her.

Ray let the man go. They didn't exchange any insurance details, but there wasn't much damage done to the Datsun anyway. She doubted the driver of the Benz would ever rear-end anyone again.

Ray and Abby drove home without another word.

Later, as they lay on top of the covers of their bed, watching the ceiling fan turn, Ray told her he was sorry.

In the dull light of the bedside lamp, he had looked lost and childish. More scared, even, than the man in the street had looked.

'What was that?' Abby asked. 'I've never seen you lose control like that before.'

He blamed his outburst on the stress of being a new father. The false labour had shaken him. He was tired, that was all.

'Promise me nothing like that will ever happen again,' she had told him.

'Ab, you don't need to worry about me.'

'You scared the shit out of me tonight,' she said. 'So promise.'

'I promise,' he said.

She kissed him softly on the mouth, then rolled onto her side, partly because it was the only way she could get comfortable, and partly because she didn't want to look at her husband anymore that night.

She lay awake for a long time, long after she turned

out the lights. She stood in the dark garage, her hand on the pull-string switch, and stared in jarring, frightened wonder as the luminol lit up like phosphorescence on the wall of an underwater cave. The chemical, activated by the blood entangled in the fibres of Ray's clothing, glowed blue.

There were splatters on the front of the shirt, more on the boots, and a concentrated puddle on the left leg of the cargo trousers.

Abby felt untethered.

As the blue glow of the luminol faded and the darkness of the garage enveloped her once more, she pictured the man who was driving the Benz that night. He was sobbing, wide-eyed. He was sorry. So sorry. And so was she.

What now? she thought. *What the fuck now?*

21

THE WIDOW

Annabel Stemple's son lived on a little-travelled road called Sunset Strip, that cut between Neef Steet and Old Harbour Road. When Kate first started coming to Belport a decade ago, it had been one of the most exclusive areas on the island. Since then, most of the houses that lined the street had been sold off and were in various stages of subdivision. Now it was a world of half-built homes, chain–link fences and big squares of dead land.

Kate followed her GPS to a small house set back from the road across a wild yard shaggy with weeds, dead leaves and fallen branches. There were a dozen paint-chipped gnomes scattered over the lawn, most of them overturned or half swallowed up by nature. The house appeared to be on a slight lean, with grass sprouting from the gutters and one window boarded up with pallet slats.

For a moment she questioned her decision to come here alone, but it would no doubt be a waste of time telling the cops what she'd learned from Chatveer, and she couldn't stand the idea of Eckman talking down to her again. As for Fisher, he'd go in like a sledgehammer and make everything worse. But the real reason was that she wanted to discover John's secrets – whatever they were – before anyone else. If she knew the truth, she might be able to protect Mia from it; despite what John had told her, there might still be some monsters better left hidden. There were two cars parked in the driveway: one, an ancient blue commodore, was plastered with bumper stickers. One read, *Want to see god? Then keep tailgating me!* Another, *Vaccines cause adults.* Then there were such classics as *My other car is a Porsche, Honk if you're horny* and *Caution: I brake for nobody.* In the middle of it all was a Southern Cross decal. The second car was mounted on cinder blocks and missing both its rear tyres.

She parked the Lexus across the street and started towards the house. She walked through the front gate and crossed the front yard briskly – if she lost momentum she might chicken out – and knocked loudly on the front door.

Ten seconds passed, then twenty. Nobody came to the door, so she knocked again, louder this time.

'Jesus, fuck,' called a voice from inside. 'I'm coming, I'm coming.'

The front door popped open and a man appeared, his features dark and distorted behind a tattered old screen door.

'Yeah?' the man asked.

'Are you Marcus Stemple?' Kate asked.

The man yawned, scratching his balls. 'What are you selling? Insurance, charity or religion?'

'I'm not selling anything,' she said, keeping her tone light. 'My name is Kate Keddie. You knew my husband, John. He was a physician at Trinity Health Centre. He looked after your mother.'

He opened the screen door and stepped out onto the verandah to get a look at Kate. He was a slim man, somewhere in his late twenties, with long limbs connecting to a solid, compact torso, like a daddy-long-legs spider. His face was vampire-pale, his hair black and greasy. His eyes were deeply set and etched with worry lines.

He let the screen door fall shut behind him. It slammed loudly, startling Kate.

'What are you doing here?' he asked.

'John came to Belport a couple of weeks ago,' she said. 'Then, four days ago, he was killed.'

Marcus belched, then nodded. 'Yeah, I heard something about that. It's got everyone in town on their toes. What's it got to do with me?'

Kate took David Stemple's obituary from the pocket of her jeans and handed it to him. Marcus read it, expressionless. He then folded the obituary and handed it back.

'I've never seen this before,' he said. 'It's twenty-three years old. Where'd you get it?'

'I found it among John's things.'

'Why would he have it?'

'I was hoping you might be able to help answer that.'

Marcus shaded his eyes with the palm of his hand and looked into the street. Kate's Lexus stood out against the grey landscape like a shiny sore thumb. 'Did you come out here by yourself?'

It was an unsettling question, but Kate nodded.

'I suppose you can come inside,' he said. 'But I don't get many visitors so I don't have any coffee or tea or scones or anything.'

'That's fine,' Kate said.

Marcus Stemple's home was sparse and felt almost transient. There were no pets and no plants. The only items of furniture were a wooden desk and chair, an armchair by the window that the Salvation Army would reject, and a coffee table covered with empty beer bottles, ash trays and an extravagant glass bong. The walls were the colour of burned mustard, and a musty, second-hand smell hovered in the air.

He collapsed into the armchair. Its cushions exhaled dust. Kate sat in the stiff wooden chair beside the desk, on which stood a grimy Royal Epoch typewriter.

'Are you a writer?' she asked.

'I wouldn't use that old bastard if I was,' Marcus said.

'That was my dad's. Most of this stuff was.'

'How long have you lived in Belport?'

'Oh, I don't live here. If I *lived* here, I'd have to kill myself. I'm just passing through. About two or three years ago, I got into a little trouble.' He placed a pair of mocking air quotes around the words *a little trouble*. 'I lost my job because my boss was an arsehole. Ran out of money. And since my mother refused to set foot in this place but also refused to sell it, I figured the old shithole was as good a place as any to figure things out.'

Two or three years is a long time to be passing through a place, Kate thought.

'I was sorry to hear about your mother,' she said.

'Did you know her?'

'No, but from what I hear she and John were close. I heard about what happened, how she wrote John into her will.'

Marcus licked his lips. 'From the look of the Lexus across the street, I'd say it's not the first time he put the squeeze on one of his patients. To swoop in right at the end of someone's life like that and manipulate them out of their hard-earned – that's a pretty fucked-up side business. You think that's why he got topped?'

Kate flinched, and worse, Marcus noticed.

'John wasn't like that,' she said. 'If your mother offered him anything it was because she wanted to.'

He stood quickly, and for a moment Kate thought he

was lunging towards her. But then he moved past her and into the adjoining kitchen. An unwashed, sweaty smell went with him: a wave of what Mia would describe as *stank*.

The kitchen was cluttered and nicotine-stained. The sink had been removed, revealing a rectangular cavity full of rusty pipes and cobwebs. An ancient refrigerator hummed like a drunken busker.

He grabbed one of the beers, came back into the living room and fell into the armchair again. He fixed her with a look that seemed to say, *I'm a busy man, so either get on with it or get out.*

'Did you ever meet John?' Kate asked.

'Sure.'

'When?'

Marcus shrugged, drank and thought it over. 'About two weeks ago.'

'Two weeks ago? Are you sure?'

'Uh huh. The doc sat right where you're sitting now.'

Kate gripped the arms of the wooden chair like a nervous flyer, as if she might still be able to pick up the vibrations made when John sat in it. 'He came here, to the house? Do ... do the police know that?'

'Why would they?' Marcus asked, then belched.

'They were trying to create a time line, that's all. Trying to figure out John's movements on the island before he ...'

'Nobody asked me anything,' he said. 'And if you're thinking what I'd probably be thinking, no. I had nothing to do with what happened to him. Wishing someone was dead is a long way from making it happen.'

'Oh, no, I wasn't—'

'Yeah, you were.'

'Why did John come here?' she asked.

'Never quite figured that out,' Marcus said. 'He was either here to help me or blow me. Or maybe both.'

'What do you mean?'

He chuckled to himself. 'He came on pretty strong, is what I'm saying. He came around here looking to make amends. He apologised – and, look, I never wanted to get the guy fired, I just didn't like the idea of him taking advantage of my mum, and that's what I told him. As far as I was concerned, that should have been that.'

'But it wasn't?'

He picked at the label of his beer. 'He tried to pay me back the money Mum had left him. He said I needed it more than him. I'm not some fucking charity case, which is also what I told him. But the guy wouldn't let up. He was … full-on.'

'How do you mean?' Kate asked.

'He made out that I needed the money, but it was more like he needed to give it to me. He was all fucked up about Mum's death. More than me, even. He was *obsessed*. And he was looking for somewhere new to send that obsession.'

'Maybe he felt guilty about Annabel writing him into her will,' Kate offered.

'He was guilty about something, that's for sure,' he said. 'Trust me, people like us can smell our own.'

He leaned back in the armchair to look down the narrow hallway, out through the screen door and over Sunset Strip.

'Did you and John talk about anything else?' she asked.

Marcus lifted the longneck to his lips and sucked like a baby lamb. He swallowed hard, then wiped his mouth with the back of his hand. 'He had a lot of questions about my dad.'

'What kind of questions?'

'He wanted to know what I remembered about him and about when he died. I was only five when it happened, so all I really remember is my mum crying a lot, and us going to stay with my aunty Rita in Mollymook and her annoying fucking yappy dog.'

'Why was John so interested in your dad?' Kate asked.

'You'd have to ask him that. There's a ouija board around here somewhere, if you'd like to try.'

'How did your dad die?'

Marcus paused mid-swig, set the bottle down on the coffee table, and glared at her. 'You don't know?'

'All I heard was it was sudden,' she said.

'*Sudden*,' he echoed. 'Yeah. You could say that.'

22

THE WIFE

Abby listened to the rain drum against the roof of the Volvo, working up the nerve to go inside. She was parked on Old Harbour Road, opposite Deepwater Living, Bobbi's apartment building.

She took a few deep breaths, forced herself out of the car and started toward the building. Six or seven ravens perched on the chain-link fence that separated the apartment block from an empty block of land next door. They watched her. One of them squawked at her in a tone that sounded personal.

She found Bobbi's apartment number on the intercom list. 2-D. Someone had added *ykes* in black texta, making it *2-Dykes*. A chill ran through her. It was tempting to think of Belport as a progressive little microcosm, separate from the mainland and immune to its prejudices, but then something like this came along and reminded her such thoughts were naive. She thought about what went on inside the old ferry terminal and didn't suppose a place like that would need to exist if Belport was as accepting as she thought it was.

Buzz. The intercom spat static, then a sweet, soothing voice said, 'Yes?'

It was Bobbi's girlfriend, Maggie.

'It's me.'

'Could you be a little more specific?' Maggie asked. 'I wouldn't ordinarily ask, but there may or may not be a murderer loose on the island.'

'It's Abby.'

'Abby! Get your arse up here. The remote unlocking doesn't work, but luckily for you, neither does the security gate.'

The front gate gave with just a gentle nudge. Abby navigated around a small garden of ferns, then skipped up two short flights of external stairs to Bobbi's apartment. Maggie was waiting for her on the second-floor landing, resting one hand on her hip and the other on her heavily pregnant belly. She was dressed in maternity jeans and an XL white T-shirt. Pregnancy suited her.

'Come here, Ab,' she said. 'It's so good to see you. In fairness, I've been cooped up inside for weeks so it's good to see *anyone*, but it's especially good to see you.'

She showed Abby inside. The apartment was warm and bright. There were potted plants on every surface and more out on the balcony.

'I'm halfway through second lunch,' Maggie said. 'Or maybe it's first dinner. Either way, there's plenty, if you're hungry.'

'No thanks,' Abby said.

Maggie slid herself into the breakfast nook and chowed down on vegemite toast. Abby sat with her.

'Is Bobbi around? I know she's been working nights lately, so I thought I'd catch her before she goes on duty.'

'She's just getting out of the shower; she'll be out in a minute. Isn't all this murder stuff crazy? I hate the idea of Bobbi going out there. I didn't mind the idea of sharing my life with a cop when the biggest thing to happen was Bert Sercombe getting busted shoplifting tampons from the pharmacy.'

'Did that really happen?'

Nodding, Maggie laughed. 'Clare had sent him out for them. He had the money. He was just too embarrassed to take them through the register. It's the most pathetic thing a man has ever done. But you didn't hear that from me.'

'Mum's the word,' Abby said. 'And try not to worry about Bobbi. She's tough.'

If Maggie had seen Bobbi in the car with the tequila, she might not have agreed so easily. 'I know,' she said. 'She's basically Sarah Connor.'

Joe slunk coolly into the room, yawned and helped himself to Maggie's lap. Joe was a beefy cat, an apartment stray that Bobbi had started feeding a couple of years back. He had officially moved in soon after. Maggie winced as he kneaded at her legs to get comfortable.

'I thought you and Joe hated each other,' Abby said.

'When I got pregnant, I had to stop changing his litter tray because cat turds can carry this nasty parasite called toxoplasmosis, which can cause birth defects.' She rubbed her palm over her belly. 'There's something about not picking up someone's shit that puts you on the same level. Joe respects me now.'

'*Toxoplasmosis*,' a voice mocked from the hall. Bobbi padded in from the bathroom, dressed in her crisp powder-blue uniform, drying her hair off with a towel. Her eyebrows were still wet from the shower. They looked more commanding than usual. 'Be honest, Abby, don't you think that sounds made up?'

'Bobbi thinks the whole cat-turd thing is a conspiracy to trick her into cleaning out Joe's litter all the time,' Maggie said. 'Personally, I think it's a pretty good trade-off when you consider what I'm going through over here. Morning sickness, bloating, frequent urination, haemorrhoids. I can go on.'

'And on and on and on,' Bobbi said, giving Maggie a peck on the cheek. 'How do I look?'

'Babelicious,' Maggie told her. 'So you're stuck at the information caravan again tonight?'

Bobbi prepped some coffee in a thermos at the kitchen counter. 'All night.'

'I drove past there, and it looked pretty packed,' Abby said. 'How's it going?'

'As an exercise in gathering gossip, it's working great. As far as generating any actual leads, I don't know yet. Time will tell, I suppose. Is everything okay, Ab? You look … weird.'

Abby's instinct was to open her mouth and tell her everything was just fine, but if that was true, she wouldn't be there. In the time it took her to think of an answer to that question, Bobbi exchanged a telepathic glance with Maggie, who quickly took the hint.

'If you'll excuse me now, I need to make my eighty-seventh daily trip to the loo.'

She hoisted herself out of the breakfast nook with a grunt and waddled into the bathroom, which was still steamy from Bobbi's shower. Joe made himself comfortable in the warm space she'd left.

'If this is about the call, it's all been straightened out,' Bobbi said. 'I buzzed the office earlier. Ray went into the station on his lunchbreak and cleared it all up. I should have known the call was about a caretaking job. Sorry if I freaked you out the other night.'

'That's good,' Abby said. 'But it's not why I'm here. Bobbi, I need to talk to you about something. But before we get into it, I need to know I'm talking to Bobbi the Friend, not Bobbi the Cop.'

'I'm always your friend first.'

'Promise?'

'I promise,' Bobbi said.

'I need you to give me a day, twenty-four hours to get my ducks in a row. Then Bobbi the Cop can do what she needs to do.'

A grave look came to Bobbi's face. She sat down in the nook opposite Abby, forehead knitted with concern. 'What's going on?'

'The other night in the church car park, you told me something,' Abby said. 'You said that in a town as small as this one, someone knows something. Do you remember that?'

'A lot of that night is foggy,' she said. 'But yeah, I remember that. Why?'

'Well, as it turns out, you were right.'

Gloomy afternoon was shifting into drizzly evening when Abby got home. She pulled the Volvo into the driveway, stepped out and winced when she spotted Dorothy Fancher coming towards her.

Dorothy was a slight woman, her face strewn with worry lines. She and her husband Teddy lived on their street. Teddy hardly said a word, but Dorothy never stopped talking. You could get caught talking to her for hours about absolutely nothing. Ray called her the human vortex. He once joked that all the people who

CHRISTIAN WHITE

went missing in the Bermuda Triangle really just got stuck talking to Dorothy.

Abby gave her a quick wave and started towards the house.

'Oh, Abby,' Dorothy called. 'Do you have a minute?'

'One minute?'

Dorothy strode across the front lawn, hunched beneath an umbrella. She cast a glance at the drooping she-oak in the front yard that she'd gently reminded Abby – six times – needed to be cut back. If it wasn't the she-oak, it was the lawn they let get too long, or the bins they sometimes forgot to bring in after garbage day.

'Would you be a dear and ask your husband to stick to the speed limit when he's driving past our house? You know me, normally I wouldn't mind, but there's a pothole that the council hasn't got around to fixing yet, and when it rains it fills up with water, and when your husband drives past doing eighty in a sixty zone, he sprays mud all over the nature strip, and it drowns the grass seed, and—'

'I'll let him know,' Abby said. 'Anyway, I should get in out of this rain.'

'Mmm, I noticed you forgot your umbrella. You really should keep one in the car in case of an emergency. You're still a city girl at heart, I suppose. You'll figure it out one of these days. Where was Ray off to in such a hurry, anyway?'

Abby felt herself being pulled into the human vortex, so she took a step towards the house and looked at her watch, as if she had somewhere to be. Then she hesitated. 'Wait, when was this?'

'Not twenty minutes ago,' Dorothy said. 'He was driving like Juan Manuel Fangio. Like I said, normally I wouldn't mind but—'

'I have to go,' Abby snapped.

'Oh, your generation move a mile a minute,' she said. 'What do you have on? A party? Not great weather for a barbecue if that's what you had in—'

'Uh huh, bye,' Abby cut her off. She felt Dorothy's eyes on her back as she hurried up the driveway.

Where was Ray off to in such a hurry? It was a good question. She entered the garage through the side door, turned on the light and looked over at her workbench.

She could remember returning Ray's clothing and workboots to the box, but she couldn't remember putting it away. She had left it on the bench, she was sure of it. But it wasn't there now, and neither was Ray.

She stood there awhile, deliberating. The box and all its contents were probably at the bottom of Elk Harbour right now. She felt her skin flush hot, then run so cold it made her shiver. Since the murder, she had been living in a state of heightened panic, and had at times wondered if it might all become too much – if her spirit might simply slip away from her body, from her reality, from a world that once felt safe and predictable but now made her feel like a stranger.

But under all of that, a new seed was budding. She felt a strange and very strong sense of something else: relief. The *evidence* – and that is what it was – was gone, and with it, all tangible connection to the crime. She thought about the blue glow of the luminol and wondered if she might one day find a way to live with it. She might even be able to trick herself into believing she imagined the whole thing. She might be able to repress the memory itself, to push it down somewhere so deep and dark that even she couldn't—

The sound of a car pulling into the driveway cut through her thoughts. It sounded like Ray's truck. If that was true, then a difficult conversation was about to happen. She slammed the palm of her hand against the roller door's *Open* button and it clicked to life, rising an inch at a time, slowly revealing the landscape beyond.

There was one police cruiser in the driveway – that was the car she'd heard – and two more parked on the nature strip, wheels already sinking in the wet soil around the drooping she-oak. Doors were open. Officers were spilling out in windbreakers and heavy black boots. Cherry lights were flashing against the dull late-afternoon gloom. Dorothy Fancher was huddled beneath her umbrella, watching it all with a giddy look in her eyes.

The officers were wearing gloves and carrying empty bags and boxes marked with big red letters: *Evidence*. One of them, a hefty man with deep-set eyes and trousers that swished together as he walked, walked up to the front door, wiped his feet on the welcome mat, and let himself into the house. It felt like a stranger's hands riffling through her underwear drawer.

'Hey,' she screamed. 'Hey!'

Another, rosy-cheeked, constable glanced over, then walked quickly towards the house. Abby marched through the rain. 'Stop! You can't go in there. What the hell do you think you're—'

'Ab,' came a voice.

She turned to see Bobbi coming sheepishly towards her. Abby counted off the reasons she shouldn't attack this woman where she stood, but she couldn't hold onto a single one of them. She was existing in a single moment of hot rage, where reason and logic and the law were abstract, faraway objects.

'What the fuck, Bobbi,' she spat. 'What the actual fuck!? You couldn't give me a day. One fucking day.'

'Wait.'

'I guess you made your choice between Bobbi the Friend and Bobbi the Cop, you fucking—' She almost said *dyke* and hated herself for it. The word seeped out from somewhere deep and vicious. 'How could you do this to me, Bobbi?'

'Stop,' she demanded, raising the palms of both hands. 'Just stop. And listen. It's very important you get your shit together right now. We can scream at each other later all we want, but not in front of my colleagues, and not in front of your kids.'

'Jesus. The kids.'

'You can take them to my place. I'll call Maggie and let her know what's going on. They can stay there until we're finished.'

'Finished with what?'

Bobbi took a deep breath and looked at Abby with deep sympathy. 'Until we're finished with a search of your home, property and vehicles thereon.'

Two skinny constables in long raincoats slipped into the garage. An absurd and absurdly funny question popped into Abby's head: what would they think of all her taxidermy equipment? What would they think of Trevor the half-skinned ringtail, wrapped in a Buy & Bye shopping bag and stashed inside the bar fridge?

'We'll be as low-impact as possible, Ab,' Bobbi said. 'I promise.'

'Your promises aren't worth much anymore, *Officer*. You're crazy if you think I'd let my kids anywhere near your apartment and crazier if you think I'll ever trust you again.'

'Don't make me the enemy, Ab, and get it together.'

'Don't tell me what to do.'

'Look, I know you're scared, but you need to calm—'

'I want to see a warrant.'

'Abby.'

'You have no right to be here. I want to see a search warrant and I want to see it—'

'We don't need a search warrant,' Bobbi said in a short, sharp tone. Her patience was wearing thin. 'Ray gave us permission to search the house.'

Fresh rain fell. Abby stood on the grass and let it fall. '… What did you say?'

'I didn't tell anyone about what we talked about,' Bobbi said, lowering her voice and leaning in closer. Her hair was soaked, clinging to her cheeks. 'Abby, as soon as you left, I got called in. I was despatched here straight away to perform an evidence search. Ray's at the police station. He turned up with a box full of what he claims is evidence.'

'No, that doesn't make sense … You're lying.'

'I'm not.'

'You're lying!' Abby reached out with trembling hands and shoved Bobbi, hard.

Bobbi stood her ground but she didn't fight back. Abby shoved her again, but this time, in almost the same movement, she collapsed into her arms and began to cry.

Bobbi held her and kissed her softly on the forehead.

'I wish I were, hun, but Ray confessed,' she whispered.

'… No.'

'Yes,' she said. 'He confessed to the murder of David Stemple.'

23

THE WIDOW

'Dad was murdered in the winter of 1996,' Marcus Stemple said, massaging the arm of the dusty armchair with his fingers. 'Blunt force trauma. Someone hit him across the head with a brick, then dumped his body in the water.'

'God,' Kate said. She was leaning forward in the wooden chair that John had sat in just two weeks earlier. 'I'm sorry.'

Marcus, who had nearly reached the bottom of his longneck and was glancing over at the fridge in anticipation of his next, looked back at her and shrugged. 'What are you gonna do, right?'

Kate was struck with an unnerving idea: she might have been looking at a future version of her own daughter. Mia was older than Marcus was when his father died, but it was too easy to imagine her following the same path of substance abuse and self-destruction.

I should be with Mia, she thought, with a sudden twang of guilt. *I should be home with my daughter and instead I'm out here in the middle of the ocean, chasing John's ghost.*

'What happened?' Kate asked.

Marcus drained his beer, found a half-smoked cigarette in the ash tray and lit it. 'I don't remember many details. That whole time in my life just feels like some movie I watched when I was a kid. I was ten or eleven before they told me he was killed.'

'Your mum kept it from you?'

'She refused to talk about it.'

'Maybe she was trying to protect you,' Kate said, and thought about monsters under the bed.

'Maybe, but it's never a good idea to keep something like that from a kid. All it does is send them off to find out themselves, which is what I did. Some of what I've learned came from family or looking at old newspaper articles, but mostly it was from talking to old-timers down at the Belly. Everyone remembers when it happened, and everyone remembers why he was killed.'

'*Why?*'

He sucked on the cigarette hard and fast, as if he was hoping to develop lung cancer before dinnertime. 'Dad got killed because he was a fag.'

Kate flinched. 'Excuse me?'

'His body was found floating in the water off Beech Tree Landing. He was killed in the old ferry terminal that used to be out there, then dumped off the jetty into the sea.'

'Beech Tree Landing? Are you sure? That's where John's body was found. There must be a connection.'

Marcus raised his eyebrows. 'If there is, you might not like it.'

'What do you mean?'

'The terminal was a gay beat,' he said. 'Men used it for sex. That's what my dad was doing out there that day. Cruising for it.'

He sucked the last of his cigarette, stubbed it out forcefully in the ash tray and fetched himself another longneck. He popped the lid and sculled a third of the bottle before closing the fridge, then hovered in the next room.

'Are … are you sure?' Kate asked.

'Only one way to be sure, I suppose. Like I said, I have that ouija board somewhere if you want to ask him. I'm serious, you know. I saved up my pocket money as a kid and bought the official Psychic Circle Spirit Board. I'd have to wait until after Mum went to bed because she hated all that stuff. I'd sit there in my bedroom with the board and a notepad, all set to take down the messages from the other side.'

He pulled the longneck to his mouth, glanced down at it as if the taste had soured, then set the bottle down on the kitchen counter with a loud thud.

'I guess Dad was the silent type,' he said. 'Because his ghost never told me shit.'

Marcus's mood had darkened – something she wouldn't have thought possible – and Kate sensed it was time to leave.

She noticed her phone buzzing softly from inside the handbag she'd slung over the side of the chair. There were two missed calls from Fisher. He was probably wondering where she'd got to. 'I have to go. Thank you for your time.'

He looked at her longingly for a moment. Did he want her to stay, or did he want something from her?

'What is it?' she asked.

'Dad's obituary,' he said, sheepishly shifting his weight from his left foot to his right. 'Mind if I hang onto it?'

There was a good chance David Stemple's obituary was evidence, but then she thought of how Eckman had said John's body belonged to the police – how it had made her feel. She took the folded paper from her pocket and placed it on the coffee table, between an empty cup of stale noodles and the glass bong.

Marcus nodded his thanks from the kitchen doorway, and asked, 'Why did you come here?'

'To figure out John's connection to your father,' she said, honestly.

'If you have a theory, I'd love to hear it.'

As it happened, she did have a theory. From the outside

looking in, she must have looked cool and composed, but inside, her mind was scrambling like a crab.

'When John was younger, he started having these nightmares,' she started. 'Worse than nightmares, actually. Night terrors. It turned into a full-blown sleep disorder, and he started seeing things. Hallucinations. He saw a man with …'

'What?' Marcus asked.

She remembered the sketches she found in John's notepad, remembered the Visitor – a heavy black jacket, a pair of tennis sneakers, and—

'Moths,' she said. 'He saw a man with moths spilling out of a split in his head.'

Marcus said nothing. He didn't move a muscle. He didn't even blink. He just waited silently for Kate to go on.

'I think John knew something, or saw something, or heard something, or discovered something. Whatever it was, he must have supressed it for a while, learned to live with it.'

'For a while?'

'Your mother's death was the leaf that dammed the stream,' Kate whispered dreamily, recalling Holly Cutter's words. 'When Annabel died, John turned dark. He didn't tell me about it. He didn't tell *anyone* about it. But he must have come back to Belport to work through that darkness. I think that's why he came to see you, and

I think that's what got him killed. John had information about your father's killer.'

Marcus exhaled, long and slow, like a deflating air mattress. 'If your husband had evidence that would help solve the murder, he was about two decades too late.'

'What do you mean?'

'My dad's murder isn't unsolved,' he said. 'They caught the guy who did it a few days after it happened. He's serving twenty-five-to-life at South Hallston Correctional Facility.'

Kate's mind was floundering, but it caught onto a single word. 'Did you say Hallston? H-A-L-L-S-T-O-N?'

Fisher was standing beneath the awnings outside his room at the Blue Whale Motor Inn, staring into the cold rain.

'I've been trying to call you,' he said when Kate parked the car and climbed out, hurrying under the awnings to join him. 'Where were you?'

'With Marcus Stemple,' she said.

'Stemple? As in …'

'David Stemple's son.'

As the rain grew heavier, she explained what she had learned from her visit with Marcus. Fisher lit a fresh cigarette, smoked and listened.

'My God,' Fisher said when she was finished. He frowned, searching his memory. 'I remember there was a man who was murdered here, but I never knew the victim's name. Or, at least, I didn't know it til now. When was the obituary from? 1995?'

'August 1996.'

He nodded. '1996. It was big news. He was a holiday resident, like us, killed by a local man – God knows what Stemple was doing here in August. Still, people saw it as an attack against tourists, and the day tourists stop coming to Belport is the day it may as well sink into the ocean.'

For the most part, Belportians treated Kate kindly during her stays, but there was a palpable tension below the surface. Smiles and greetings often felt hollow, there were heavy sighs behind her in the long line at the Buy & Bye, and the occasional hand-painted sign hung outside a shop on Bay Street that read, *LOCAL PARKING ONLY*. The locals needed tourists, but that didn't mean they had to like them.

'We spent the next few summers up in Noosa after it happened,' Fisher said. 'But eventually we went back. It wasn't quite the canary down the coalmine some people thought, but Belport was never really the same after that. John would have been a teenager when it happened. I'm surprised he even remembered it, so I can't imagine why he'd be so … invested in the family.'

Invested was a polite way to put it. *Obsessed* might have been more accurate.

'Is it possible he witnessed something?' Kate asked.

'It was the off-season; we weren't even here.' He looked at her, held her gaze a second, then turned back to the rain. 'It's time for me to go home, Kate. That's why I called you. There's nothing left to do here, and Pam needs me. She's … she's not coping. Not that she'd ever admit that, but I can tell. You don't have to come with me; I can catch the ferry back to the mainland and the bus home after that, but I think you should.'

He didn't add, *Mia needs you*, but Kate was pretty sure he was thinking it. Instead, he gazed into the rain and did something startling: he smiled. It had been a long time since she'd seen him smile, long even before John disappeared. 'Before you got here, I was thinking about the time John fell asleep during mass. Did he ever tell you about that?'

'No,' Kate said, but now she was smiling. Whatever it was that Fisher had caught, it was contagious.

'It was the night after his high-school graduation, and he was wildly hungover,' he said. 'He couldn't keep his eyes open. Usually it wouldn't be so bad, because Pam gets so wrapped up at mass that you could strip naked and run up and down the aisles and she wouldn't notice. But John started snoring. Then, before Pam could say anything, Father Chang stopped halfway through his sermon, looked at John, and said, *I've always encouraged young John to follow his dreams, but this isn't what I had in mind.*'

Fisher laughed. It sounded so unfamiliar.

'Do you remember his apartment in Elwood?' Kate said. 'The first time I ever went around there, the kitchen looked spotless. But when I opened a cupboard to look for a glass, I saw he'd just stashed all his dirty dishes under the sink.'

Laughing, Fisher asked, 'What did you say?'

'Nothing. I just shut the cupboard door and acted like nothing had happened. But when we got a place together, I made sure it had a dishwasher.'

'When John brought his first girlfriend home to meet us, he called ahead first. They'd been dating nearly four months, so it seemed like things were looking serious. But when he called ahead, he told us that she thought his name was James. She must have misheard it when they first met or something, and rather than correcting her, he just let her keep calling him James.'

'No!'

'Swear on my life,' he said. 'It gets worse: he was calling ahead to ask that when she was around we all call him James too!'

'What did you do?'

'What could we do? We called him James the whole time. Thankfully it didn't last too long!'

He threw his head back, tears in his eyes, shaking his head. It felt good to watch him laugh, and even better to laugh herself. Slowly though, reality drifted in again, like tear gas.

'I wish he'd let me in,' she said, driving a dagger into the heart of Fisher's good mood. 'Whatever he was chasing out here, I just wish he'd asked for help.'

Fisher's smile vanished. 'He did.'

'He did what?' she asked.

'John called me, Kate. On the morning he left to come here. I didn't know it at the time, but I checked it against my phone log later. He told me he was on his way to the airport, that he was about to fly out to London for the palliative care research colloquium. The same lie he told you. But he was quiet, and strange.'

'Strange how?'

'You were married to my son long enough to know he rarely went directly at a thing. He danced around a subject until you talked it out of him. He was doing the same dance when he called. There was something on his mind. He … wanted to talk.'

He dropped each word slowly, like stones from a bridge, watching them tumble through the air and disappear in a splash.

'I was at Woolworths with a shopping list as long as my arm,' he went on. 'I was in the pasta section, trying to find something that was gluten-free because Pam's been on a no-gluten diet and those labels are so small, and I'd been getting calls from the Porsche club all morning because the new president is a bloody fool and … I was busy, Kate. Too busy to talk to my son. If

I had acted like his father … Instead, I acted like mine.'

Be a man, Kate thought.

'This isn't on you, Fisher,' Kate said. 'It's not on me, either. Like you said, he had friends, colleagues, Pam. He had a support network that he *chose* not to use. That can't be on us.'

Fisher dabbed his eye with the sleeve of his jacket. 'He was lucky to have you, Kate.'

'He was lucky to have both of us,' she said.

He put his hands into the pockets of his jacket and turned to head into his motel room. 'Will you be ready to leave in the morning?'

'I'll ride over with you on the ferry and drop you at the train station in Geelong,' she said. 'But I'm going to stay for another day or two.'

'Are you sure that's the right decision?'

'Marcus mentioned something I want to look into on the mainland. Do you remember the Post-it Note we found in the kitchen of the holiday house, *S. Hallston, 2pm*? Turns out, S. Hallston isn't a person. It's a place.'

She wasn't through chasing John's ghost yet.

24

THE WIFE

Abby was shown into a small, featureless room at Belport Police Station. The walls were stark and there were no windows. A single light globe buzzed overhead, locked inside a small metal cage. There was a steel table in the middle of the room, and two white plastic chairs on either side. She sat down and waited for her husband.

Ray was led in close to twenty minutes later, looking ghoulish, smelling of wet dog and week-old jeans. He was dressed in a faded grey T-shirt and loose-fitting trackpants – the clothes he was wearing at the time of his arrest – but his shoes were gone. Instead, he wore socks and blue paper slippers, which made him look almost whimsical. His eyes were like a rain-drenched sheet of glass.

He sat down across from her, frowned and said, 'Hi, babe.'

'Are you okay?' she asked.

He shrugged. 'I just spoke to the lawyer, Bob. He thinks they'll be moving me soon, ahead of the trial. He wants to sit down with you next week to go through everything, so I gave him your details.'

She was trying to listen to every word but found them hard to grasp. This couldn't be their life. It was as if he was describing something he heard from a friend of a friend about an unlucky family whose life had been derailed.

She placed her hand on the steel table, open-palmed, waiting for Ray's. He didn't offer it.

'How are the kids?' he asked.

'Confused, angry, but not necessarily in that order,' she said.

He seemed reluctant to ask the next question but asked it anyway. 'How are *you*?'

'Confused, angry, but not necessarily in that order,' she repeated. 'I came in here wondering if I should apologise – for hounding you, for digging your clothes out of the garbage, for suspecting you in the first place.'

'I took my own bucket down the well, Ab.'

'You're fucking right you did. I *am* sorry about those things, Ray, but what you did is so far beyond any of that. What you did is beyond real life and ...'

'... What?'

'It might be beyond forgiveness, Ray.'

He bowed his head, stared hard at his fingernails. There was a pale white ring where his wedding band used to be. The police must have removed it. She imagined him getting handed a small yellow envelope sometime in the future, when they were on the other side of this thing. The ring would be inside. He'd take it, turn it over in the palm of his hand, then slip it on.

Will it still fit? She wondered. *And when will that be? Ten years, twenty, fifty?*

'You know what really pisses me off?' Abby asked. 'What really pisses me off is, I still love you. I still love the hell out of you, in fact.'

'I love the hell out of you too,' he said.

They looked at each other across the steel table. Abby felt a deep and helpless longing, down in her bones. She'd never felt anything like it.

'Are they listening to us?' she asked, checking the corners for security cameras or listening devices.

'It doesn't matter if they are,' Ray said. 'I told them everything. I told them the truth.'

'You told them you killed that man,' she whispered.

'… Yes.'

Never had a single word hit her so hard. If she hadn't been sitting down, she might have collapsed. She pictured an egg that could never be un-scrambled, a glass that could never be un-shattered.

'You look like you were expecting another answer,' Ray said. 'But you knew, Ab. You knew the whole time. So why do you seem so surprised?'

'Because I once saw you weep without shame during an airline ad. I've seen you add lavender oil to your bathwater. I've heard you laugh like a crazy person when you watch *Funniest Home Videos*. Because it's you. Because even after everything, all I wanted was for you to tell me I was wrong. This whole time, that's all I wanted.'

She closed her eyes. Hot, salty tears had come to them, pulled from some deep, black well. They fell down her cheeks in fat, unapologetic drops. 'Why did you do it?'

Ray folded his hands on the table, looked Abby in the eyes and began to talk.

'Let me start with those magazines you found,' he said. He paused, as if he was expecting the right words to arrive when he needed them. Then, perhaps realising what Abby already knew – that there were no *right* words – he shook his head and pressed on. 'I've always been attracted to women, so it's not like I'm, you know …'

'Gay.'

He nodded. 'Those magazines were just something I was curious about. I suppose part of me has always … worried I was that way inclined. I mean … I'm sorry, this is so fucking hard.'

Abby thought about Bobbi's rainbow flag analogy.

'You were curious about your sexuality,' she offered. 'That's fine, Ray. That's normal. I don't think anyone's really all the way straight or gay. But have you ever acted on your curiosity? I'm not talking about looking at a bunch of skin-mags. That, I'd call research. But have you ever taken that research into the field, so to speak?'

Ray's face reddened. He shook his head. 'Not until David Stemple.'

Abby leaned back in her chair, almost instinctively, as if bracing herself for what was about to come.

'Most days I eat my lunch down at Beech Tree Landing,' Ray said. 'I park at the top of the furthest boat ramp, eat my ham-and-cheese, drink my coffee. Sometimes I listen to talkback, but mostly I just watch the water. It's peaceful down there. At least, it used to be.'

'I didn't know you did that,' Abby said. 'Why don't you come home for lunch?'

He shrugged. 'I haven't been happy for a while, Abby. It's got nothing to do with you or the kids. You, Eddie and Lori are my everything, you know that. But when I'm in that house, all I think about are the mortgage repayments, and the bills, and all the broken things that need fixing, and all the renovations we said we'd do.'

He closed his eyes and took a long moment before continuing.

'Home makes me think about work, which is all I ever seem to do. Every day, every season, every year, and our savings account sits at below zero, and our debt just seems to get bigger. And I know that's just, life or whatever, but sometimes it feels like trying to knock over a brick wall by tossing eggs at it. I've watched rich fucking tourists descend on this island every year since I was a kid. They spend their money and we circle like the seagulls and then they get to do what I never have. They get to leave, Abby.'

He smiled sadly. 'Sometimes I'd imagine the ferry coming in to dock at the old terminal – the little rickety old thing they used when I was a kid. It could barely fit half-a-dozen cars, and there was no lounge or cafe. There were just a couple of plastic chairs, a vending machine and the water. Me and Mum would go to the mainland once a month or so, and I'd sit with my feet dangling over the railing, watching for dolphins. Nine times out of ten I'd see them too. Most days, when I'm eating my lunch, I imagine that old ferry coming in to dock, and I imagine myself getting on it, chugging off the island, on and on into the sunset.'

'Why haven't you ever talked to me about this?' Abby asked.

'Come on, Abby, I'm not one of your girlfriends. I'm not Bobbi. Men aren't like that.'

The light globe above their head flickered.

Ray cleared his throat and continued. 'The day it happened, I was having my lunch at the landing as usual. That's when he turned up. David Stemple. I didn't know that was his name then, and I didn't know it was the same guy who'd called looking for a caretaker. All I knew was he was driving a fifty-thousand-dollar car and looked like he'd never worked a day in his life. He parked his car right next to my truck. There must be fifty slots down there, all of them empty, but he parked right beside me. Thinking back, I guess that's code or something.'

'Code?'

'When he got out, he looked over at me, right in the eyes, and nodded. It wasn't until he got halfway out to the ferry terminal and looked back that I realised what he wanted from me, until I remembered what people use that place for.'

Abby remembered what Ray had told her at the kitchen table, when she'd asked him about the terminal being a gay beat. He'd gone on about the crocodile in Blue Lake, the lighthouse drug ring, the family of deformed dwarves that haunted the saltmarsh. *Rumours are like holey buckets around here*, he'd told her.

'I can't tell you exactly why I followed him into the ferry terminal,' Ray said. 'But I did. When I got inside, he was sort of lurking in the corner. He didn't say anything to me, and I didn't say anything to him. It was like some sort of base instinct took over. I went over to him. He ...'

'What, Ray?'

'He put his hands on me. And for a couple of seconds, and that's all it was, it felt right. But then all of a sudden, it didn't. I saw that he was wearing a wedding ring, and I thought about what I was doing and about what I could lose if I did it. I thought about you, Ab.'

'What happened next?' she asked.

'I can't remember all the details. I know I pushed him away. At first, he didn't want to take no for an answer, so I pushed him harder. He fought back. I lost control. I don't know how else I can explain it. Something just flicked inside my head.'

The Switch, Abby thought.

'He must have got me on my back somehow, because that's when I saw the brick,' he said. 'That's when I—'

'Stop,' Abby said. 'I don't need to hear that part.'

For a long moment, they said nothing. The silence between them grew like the distant scream of an air-raid siren. Abby read her husband's face while processing everything he'd just told her. A single word emerged suddenly, breaking through the surface of her mind like a breaching whale.

Bullshit.

She didn't believe his story. It wasn't that she was in denial – at least that's not how it felt. She knew it in her bones. Just as she had known he was lying to her at the foot of the fallen gum tree, she knew he was lying now.

'Promise me something,' Ray said.

'What?'

'Survive. You, Lori, Eddie. Promise me.'

'If there's one thing this family knows,' she said. 'It's how to survive.'

On her way out of the station, Abby noticed the woman she'd sold cigarettes to at the Buy & Bye. She was standing in a dimly lit alcove beside the front entrance, feeding change into a vending machine. A young boy was with her, clinging to the pocket of her jacket with one hand, with his other pressed against the glass, gazing in wonder at all the confectionary that hung beyond it. He couldn't have been more than five or six, with jet-black hair and a ghostly face.

'What can I get, Mum?' he asked in a small voice.

'Whatever you want, Marcus,' the woman told him.

As the boy scanned his options, his eyes widened. They were luminol blue.

25

THE WIDOW

After dropping Fisher at the train station on the mainland, Kate carried on to the highway until she reached the exit for South Hallston. She had been behind the wheel for almost four hours. When the colossal concrete structure of South Hallston Correctional Centre appeared on the horizon, she felt a rush of nervous energy sweep through her until she could feel it in her fingertips.

There was a line of vehicles banked up behind a bright-red boom gate built into the perimeter fence. A sign above the glass booth read: *VISITOR SECURITY CHECKPOINT 1*. Kate joined the queue. A motorbike with exaggerated handlebars pulled up behind her. The rider was a middle-aged woman in a tattered red leather jacket. She met Kate's eyes through the rear-view mirror, then gave her engine a few obnoxious revs.

The line moved slowly, as each driver's ID was checked against the visitor list by a prison guard at the booth. Kate had called ahead to have her name added to the list, but there was still no guarantee Ray Gilpin would agree to meet with her. She might have driven all this way for nothing.

'Good afternoon,' Kate said when it was her turn at the booth. The prison guard was a chunky man in a black, short-sleeved work shirt and a white baseball cap with *Corrections* printed across the peak. A heater glowed behind him.

Kate handed over her ID. He checked his computer screen, nodded, then gave it back. Chant-like, he said, 'No hats no sunglasses no revealing clothing no gang colours no offensive language.'

'No problem,' she said.

'Drive through please.'

She did as she was told. The narrow road opened into a wide car park. She sat in the car for a few minutes, engine idling, watching the front door and mentally preparing herself for the gauntlet of security checks she was about to run, and the man waiting for her on the other side. Collecting herself, she walked towards the reception hall. It was stuffy and overheated inside and smelled like mice and man-sweat. The first thing she saw was a noticeboard beside the front desk. Pinned behind plexiglass were brochures and flyers offering legal advice, support groups and helplines. Someone had made a hand-painted sign in big green block letters.

The idea of being with him tomorrow is enough to
get me through today
— Old Prison widow saying.

Kate showed her ID to a prison guard behind the front desk, an almost impossibly pale man. He waved her into the next room, where a metal detector waited. After that came a sniffer dog, a personal search by a prison employee – 'hair back, mouth open' – and finally she had earned the coveted South Hallston Visitor Pass, displayed in a lanyard around her neck.

Through a heavy glass door, Kate entered the visiting hall, where everything was bolted to the floor – the tables, chairs, even the vending machines. The walls were painted in soft pinks and blues to fool the inmates into believing they were trapped inside a creche and not a prison. She found a free table against the far wall and sat down, listening to the chatter of inmates and their visitors. The nervous excitement reminded her of the day at the airport.

Soon, a man entered the hall and looked around, searching for someone. Kate was the only person sitting alone, and he caught her eye across the room. There was a flicker of something in his face – it might have been recognition, but she couldn't be sure. She raised her hand in a brief wave and he began to shuffle towards her table. It made her picture an old boat drifting at sea with nobody inside.

He was somewhere in his sixties but looked older than he should have. It wasn't just his hair that had turned grey, but his skin too. He was clad in heavy denim and wore boots without laces. Deep wrinkles crisscrossed his forehead, and he was either bald or had shaved his head with a razor, or both. He was desperately thin, with coathanger shoulders and saggy jowls that dangled loose beneath his chin. He would be a tall man if he walked upright, Kate thought, but instead he walked with his shoulders slumped forward.

He reached Kate's table and regarded her with caution.

'Are you Ray Gilpin?' she asked.

'Yeah.'

'Thank you for agreeing to meet with me.'

He shrugged. 'It's not like I had to move anything around to fit you in.'

He sat down and glanced around the hall, watching his fellow inmates and their visitors. The rumbling sound of their chatter filled the room.

'Your name was Kate?' he asked.

'Kate Keddie,' she said. 'I think my husband came to see you recently. I'm not sure when, but it would have been sometime over the past few weeks.'

He shook his head. His sagging jowls wobbled like a turkey neck.

'Are you sure?' Kate asked.

'Positive. So, is that it?'

'Can I show you a picture of him? Maybe it'll jog your memory.'

'My memory doesn't need jogging. I can count the number of visitors I get on one hand.' He raised his right hand into a two-fingered Scout salute. 'Come to think of it, I don't even need the full hand.'

Several times on the long drive to South Hallston, Kate had doubted herself – it was a long way to come for some words scribbled on a Post-it Note – and she doubted herself again now. But she had shed her cocoon. She was something new now. Something stronger. 'I know he came here to see you,' she said coldly. 'I just don't know why. You can either tell me, or I can leave. But if I leave, my next stop is the police. They won't have any trouble accessing visitor records, and then you can talk to them.'

'The police?'

'My husband is dead,' Kate told him. 'John was murdered on Belport Island a few days ago.'

Ray flinched. His muscles tightened. 'I had no idea …' he said, looking past her. 'How?'

'Someone lured him to Beech Tree Landing,' she said. 'Then they slit his throat, close to the exact same spot where David Stemple was killed.'

He met her eyes. 'Jesus. I'm sorry to hear that.' It sounded like he meant it.

'He did come to see you, didn't he?' Kate asked.

There was a moment of confused silence. Watching him, Kate felt sure he was about to deny all knowledge again. Then, unexpectedly, his face softened. He nodded and looked away.

'Why did you—'

'Look,' he interrupted, 'I'm sorry you're going through this, but you're not going to get any big revelations here. I hadn't seen him in years.'

'Years? You'd seen him before?'

Ray made the face of someone who had just accidentally ruined a surprise party. He began speaking more cautiously. 'He was one of the regular summer kids,' he said carefully. 'I did maintenance on a lot of the holiday places, so I knew most of them. By face, anyway.'

Kate considered probing further, but she could see him closing up again. She had to get to the point before it was too late. 'Why did John come to see you?' she asked.

He spread his fingers on the steel table and stared at them, as if feeling for vibrations from long ago. 'To tell me David Stemple's widow had died.'

'Annabel,' Kate offered.

'She was younger than me, but she had issues with her lungs. Pulmonary something.'

'Why would he do that?'

'I wasn't sure myself for a while,' he admitted. 'It wasn't until after John left that I figured it out. I think he wanted me to know her suffering was over. Not just the pain of her illness, but the pain … the pain I caused her.'

'John knew something about the murder, didn't he?'

Ray glanced over at the next table. Kate recognised the woman there; it was the motorbike rider who had followed her off the freeway on her growling, overstated machine. With her helmet gone, a head of stark white hair hung down over one shoulder. She sat across from a stocky inmate, who was leaning forward on his elbows, holding the woman's hands tightly in his own. Both had stopped talking and were staring at her.

She lowered her voice. 'He had information about David Stemple. He witnessed something or knew something somehow.'

'What makes you say that?'

She thought about John's night terrors, about the Visitor, and said, 'It doesn't matter. I'm right, aren't I?'

He closed his eyes and took his hands off the table, placing them under his legs. The white-haired biker at the next table was crying softly now, working up to a goodbye with the stocky inmate across from her. Ray watched them for a moment, frowning, then turned back to Kate.

'I was never a big reader before,' he told her. 'But when I came here I started to read a lot. There's not much else to do here, and not that many options in the library. I tried reading Tolstoy but couldn't get into it. Vonnegut and Salinger were both pretty good. Didn't mind Jane Austen either – bet you're surprised to hear that one?

Kate said nothing.

'Right. Well, lately I've been having a read of some Greek mythology. Have you ever heard of Orpheus?'

Kate shook her head.

'In this story, Orpheus is married to a beautiful woman named Eurydice, but she's bitten by a snake and dies, so Orpheus travels into the underworld to save her. Hades, the god of the underworld, agrees that Eurydice can follow Orpheus back to the realm of the living on one condition: as they walk through the caves, Orpheus can't look back. Not once. So guess what old mate does?'

'He looks back?' Kate offered.

'Orpheus looks back. Eurydice is pulled back into the darkness forever, while Orpheus is torn to shreds by vicious, hungry beasts. The story really got to me. I'm up for parole in fourteen weeks, three days, two hours and …' He paused to look at the clock on the far wall. 'Eighteen minutes. I've been in this place for more than two decades. Want to know how I survived?'

'How?'

'I stopped looking back. For the first few years it was hard to do anything else, but it got easier as time went on. Then, I hardly thought about the past at all. It might be denial, but it's got me here in one piece, so who gives a shit what you call it.'

'What's this got to do with John?' Kate asked.

'When John came to tell me about Annabel Stemple's death, I told him what I just told you: I'd stopped looking back a long time ago; he should stop looking back too.'

Without another word, he stood up and walked away.

26

THE WIFE

'I can't be in this house right now,' Lori said. Abby had returned home to find her waiting at the bottom of the stairs with her suitcase packed. She was draped in layers of black: torn black jeans, oversized black T-shirt, scuffed and worn Doc Martens. Her hair was high and tight, her face as soft and white as fresh snow. Abby's face, in comparison, was like snow freshly trod on, pummelled down by dirty boots and rain, grey and puffy and aching.

'Well, unless you have enough pocket money saved to afford a suite at the Blue Whale, you don't have much of a choice. Go back upstairs and unpack.'

'I called Bobbi,' Lori said. 'She and Maggie said it's okay if I stay there for a while. A few days, maybe a week.'

'No.'

'Mum.'

'This isn't a discussion.'

'I can't stay in this house because it terrifies me,' Lori snapped. A single black line of mascara streaked down her left cheek. 'I'm scared. I'm scared of what everyone must be saying about us. I'm scared of the police. I'm scared of … Dad. I'm trying to tell you I'm not okay, Mum.'

Abby tried to hug her daughter, but Lori recoiled.

'I don't want a hug,' she said.

'Then what do you want?'

'I don't fucking know,' she shouted. 'I want this not to have fucking happened. I want a dad who didn't … I want … I just want a ride to fucking Bobbi's house.'

Abby stared at her daughter and saw a woman with child's eyes. 'Go put your suitcase in the car.'

'Yeah?'

'Yeah,' Abby said.

Surprised to have won the battle, Lori brushed a loose strand of hair from her face and gathered herself.

'Where's your brother?' Abby asked.

'He's in the backyard, regressing.'

'What do you mean?'

'Go see for yourself.'

Abby went to the window and looked out. In the rear left corner of their property line, wedged between the fence and a drooping she-oak, was Eddie's cubby house. In truth, it was less of a cubby and more of a lean-to: a sheet of corrugated iron for a roof, a strip of carpet for a floor and a few scattered milk crates as furniture.

Eddie hadn't used the cubby since he was twelve, and Ray had talked about dismantling it. He called it an eyesore and he was right, but Abby couldn't bring herself to allow it to come down. It was one of the final relics of Eddie's childhood, and she hadn't been ready to see it go. Now, she saw Eddie might not have been ready to see it go, either. He was sitting on one of the milk crates, socked feet on damp earth, reading an *X-Men* comic book.

Abby went out into the yard and joined him.

'Mind if I pull up a crate?' she asked.

Eddie looked up, shrugged, then looked back down at his comic book. Abby joined him, doing her best to ignore the stale smell of mould in the air.

'Did you see Dad?' Eddie asked.

'Yeah. He's okay. He misses you and Lori.'

'Will he be coming home soon?'

'I don't know, Eddie. I don't think so.'

'He didn't hurt that man, Mum. Everyone's saying he hurt that man, but he didn't do it. He wouldn't.'

'Your father confessed, Eddie.'

'He's lying.'

'I know this is hard, but we need to—'

'Why couldn't you just leave it alone?'

'Eddie.'

He glared at her. 'This is your fault.'

From somewhere just beyond the garden, she heard the pounding sound of surf against sand. Order and certainty and control were shifting like the tides. She felt sick and tired. '… That's not fair.'

But it wasn't a lie, either.

Eddie stood. Then, in a sudden rage that seemed to sweep up from nowhere, he flung his comic book hard into the trunk of the she-oak. The comic slapped facedown against the wet grass, pages splayed like the wings of a dead bird. It made Abby flinch, and for a moment she saw Ray's face on Eddie's.

What have you left us with, Ray? she thought.

Lori and Abby didn't talk on the ride over to Bobbi's place. Lori pulled her feet up onto the seat, hugged her knees, and stared out the window. The island looked different – more sinister. The shadows between the trees lining the street looked darker; the empty houses beyond more full of secrets. Even the Deepwater Living apartment block, which Abby had visited a hundred times, today looked haunted. The four-storey mess of balconies and rain gutters looked mad, like staircases to nowhere. It reminded Abby of the Winchester Mystery House, a mansion she'd read about in California, whose owner claimed ghosts designed the home by whispering to her in the middle of the night.

Bobbi was waiting at the security gate and greeted Lori with a tight hug.

THE WIFE AND THE WIDOW

'Go on upstairs,' she said. 'Maggie's setting up a space for you.'

'Thanks, Bobbi,' Lori said. She turned to Abby, offered a brief embrace, then headed through the gate and up the stairs to Bobbi's apartment.

Abby and Bobbi stood in silence for a moment.

'Are you alright?' Bobbi asked.

'Bobbi, the way I acted, I lost my shit and I'm—'

'We're cool,' she said. 'We're always cool.'

'Promise?'

'Promise,' Bobbi said. 'You want to come up?'

'I should get back to Eddie,' she said. 'Thanks for looking after Lori. The second she starts to drive you crazy, just call me.'

Abby hesitated. She looked across the street to where she'd parked the car and sighed. 'What do I do now, Bobbi?'

'Now, you keep moving,' she said. 'You eat, you take a bath, you shave your legs and you keep looking forward. Guilt, fear, grief, they're all like moss, Ab. If you slow down long enough it'll start to grow, and it won't stop until you're covered.'

'Eat, take a bath, shave my legs,' Abby echoed. 'Survive.'

Night fell. Abby went upstairs to Eddie's room to ask if he was hungry, but he refused to come to his door. She slumped back downstairs, dug out a frozen box dinner and heated it up. She poured some red into the biggest glass she could find. It was cold enough to hurt, so she started a fire and stared into it. The house was too quiet. In the silence, it was too easy to imagine a colossal wave rising from the ocean and crashing down over the island, carrying with it all the mistakes of her past. The events of the past few days flickered in her mind, like sunlight through leaves.

Feeling lonely and overwhelmed, she tried desperately to keep from getting lost in a wild tangle of thoughts. The luminol on Ray's clothing. The two men embracing on the front of *Y-Mag*. The ferry terminal. Ray's confession. *Ray's confession.* That was the loudest thought of all. It slunk and slithered around her, like the slowly circling tentacles of an inky creature from the bowels of the ocean and—

Clunk!

All the power in the house shut off. The room fell suddenly and unnaturally quiet. There was no buzzing lamp in the hallway, no humming refrigerator in the kitchen. There were only the sounds of crackling flames and distant insects. Abby sat in the firelight for a moment, catching up, then went over to the window. Blackouts were common in Belport at this time of year, when the weather was bad, but the night was clear, and the lights were on in Dorothy and Terry's cottage at the bottom of the hill.

'You alright up there, Eddie?' she called.

She heard his bedroom door open, then close, followed by footsteps along the upstairs landing, then Eddie, silhouetted against the dark hallway, appeared at the top of the stairs. 'What happened?'

'Power went out,' she said. 'I'll check the fuse box. Wait in here.'

She crept out into the hall and down the corridor, and quietly opened the front door to a chilly blast. She was used to Milt Street looking deserted, but tonight there seemed to be too many shadows and dark things to hide behind. She felt watched. The fuse box was mounted on the side of the house beneath a narrow awning. It was barely more than a dozen steps from the door, but tonight it felt very far away.

Down the verandah steps, onto the damp lawn; she used a penlight they kept on a hook by the front window. Its beam was pencil-thin and pathetic. Rather than lighting her path, it seemed to make everything around it darker.

A couple of metres before reaching the fuse box, she froze.

The little white wooden door was wide open. Someone had flipped the latch and left it that way.

Alarmed, she spotted the figure of a tall man on the periphery of her penlight. He was big, broad and stood perfectly still. Watching her.

'Who's there?' she asked, trying her best to make her voice sound big and brave. 'What do you want?'

There was no answer. The figure in the dark remained still. For a moment, Abby feared it was David Stemple's ghost, back to take his revenge, grinning maniacally in the dark. Whoever was standing in the narrow walkway beside the house was well over six feet tall, with bulky shoulders, a narrow head and heavy sleeves that flapped in the wind.

'I can see you,' she cried. 'Who are you?'

No answer.

She could run, but she was sure this man would chase her down. Instead, after summoning everything she had, she took one long stride forward and raised the penlight.

'Fuck me,' she said.

The figure in her yard was a beach umbrella. She'd forgotten that was where they stored it during winter. She braced her hands on her knees and exhaled. A killer wasn't here for her after all, but the fuse box *was* left open. She didn't imagine that.

Moving fast now, she shone her penlight inside the box. The main switch had been thrown. She switched it back and power returned to the house. Light poured out from inside, illuminating the side yard and a shaggy, unkempt section of garden. Abby scanned it, half expecting the man she imagined lurking there to leap out brandishing a dagger. Instead, standing among the foliage, she spotted a teenage boy.

'Christ,' she said, gasping.

The boy stared quietly back at her. He was quite a good-looking kid, fifteen or sixteen, with delicate features and thick black hair, slicked back in a way she didn't see very often nowadays. He wore blue jeans and a light-blue windbreaker. He was shivering.

'I'm sorry,' he said. 'I didn't want to use the front door in case the cops were watching the house, but I needed to see you.'

'Who are you?'

He took a step forward, into the soft light falling out through the living-room window.

'I'm John Keddie,' he said. 'Do you remember me?'

27

THE WIDOW

Kate pulled the car into the vehicle loading area at the mainland ferry terminal, waiting for the second-last boat of the day to arrive and take her back to the island.

She spent most of the trip outside, on the ironically named *sun deck*, her gloved fingers curled tightly around the railing, watching Belport Island loom closer and closer. The ferry lifted wildly and fell suddenly, but it didn't falter.

The fresh air helped clear her mind. She had spent too many hours in the car.

She had thought a lot on the drive back from South Hallston Correctional Facility, mostly about home. Mia. She missed her little girl. It had been days, not weeks or months, since she last saw her, but her heart ached when she thought about it.

Even now, out on the sun deck, she wondered if coming back to Belport was the right move. Deep down she knew she didn't have much of a choice – she *had* to find out what happened to John. How could she go back to Mia and build any sort of normal life with these questions chasing her?

Still, the urge to take the Melbourne exit off the freeway had been strong. She'd have been halfway home by now if she had.

Her things were still in her room at the Blue Whale, but she could have checked out easily enough over the phone, popped her room key in the mail and had the motel staff post her things.

Then all she'd have needed to do was look for a good real estate agent to sell the holiday house, and she might never have had to come back to the island again. Hell, the agent wouldn't even need to be *good*. Anyone could sell real estate in Belport. All they'd need to do was clean the place up a bit, air it out, maybe hire someone local to throw a fresh coat of paint on the walls and—

A bulb flashed in Kate's mind. Ray said he worked in maintenance. She remembered going back to the holiday house, remembered the three-piece sofa, the furry blue rug that Mia sat on to watch TV, and the fresh white paint that had been slapped against the wall on the far right corner of the living room.

She had run the palm of her hand across the sticky paint and wondered what on earth John had been thinking when he covered up the dozens of names and heights that were written underneath. The answer came suddenly now: John wasn't thinking anything because he hadn't been the one holding the brush, no more than he was the one who tripped the house alarm.

Finally, she thought of the maintenance truck she'd spotted parked on the street, and pulled out her phone.

'Island Care?' Detective Eckman asked. They were back in the small interview room at Belport Police Station with the cramped view of a concrete laneway. Kate sat opposite Eckman at her coffee-ringed desk. 'What's that got to do with any of this?'

'I looked it up.' From the company's outdated website, she'd discovered that Island Care was an off-season caretaking service specialising in general maintenance, storm damage repair and winter surveillance. At the bottom of the page was the contact information for an Ed Gilpin. 'There aren't many maintenance companies in this town, and *this* one is run by somebody with the same surname as the man who murdered David Stemple. It has to be the van that I saw near the house.'

'I don't follow.'

Kate told Eckman about finding the obituary locked in the attic of the holiday house, about John's connection to Annabel Stemple, and about her visits to Marcus Stemple and South Hallston. Eckman listened carefully, leaning on one elbow, chewing a little harder on the end of her pencil each time Kate dropped a new detail. She looked surprised.

You underestimated John Keddie's widow, Kate thought. *Just like everyone always has.*

'Ray Gilpin's nephew or whatever broke into the holiday house to paint over a wall in the living room,' Kate said, when she had reached that part of her story. 'His name must have been one of a dozen or so kids who had their heights marked on the wall. I *knew* the paint was important. He and John knew each other as kids, I'm sure of it. They would have been around the same age.'

Eckman took the pencil from her mouth and looked at her teeth marks sceptically. 'First off, he's Ray's *son*.'

'You know them?'

'Second, why would he paint over his name?'

'To erase his connection to John.'

'You think he had something to do with John's murder?' Eckman asked, setting the pencil down.

'All I know is that he has something to do with all this. He's connected, the way everyone on this damn island is connected. He was parked outside the house. He helped me open the lock-box I found in the attic. He saw what was inside.'

'To be clear, this is the lock-box you took from an active crime scene, right? That's called *evidence*, Mrs

Keddie. Evidence than you didn't just contaminate, but evidence you withheld from the police.'

'Evidence you missed,' Kate said. 'Evidence that I found in my own house.'

'Your house is a crime scene.'

'I'm well aware of that, Detective. My house is a crime scene and my husband's corpse is police property.'

Eckman sank in her chair. Her jaw flexed, then relaxed. 'Where's the obituary now?'

'I don't have it,' Kate admitted.

'Where is it?'

'Marcus asked if he could have it, so I gave it to him.'

Eckman sipped stale coffee from a ceramic mug and shook her head. 'I don't want to argue with you, Mrs Keddie. I'll talk to Ed and Marcus Stemple, and I'll follow up on everything we've talked about, but you need to take a step back now. I can't have you running around the island like this is some sort of suburban procedural TV show. I just can't. You understand that, right?'

'I need to be doing something,' Kate said.

Eckman's expression softened. 'I know this isn't what you want to hear, Mrs Keddie, but the best thing for you to do is go back to Melbourne. Spend time with your daughter. Wait. Survive. Then repeat.'

Kate smiled sadly. 'Please stop calling me Mrs Keddie. It's Kate.'

'Barbara,' Eckman said. 'But everyone calls me Bobbi.'

Eckman was right. It was time for Kate to go home. Mia needed her mother, and just as much, Kate needed her daughter. If she packed and checked out of the Blue Whale quickly enough she'd make the last ferry back to the mainland. But there was one thing she needed to do first.

She followed Bay Street back down to the boardwalk carnival and turned left, following the promenade. She turned down Old Harbour Road and drove along until the houses gave way to ragged thatches of coastal woodland.

Soon enough, she arrived at Beech Tree Landing, where someone had lured her husband, slit his throat and let him roll into the sea behind the wheel of his car. He'd hated this place, this island. It seemed painfully unfair that he had to die there.

The landing had thirty or so extra-long parking spaces to accommodate people's boat trailers, and every one of them was empty. She drove diagonally across them and parked at the top of the furthest boat ramp.

In the water beyond stood a dozen or so wooden pilings rising from the sea like blunt teeth – the remains of what must have been the old ferry terminal, where David Stemple met his end.

She looked across the face of the water and thought: *this is where it happened, this is where I was made a widow.* The last word hit her hard. She was a widow. Worse, she was a widow who never really knew her husband.

She threw open the door of the car and stepped out into the wind. She marched to the bottom of the boat ramp, far enough so her sneakers touched the water, and screamed.

When she was done screaming, she folded to her knees on the damp concrete. Grief poured out of her, hot and wet and salty. She wished that she could leave the grief here in Belport, but knew she'd be carrying it home.

If Kate had driven away from Beech Tree Landing thirty seconds earlier or later than she did, everything would have been different. She wouldn't have arrived at the intersection of Old Harbour Road and Elm just as Ed Gilpin's work truck – *MAINTENANCE* stencilled along the side panel – rolled past. She would have turned right, driven back to the motel, and caught the last ferry back to the mainland.

Instead, she turned left, and followed Ed deeper into the island.

28

THE WIFE

Abby put the kettle on and sat John down at the kitchen table. God knew how long the kid had been out there in the dark, creeping around the house. The knees of his jeans were muddy, and there were pine needles caught in the collar of his windbreaker, which he'd left in a pile on the floor beside his shoes.

John had been to the house before, once or twice, she now realised. He was one of Eddie's summer friends. There was a big group of teenagers around the same age that knocked around together during the on-season. It was hard to keep track of who was who, and John didn't stand out any more than the rest of them.

'I think I might have trampled a garden bed when I came over the fence,' he said. 'They were agapanthus, I think. Sorry. I'll pay for the damages.'

I'll pay for the damages. Abby wondered if she'd ever heard those words from a mouth so young. Come to think of it, she could say the same thing about *agapanthus.*

'You came over the fence?' she asked.

She put a glass of water on the table for him and he gulped it. When he'd drained the whole glass, he stifled a burp, and nodded. 'From Elk Harbour, rather than coming up Bay Street, I walked up Hat Island Road and through the bushland there. I forgot to bring a torch, but I know those trails pretty well and there was enough moonlight to see for most of it. I followed the sound of the surf until I hit the sand dunes, then came in through the back.'

'Over my agapanthus.'

'Again, I'm really sorry about that. But I was sure the police would be watching the house.'

'You mentioned that,' she said. 'Why would it matter if the police saw you? You're not here to see Eddie, are you?'

He wet his lips and looked down into his lap. 'No. I … I saw on the news that Mr Gilpin had been arrested. That's … They got that wrong. That's not how it happened.'

'How what happened?'

'It's not how that man was killed.'

'… And how do you know that?'

He looked up and to his right. Eddie was standing in the kitchen doorway, crying. The kettle began to whistle loudly. Abby stood frozen in place for a moment, then turned off the stovetop. She watched the boys as the screeching kettle faded into silence.

'What are you doing here?' Eddie asked John. When John didn't answer, Eddie turned to his mother with the same question. 'What's he doing here?'

'We have to tell, Eddie,' John said. John looked back down into his lap. His posture reminded Abby of melting snow. 'We have to.'

'Tell me what?' Abby asked.

'... Mum,' Eddie said.

Abby steadied her hands. She swallowed the ball of panic that had climbed up her throat and opened the pantry. She took the tin of Milo down from the pantry and prepped two mugs.

'Sit down, Eddie,' she said. 'It sounds like we need to have a talk.'

Reluctantly, he took a seat across from John. Abby felt hot and bitter, sad and fearful. Part of her – and it was a big part – didn't want to hear what they had to say. Even before they started talking, she knew it would change everything. But slowly, tensely, painfully, like pulling a leech from the skin, she drew their story out of them.

The boys talked. It sounded a lot like the truth. She filled some of the gaps by asking questions, others by using her imagination. Images came to her. Skin. Water. Blood. As Eddie and John explained, she saw the events of that day unfold in her mind's eye, as vivid as if she'd been right there with them, watching from the corner of

the ferry terminal shook in the harbour breeze. The walls shifted and the wood moaned around them like a tired old beast. Dusty beams of light fell in through the dirty window, casting them in light the colour of whipped butter. It was late morning, a school day.

'There's no way in hell I'm spending the night in here alone,' John said.

Eddie taunted him with chicken sounds.

'Don't be an arsehole,' John told him. 'Would you stay out here with me?'

'Sure,' Eddie said. 'We'll have to come up with a lie to tell my parents, but it doesn't have to be a good one. They won't notice.'

John had already lied to his parents. He told them he was spending the next three nights on school camp. Instead, he'd snuck away from the city at dawn, hopped a train, bus and ferry, and arrived in Belport mid-morning.

Eddie was all too happy to skip school to spend the day with him. All John had said on the phone was that he needed to get away for a while, but Eddie was certain there was another reason, and he was almost certain he knew what it was.

John had brought along his sleeping bag and had planned on sleeping in one of the utility sheds at the deserted foreshore campgrounds. But each shed had been chained, padlocked, and marked with a sign that read, *Smile, you're on camera!* Neither of them had been able to see a security camera, but the risk seemed too high, so Eddie had suggested the terminal.

'What the hell even is this place?' John asked, looking over at the soiled and stained mattress in the corner. There were loose bricks and broken glass on the ground, graffiti sprawled across the walls – *For free cock call this number*; *Judy Bray is a fucking whore*; *Weed is gay* – and a used condom hanging from one of the rafters. Someone must have flung it up there when they were done.

'It used to be the main port on the island,' Eddie said. 'I remember it from when I was little. Now they have the new one in over at Elk Harbour.'

'*Call Barry for the best blowjob in Belport*,' John said, reading from the wall of graffiti.

'Yeah, now this place is a beat.'

'What's a beat?'

'Like, a meeting place for fags.'

'Great,' John said. 'Now I'm definitely not spending the night here.'

'Why don't you just stay at my place?' Eddie asked.

'Because your parents would want to know what I was doing here in the middle of the week. They'd probably want to call my parents, and if *they* found out I was here they'd never let me leave the house again.'

Eddie stuffed his hands into the pockets of his hoodie

and kicked an empty beer can. It shot across the terminal and landed with a *clang* that echoed around the room. He looked at John, wondered if he should ask, decided he probably shouldn't, but then went ahead and asked anyway. 'Why are you here?'

'Because if I stayed in that house any longer, I'd go crazy and murder my family with an axe,' John said, with a wry smile. 'My parents are doing my head in, that's all. Dad's at work all the time, and when he does come home, he just sits in front of the TV like a robot. And Mum is just so fake I can't even stand it. She goes on and on about how important it is that I study and get into a good uni, when she never made it past high school.'

'I like your mum,' Eddie said. 'She's nice.'

Eddie had been to John's holiday house a handful of times during the summer, and Pam had always been good to him. She even marked his height against the wall of their living room, alongside John and his cousins.

'Yeah, but she's only nice because she has to be,' John said. 'Because the Bible tells her to. That's what I never get about Catholics. If we're just doing things because we're scared of God, then it shouldn't really count. Anyway, she wouldn't be so nice if she knew where I was.'

'Belport?'

'A fag meet-up joint,' John said. 'You know what the Bible says about being gay?'

'*If a man lies with a male as with a woman, both have*

committed an abomination,' Eddie said, quoting Leviticus.

John raised his eyebrows. 'How do you know that?'

'I looked it up at the school library.'

'Why?'

'I was curious,' he said. 'You know what else the Bible says you're not meant to do? Wear torn clothes, get a tattoo, eat bacon ...'

John laughed. 'Eat bacon? You made that one up.'

'You can't eat a pig or touch its carcass because it doesn't chew cud, or something.'

'That's completely mental,' John said. 'How come you know so much about religion when your parents aren't religious?'

Eddie gave his ear a tug and shrugged. 'Maybe that's why. We were never taught about God and heaven and all that stuff, so I guess I wanted to see what all the fuss was about. So, what do you think?'

'What do I think about what?'

'You think God sends gay people to hell?'

John looked Eddie in the eyes, deep in the eyes, and shook his head. 'No. I don't.'

'Me neither.'

Eddie kissed him.

'The fuck are you doing?' John snapped. He shoved Eddie backwards. 'Get the fuck off me.'

'I ...'

'I'm not into that shit, Eddie.'

'Well neither am I,' Eddie said, forcing a laugh. 'It was a joke, because of where we are and—'

'Bullshit.'

Eddie rubbed his eyes with the heels of his hands and muttered, 'Fuck, fuck, fuck …'

'I'm gonna go.'

'Wait.' Eddie blocked his way. 'John, just wait.'

'Let me pass, Ed.'

'I'm sorry, okay. It was a joke. I was trying to be funny.'

'Funny,' John echoed. 'Okay.'

'You're not going to tell anyone, are you? Craig and Gordy and those other guys?'

'Let me *pass*.'

'I thought …'

'Get the fuck out of the way, Eddie.'

'I thought you wanted … I thought you were into …'

'I'm not.'

'But—'

'I'm not, Eddie,' John said. 'I'm not like you. I'm not a …'

'A fag?'

'That's not what I said.'

But that's what Eddie heard. His anger flared.

Eddie had shoved John. John shoved him back. Then, in the blink of an eye – just long enough to throw the Switch – Eddie threw a punch. It connected with John's chin – not hard, but hard enough to send John stumbling back, pinwheeling for balance. A flash of chaos came next, a mad and awkward burst of childish violence.

They pushed, pulled and punched, cursed and gasped and cried. They became a tangle of limbs, but somewhere in that tangle, Eddie kissed John again. This time, John let him.

Thunder growled in the distance. The squawking of seabirds and the pounding of waves drifted in through wide cracks in the floorboards, and through the front door, which hung open on one hinge.

Eddie slid to his knees, fumbling dumbly with John's belt. He unbuckled, unbuttoned, and unzipped.

It was awkward and uncomfortable, wonderful and perfect. John moaned, bit down on his bottom lip, tasting blood and toothpaste. He threaded his fingers through Eddie's hair and guided him up and down, back and forth, following the rhythm of his body, the rhythm of the waves outside.

John looked out through the dusty, yellowing window. A fat brown moth clung to the glass, then flicked its wings and flew through a hole in the ceiling. John's focus shifted then. He looked out over the landing and drew in a tight, sudden breath. There was a car parked over by the boat ramps. A dark-blue BMW. It hadn't been there when they'd come in, had it?'

'Eddie, stop. There's a car out there. I think there's

someone … here.'

John glanced over at the door. A man stepped into the terminal. He was tall, with the bulky, solid build of a rugby player. His hair was cropped short. He wore white canvas tennis shoes and a heavy black coat. He was watching them.

Eddie turned away from John and saw the man. He gasped and scrambled to his feet. John yanked the fly of his jeans up and buckled his belt.

The boys couldn't be sure what he was doing there, but there was no other reason they could think of: he was *cruising*. He had brought along a six-pack of beer. He held one open can in his left hand, while the other five dangled from plastic rings in his right. He stepped forward, half a smile on his face. His sneakers crunched against broken glass.

'Don't stop on my account,' he said. 'I was enjoying the … Jesus, how old are you two?'

His eyes had adjusted to the low light of the terminal and he had seen two hairless, frightened faces staring back at him. He screwed up his face.

'What are you doing here?' he demanded.

'Nothing,' John said.

'This isn't a place for kids,' he said. 'You shouldn't be here.'

If Eddie had stopped to think about that – to *really* think – he might have realised that if this man was there cruising, he had a reason to keep their secret. But Eddie didn't think about it. The only thoughts in his mind were, *No. This man can't see this. This man can't see us. This man can't end this.* They buzzed in flashing, neon lights.

'Fuck off,' Eddie snapped in a small voice.

The man glared at him. 'What did you say?'

'He didn't say anything,' John said, throwing a glance Eddie's way. 'Leave it.'

But Eddie wasn't thinking straight. He was hardly thinking at all. A fog of panic had rolled into his head, joined the anger and the shame and the lust, and this man shouldn't know their secret. He couldn't.

'I said fuck off,' he blurted, louder now.

'Eddie,' John hissed.

The man looked annoyed. 'Didn't your parents tell you to respect your elders?' he said. 'Do they know you're here, *Eddie*?'

'Shut up,' Eddie said.

'They might be interested to know what their son is doing in the middle of a school day.'

'Your wife might be interested too,' John said, eyeing the ring on the men's left hand. He could feel Eddie shaking beside him.

'I was just passing by, minding my own beeswax, when I heard what sounded like a couple of kids fighting.' He stared at the boys, took a moment to consider his options. Then, perhaps deciding that an argument with two teenage boys wasn't worth it, shook his head and turned to leave. 'Whatever. This is not my problem. Your parents can sort this shit out themse—'

There was a hollow clunk and the man took two big steps backwards. His hand shot to his head. He stumbled, then lost his balance and fell backwards, onto the floor, his head smacking hard on the ground.

It took John a few seconds to piece together what had happened. The man was very still. Eddie stood over him, his fingers curled tightly around a loose brick. He must have found it on the floor, must have picked it up, must have—

'What the fuck did you do?' John hissed.

'He was going to tell,' Eddie muttered. 'You heard him. He was going to tell.'

The man's limbs jerked once. He made a gurgling sound. A rough triangle shape was missing from his forehead. A narrow line of blood seeped from it, cutting a vertical stripe from forehead to chin.

'I had to,' Eddie kept saying. 'He was going to tell. I had to. He was going to tell. I had to …'

'Jesus, Eddie,' John said. 'What have you done?'

'I had—'

'We need to help him.'

As Eddie began to pace, cry and curse, John went to the man. He was still alive, he thought, but there was a lot of blood and it kept coming. It wasn't just a seep now. It guzzled from the wound in his head in shallow bursts, keeping in time with his heartbeat.

'He's still alive,' John said.

'Come on, we have to go.'

'We need to help him.'

'We have to get out of here, John. Now!'

Eddie yanked at John's arm, but John refused to move. He couldn't move. All he could do was watch the light fade from the man's eyes.

Eddie dropped the brick and ran. His hurried footsteps echoed around the terminal. Then there was only John and the dying man. And he *was* dying. His chest rose once, then fell. The blood streaming down his face slowed to a stop. John stared at the blood. It didn't look like one whole thing, John thought, but hundreds of tiny things.

'Like caterpillars,' he muttered. 'This wasn't supposed to happen … This wasn't supposed to

happen that way,' Eddie said.

Abby sat in stunned, broken silence. Her first thought was: *I wish I didn't believe them*. Her second was one of self-preservation. She didn't wish that David Stemple hadn't met his end, only that it hadn't been at the hands of her own son. She wished it had been John. Why couldn't it have been John?

But if Abby was honest, it wasn't hard for her to picture Eddie losing it like that. She thought of him as a toddler, in what Ray had called his 'apocalyptic temper tantrums', screaming and kicking uncontrollably until, exhausted, he'd collapsed into her arms. She remembered the times – rare enough to be dismissed, but uncomfortable in the moment – when she saw that fury again: when her usually quiet seven-year-old had thrown himself to the floor of a toyshop, screaming and shaking so that she almost thought he was having a seizure. And Eddie at thirteen, after a girl at school had spread a rumour about him and he'd viciously kicked at the wall, both panicked and enraged. And finally, Eddie in the back yard, hurling a comic book into the she-oak. She thought about the Switch, and about the dark things kids inherit from their parents. Abby had been a fool to think that kind of anger just went away.

'Mum, please, say something,' Eddie said. 'I'm sorry, Mum. I fucked up. Fuck! I fucked up! I fucked—'

'The magazines are yours, aren't they?' she said, half dazed.

'What?'

'Give me a second.'

'Mum,' Eddie said.

'Shut up,' she told them. 'Just give me a fucking second.'

She glanced into the hall, to where the teenager had kicked off his dirty sneakers. She wanted to throw them in the fire. She wanted to throw *him* in the fire. She wanted to drink. She wanted to hurt something. The lights in the kitchen were suddenly too bright. There was too much sensory input. She felt overloaded, like a glass beneath running water, like a screaming, squealing, boiling kettle.

'Alright,' she said suddenly. 'What happened next?'

'Next?' Eddie asked.

'After you ran,' Abby said.

She clenched her hands into tight fists below the table. 'If you ran, how did his body end up in the water?'

'The guy had parked his car over on the promenade,' Eddie said. A startling casualness had crept into his tone. 'When I reached it, it was like, sounds came back or something. It started to rain and that sort of, snapped me out of it. The car was unlocked and … he had a car phone. I thought about calling the police. I was *going* to call the police …'

'But you didn't,' Abby said. 'You called your dad.'

Eddie nodded sadly. 'I didn't know what to do.'

She turned to John. 'What did you do?'

'I stayed with the man until he …' John said. 'I stayed there until Mr Gilpin arrived and found me. When he got there, he put me and Eddie in the back seat of his work truck and had us tell him what happened. He went out to the ferry terminal and was gone for a while. When he came back, he told us to leave.'

'Leave?'

'He told me to go home, back to Melbourne, and he

sent Eddie back here, to the house. He told us we should never talk about it. Not ever. But I … He didn't do it. He got arrested and he didn't do it, and I can't—'

'Yes,' Abby said. 'You can.'

The boys were staring at her dumbly, so she closed her eyes tightly and in the deep, still darkness behind them, she saw her husband. *Promise me something. Survive. You, Lori, Eddie. Promise me.*

Ray was right, she felt suddenly. She inhaled deeply, then, as calmly as she could manage, said, 'Here's what we're going to do. John, you'll spend the night. Tomorrow morning I'll drop you at the ferry and you'll go home.'

She looked hard at both boys.

'We're going to bury this,' she continued. 'Do you know what I mean by that? We're going to bury this someplace so deep and far away that we're not even sure it really happened. You're young. Both of you. You have long lives ahead of you.'

'But, Dad,' Eddie started. 'He—'

'Your dad made a sacrifice, Eddie. Now be a good boy and make up the couch for your friend.'

She stood up, sighed deeply, and went to the fridge to fetch a beer. She left the boys where they were and strode out onto the front verandah to drink.

Milt Street was quiet and dark. The sawhorses were finally gone from the low intersection of Brown and

Delahunt streets. It was finally dry. Dry enough to drive on, at least.

Abby sat down on the top step, wondering if she'd rescued those boys or cursed them. A new weight settled on her shoulders. She'd have to carry it a long time, she knew.

A *long* time.

29

THE WIDOW

Full dark was creeping over Belport when Kate followed Ed Gilpin's truck onto Milt Street. He pulled into the driveway of a small, two-storey weatherboard house, set back from the street across a sweep of lush green lawn. A homemade sign was posted on the grass with *Caretakers* written in big black print.

Ed drove the truck inside the garage. The roller door rattled down behind him.

Kate parked across the street and started up a narrow stone path that cut across the lawn.

The house was in desperate need of some TLC. The paint was chipped and peeling, there was a crack in the picture window above the front door, and a board had come loose below the verandah and dangled by one steel nail at a forty-five-degree angle.

The yard, on the other hand, was immaculate. There was not a blade of grass out of place. A vegetable garden ran the length of the verandah, and there were potted ferns hanging from hooks, shifting slightly in the breeze.

Kate didn't stop to think about what she was doing. If she had, she might have realised how reckless she was being, spun on one foot and hightailed it back to the car. Instead, she crept around to the side of the garage, searching for a window she might be able to spy through.

'Are you lost?' a voice drifted down from the verandah.

It was screened, so all Kate could see was the red tip of a glowing cigarette. From somewhere behind the screen, a wind chime clinked and clattered. Kate then heard what might have been a can snapping open.

A compact woman in her early sixties stepped out onto the steps, holding a beer in her left hand and a paperback in her right. She was dressed in a loose-fitting wool cardigan and pyjama bottoms with a faded pattern of stars and crescent moons. Her face was round and warm, framed by messy, stark-white hair. Her eyes were deep and dark, like Ed's.

'No, I'm not lost,' Kate said. 'I'm looking for Ed.'

'That's my son,' the woman said. 'Are you a friend of his?'

'No, not exactly. I …' She hesitated. '… I have a holiday house over on Neef Street and I'm looking for a winter caretaker. I saw the sign on the front lawn.'

It wasn't a perfect lie, but it was all she could come up with in the heat of the moment. She couldn't exactly say she was here to question Ed about her husband's murder.

'Ed will be with you in a minute,' the woman said. 'He has to wash down his truck and lay out his tools for tomorrow. You can wait for him inside if you like?

'Are you sure? I don't want to impose.'

'Oh please, I only came out here to smoke and it's colder than a fairy penguin's pocket. If you come in, I'll have an excuse to light up inside. I'm Abby, by the way.'

'Kate.'

They shook hands. The woman's fingers were dry and dusty, like moth's wings. She led Kate through the front door.

Inside, a fox mounted on polished oak stared at Kate from a side table, its face caught mid-snarl, tail up and out in the defensive position. On each of its four paws was a baby-sized Converse All Star. Behind the fox stood three blind (and dead) mice, each with its own pair of tiny sunglasses. Next to them were two dead rabbits serving as bookends to a stack of takeaway menus. A toad leaned back on its hind legs, its front hands up, webbed fingers outstretched, holding a small bowl with loose change and a set of car keys inside.

Kate gaped at them.

'Stuffed them myself,' Abby said. 'What do you think?'

'They're very … striking.'

Abby laughed. 'Now that's a lovely way of saying *weird*. I know taxidermy is an odd sort of hobby, but I try to do one crazy thing per day to keep from *going* crazy. Would you mind taking your shoes off?'

Kate did as she was asked. She stepped out of her sneakers – which were still wet from the boat ramp – and followed Abby down a short hallway and into the kitchen. It was cluttered with curiosities. A wooden ladder was suspended across the kitchen ceiling, off which dangled various utensils: a wok, a handful of wine glasses, pots, pans, and a single soup ladle. A stolen street sign – *Gilpin Ave* – was nailed above the back door. Beside that was a wooden carving of a semiautomatic machine gun and the words, *Forget the Dog, Beware the Owner.*

The kitchen was so busy, in fact, that it took Kate a few seconds to realise what was spread out over the dining table.

Arranged neatly on a pink bath towel were a box of surgical gloves, a set of tiny glass eyes, a silver knife with a scalpel blade attached and a furry, half-skinned creature that Kate couldn't identify. She took three quick steps backwards.

'It's a bush rat,' Abby said with a grin, reading her gaze. 'Marnie Conroy found the poor little bastard in the space between her wood heater and the wall. If I'd known I'd have company, I would have put him away. You want a beer?'

'No, thanks.'

'You're really going to make me drink alone?' She slammed the fridge shut. 'Just kidding. I'm used to it.'

She sat down at the kitchen table and offered the seat across from her. Kate took off her parka, hung it on back of the chair and sat.

'Ed won't be long,' Abby said.

'Does he live here with you?'

Abby necked her beer, stifled a belch, and shook her head. 'He has an apartment over on Deepwater, but he doesn't have enough space for his tools, so he keeps them here.'

'So, it's just you in this house?'

'Uh huh, which means I can drink as much as I want and fart as loud as I can. That'll change when the hubby comes home, of course. The drinking part, anyway. Not the farts.' She grinned, rocked back in her chair, and lit a cigarette. Smoke filled the room. 'I know who you are.'

'Excuse me?'

'You're the widow, right? Of that poor fella who got killed at the boat ramps?'

'How did you …'

'My husband called me five minutes after you left South Hallston and told me to expect a visit from John Keddie's widow. I should have said something when I saw you creeping around out there, but you'd gone to all that trouble making up that caretaking cover story and I didn't want to make you feel awkward. Too late for that now, I suppose.

The muscles in Kate's neck tightened. Her cheeks flushed with colour.

'How did Ray look, by the way?' Abby asked. 'He resembled a big old bag of pork crackers last time I visited.'

'He looked fine,' Kate said.

'It's nice of you to lie,' Abby said. Leaving the cigarette skilfully balanced between her lips, she took a sip of beer. 'So, what do you want with my son, really?'

'I think Ed and John knew each other as kids. I'm just here to ask him some questions.'

'About what?'

Well, I've come this far, Kate thought.

'About David Stemple,' she said.

Abby flinched at the sound of his name, but only slightly. 'What do you know about David Stemple?'

'I know that John had information about his murder,' Kate said, as coolly as she could. 'And I know that's why he came to Belport.'

Abby dragged deeply on her cigarette. She ashed into a ceramic ramekin. 'You have a daughter, don't you? What's her name?'

'… Mia.'

'How old?'

'Ten.'

'That's a good age,' she said. 'Is she here with you, in Belport?'

'No,' Kate said. 'She's in Melbourne, staying with her grandparents.'

Abby stubbed out her cigarette in the ramekin and finished her beer in three steady gulps.

'Life is funny, don't you think? We bring babies into this world, let them rip up our bodies, let them drink from us, bleed us dry, and we love them for it. We give and we give and we give. We *sacrifice*. And do you know why? Because we're mothers. It's what we do. I'm having another beer. You sure you won't join me?'

'No, thanks.'

Abby stood, struggling against a little lower back pain, and went to the fridge. 'I mean, think about it: is there anything you wouldn't do for your daughter?'

'… No,' Kate said.

'That's right,' Abby told her, smiling a sad and distant smile. 'So you understand?'

She didn't think much of it when Abby moved behind her, nor did she notice that the knife was missing from the table. Not until it was too late.

'Understand what?' she asked.

'What I *had* to do,' Abby said. 'And what I *have* to.'

30

THE WIFE

'Do you need cash for your ticket?' Abby asked.

John shook his head. 'I bought a return.'

'What about breakfast? You should eat something on the ferry. You need a couple of bucks?'

'I've got money,' he said. 'Anyway, I'm not hungry. I'm not sure I'll ever be hungry again.'

He reached into the front pocket of his backpack and pulled out a pair of woollen gloves. He slid them on and looked out over the water.

'Thanks for the ride,' he said, pushing the door open.

'Hold on, John. I want to talk to you for a second.'

He shut the door.

'I need to know you'll keep this secret,' she said. 'Ray is giving a lot so that you and Eddie don't lose a lot. You understand that, don't you? And you understand that if you tell anyone – and I mean *anyone* – it all comes undone and everything my husband is giving will be for nothing.'

'... I keep seeing that man's blood,' John whispered. He gave her a despairing look.

'Then close your eyes, John. Put it someplace out of the way, in a room behind a locked door. Then all you have to do is not go in that room. Understand? Never go in that room.'

He nodded, once. There was a good chance he'd tell his family what had happened the second he got home. Soon cops might storm her house and drag her and Eddie away to prison, leaving Lori to fend for herself. But then again, there was a chance John wouldn't say anything. It might have been blind hope, but hope of any sort had been in short supply lately, so Abby clung to it.

'Thank you, Mrs Gilpin,' John said.

'That's alright, John.'

'No, I mean it. *Thank you.*'

She looked at the boy for a moment, and hoped she'd never see him again. 'Have a safe trip home.'

John got out of the car and boarded the ferry. Abby watched him get on, then watched until the boat eased away from the island, turned in a long slow arc and headed back towards the mainland. When the boat was a white shape on the horizon, she started the car and drove home.

For the next twenty-three years, Abby lived as if waiting for a bus. She baulked at people who said things like *life's too short* and *time passes in a blur* and *Jee-zus, is it Christmas already?* Life was long, time moved too slow, and anyway fuck Christmas.

She spent her time driving out to South Hallston Correctional Facility, borrowing paperbacks from the Belport Public Library, working at the Buy & Bye, stuffing animals, smoking cigarettes on the front porch and watching the seasons come and go. Her body aged and the world changed, but her life was on hold until Ray came home.

She took her own advice, locked all the dark thoughts in a room in her mind and tried not to visit it. For the most part, it got easier. But in the dead of night, when Milt Street was quiet, she could hear them growling behind the door and scratching at the walls. It reminded her that the dark things were still there and they weren't going away.

Lori got out of Belport when she turned eighteen. She studied art history in Melbourne. She found a job on campus and moved into an apartment with three roommates. She fell in love with one of them, and when he was offered a job in Sydney that he couldn't refuse, she moved there with him and they got married.

At the wedding, when Abby asked if it made her sad that her father wasn't there to give her away, Lori said he gave her away a long time ago. Abby cried herself to sleep that night.

Eddie, who became Ed, stayed on the island to take

over the family business. He ran it well. He spent his days haunting those big empty houses on Neef Street, retreating further and further inwards. He might have wanted to leave. He might have eaten his lunch down at Beech Tree Landing as his father had done and fantasised about a boat coming in to take him away. Abby wouldn't know because they never talked about it.

Abby thought about leaving too, once or twice. A developer would probably give her three times what she and Ray paid for their place, knock the house down and put in three townhouses. But Belport wouldn't let either of them go. It was David Stemple who died in the winter of '96, but it was Abby and Eddie's ghosts that were doomed to haunt the island.

In the winter of 2019, Abby Gilpin, then deep into her fifties, was nearing the end of her shift at the Buy & Bye. Her left foot ached with what the internet had diagnosed as either gout, a corn, or foot cancer. Bay Street was practically deserted.

There was a single customer roaming the aisles: a man somewhere in his late thirties or early forties, a dusting of salt and pepper in his hair, a shopping basket under one arm. He had been standing in the medicine section for close to three minutes, engrossed in their very limited selection.

Abby thought about asking if he needed help finding something, but then she'd have to walk all the way over there on her sore foot, and besides, she had just borrowed the new Stephen King from the library and Biller wouldn't be in for another twenty minutes, so she might be able to knock off a chapter or two before he arrived.

She made it halfway through the first page when the man unpacked his basket in her check-out: bread, milk, bottled water, Mi Goreng noodles, water crackers, a box of Frosties, chamomile tea, valerian capsules, three different types of antihistamines and a bottle of Wild Turkey.

'Hello, Mrs Gilpin,' the man said. 'Do you remember me?'

For the first time since he came in, she looked at the man's face. John had been a teenager the last time they met. She had thought she'd spotted him at a distance now and then over the years – wandering down Bay Street or sitting on the beach – but had always managed to avoid him. Or maybe he was the one avoiding her. He had filled out a little and had three- or four-day growth on his face, so it took a moment to place him.

'John?' she said. Her mouth groped for more words like a fish, but nothing came out.

'It's been a while,' he said.

'What are you doing here?'

'Grocery shopping,' he said, gesturing to his shopping basket. There were dark bags under his eyes and his skin was pasty, almost yellow. It looked like he hadn't slept since the day she dropped him at the ferry twenty-three years earlier.

'I mean, what are you doing in Belport?' Abby asked, her tone unintentionally icy. Ray had told her about John's visit. He'd assured her that there was nothing to worry about, that he'd sorted it and John would be leaving again very soon.

'My wife and I have a house here,' he said. 'Actually, I'm here most summers.' Abby couldn't tell whether he misunderstood her question intentionally or not. He certainly looked dazed enough to have forgotten meeting with Ray.

'You're married then?' Abby said.

Nodding, John took out his phone and showed her his screensaver of a pretty but uninteresting brunette with a cute little girl wrapped in her arms. Abby looked into the woman's eyes and thought, *Does she know? Did he tell her?*

'How's Eddie?' John asked.

'Fine,' she said.

She began ringing up and bagging his items. She had to concentrate to keep her hands from trembling.

'I drove out to Beech Tree Landing today,' he said. 'Strange, being there without the old ferry terminal. When exactly did they tear it down?'

'Must have been a good fifteen years ago,' Abby said. 'It was a safety hazard.'

And after what happened, people said it was haunted, she thought, but kept that detail to herself.

'I've managed to avoid it, mostly. Took me nearly two weeks to work up the nerve to go out there,' he said. 'And a little longer to work up the nerve to talk to you.'

The door behind which she'd locked all the dark things rattled and shook.

'We have nothing to talk about,' she said.

'We made a mistake, Mrs Gilpin. *Abby*,' he said. 'Eddie and I were just kids, but *you* … you should have known better.'

'Keep your voice down.'

'I'm sick of keeping my voice down,' he said. 'I'm sick of keeping your secrets.'

'John, just listen—'

'No,' he said. 'I don't have to listen to you anymore, Abby. I am all shades of fucked up because I listened to you. I've had nightmares since I was a kid because I listened to you. Annabel Stemple died never knowing the truth, because *I fucking listened to you.*'

At the mention of Annabel's name, Abby was briefly transported back in time. She remembered the woman who bought cigarettes from her at the Buy & Bye, and she remembered her son, the boy with the luminol-blue eyes.

'Ray told me you went to see him,' Abby said, grasping for some kind of control. 'Did he mention he was up for parole? He'll be out soon, John. This is nearly over.'

'It'll never be over,' he said. 'And honestly, I can't understand how you can't see that. We made a mistake, Abby. We have to fix it. We have to come clean. The three of us. You, me and Eddie.'

'It wouldn't change anything,' she whispered.

'It'll change *everything*.'

A sudden gale rolled off the bay.

'Ninety-eight-sixty,' Abby said.

'What?'

'That's how much you owe.'

He glared at her a moment, then shook his head slowly. He paid in cash, then took a pen from his breast pocket and scribbled his phone number and address on the back of his receipt. He handed it to Abby.

'Come by the house tonight at eight o'clock,' he said. 'You and Eddie. The three of us can plan how we're going to move forward. But you need to understand something, Abby. This isn't up for discussion. I'm not asking for your permission and I don't need Eddie's either. I need to do this, and it can be with or without you.'

He picked up his groceries and walked out. He didn't look back once. When he was gone, Abby braced herself on her register and started to cry.

The last time she drove out to South Hallston to see Ray, they'd sat together at a steel table in the visitor hall and ate lunch from the vending machines.

'How are the kids?' he asked.

'Oh, you know,' Abby said. 'Angels and devils.'

'Has Lori called?'

'Not for a while, but she's like a sea turtle, that one. She has to come up for air eventually, and when she does, I'll strangle her with my love.'

'Give her an extra choke for me,' Ray said. 'And Eddie?'

'*Ed* is, well. Ed.'

'Is he seeing anyone?'

'If he is, he hasn't told me about it.'

'You look great.'

'I'm not sure what you're basing that on, Ray, because I don't think you've looked at me once since I got here.'

Ray, who had spent their entire conversation staring at his hands, looked up. 'There. Now it's official. You look great.'

'You're a wonderful liar.'

He smiled. It was a sturdy, genuine smile. She hadn't seen one like it in some time. 'I spoke to Bob about all the parole stuff.'

'Yeah.'

He leaned forward on his elbows and lowered his voice. 'It looks good, Ab.'

'How good?'

'You know Bob's motto: *hope for the best but expect the*

worst. But let's just say he was … quietly optimistic. I might be coming home sooner than we thought.'

Regardless of Bob's motto, Abby couldn't wipe the smile off her face.

Belport was roughly twenty years behind the rest of the world, which meant a bank of payphones still stood in a neat row outside the post office.

Abby's shift finished fifteen minutes after John Keddie left the store. Three minutes later, she pulled up outside the payphones and climbed out of a Honda (the Volvo had given up and died back in the early 2000s).

She had her mobile on her, and reception on the island wasn't bad since they cut down all those trees on Harvill Hill to erect a signal tower, but she didn't want this call traced.

She stepped out into the cold, fed change into one of the phones, and punched in the number John had given her.

'Hello?' John answered.

'Tonight is no good,' she said. 'But we're free right now.'

'You and Eddie?'

'Yes,' she lied.

'You have my address.'

'No,' she said. 'Not there. Can you meet us?'

'… Where?'

31

THE WIFE AND THE WIDOW

Any lower back pain Abby had felt when getting off her chair had apparently vanished. She moved lightning-quick for a woman her age. All Kate saw – before the knife cleaved a hot line through her skin – was a flash of grey hair and the glint of a scalpel blade.

Abby had gone for the throat. Her left hand had reached from behind and grabbed hold of Kate's face, fingers splayed outwards like talons, while her right brought the knife up and under her chin. Instinctively, Kate had managed to bring her right arm up to block the blow, but it had caught the blade. Hot blood fell in ribbons from her forearm. She tried to scream but there was no air left in her body.

'Motherfucker,' Abby spat, struggling to keep Kate in her chair.

For a moment, Kate nearly allowed herself to slip into autopilot. The temptation to submit and roll over like a frightened puppy was strong. But that was the old Kate. That was the woman who hadn't wanted to hear about the monsters under the bed, the woman who let the men in her life show her what to do and when to do it.

She had tried never to think about death, but the few times she had, she'd decided that when it came it should feel like an ellipsis: a gentle trailing off of a sentence. It should be a whisper of words, a padding of gentle footsteps. This, being killed by a deranged middle-aged woman, felt too sudden, too mad. This couldn't be how it ended.

She thought about Mia, could almost see her face, almost hear her voice.

Mum? the voice said.

Yes, monkey?

Be a big girl.

Kate rocked hard in her chair and toppled backwards onto the tiles. She scrambled back, clasping at the wet blood seeping from the gash on her arm. Abby came towards her fast, the blade of her knife aimed directly outwards like a fencing sword. Her eyes were deep and lost, and mad. They seemed to say, *Orpheus was torn to shreds by vicious, hungry beasts.*

Kate pulled herself to her feet and reached blindly upwards, groping at the pots and pans that hung from the ladder like stalactites. Her hand found the handle of a saucepan. She yanked it down and tossed it at Abby, who

covered her face with her elbow and braced for impact.
She needn't have bothered. Kate was a terrible shot. The
saucepan whipped past her, shattering the door of the
microwave.

Then, Abby was right in front of Kate, punching her in
the chest, in the shoulder, in the belly. There was no pain
– adrenalin had flooded her system – so it took her a few
moments to understand what was happening. Abby wasn't
punching her. She was *stabbing* her. Thrusting in and out,
in and out, so many times that Kate lost count.

The blade was only short, but soon Kate's white shirt
was covered in growing spots of red. She looked at her
winter parka hanging on her chair. She wished she had
kept it on. It wouldn't have stopped the attack entirely
but might have served as armour.

She felt foggy and clumsy, sluggish and terrified. Her
instinct was to pull back, but there was nowhere to go.
Her back was against the kitchen cabinets. So instead,
she thrust herself forward, knocking Abby to one side
and stumbling to the ground against the kitchen table.
She grabbed hold of it, intending to hoist herself up, but
instead collapsed it around herself, spilling the box of
surgical gloves, glass eyes and a half-skinned rat onto the
floor. The gloves fell somewhere to her left. The eyes hit
the tiles with a soft *crack* and rolled beneath the fridge.
The half-skinned and half-frozen corpse slapped down
right between her legs.

She picked it up and flung it across the room. It struck Abby in the cheek – leaving a film of yellow-brown liquid there – and slopped back to the floor.

Kate moved to stand but her vision blurred. The dozen or so one-inch nicks on her chest began to flare with pain. She grunted, spun herself onto her stomach, and began crawling and clawing her way towards the hallway.

A heavy weight slammed against her back. Abby was on top of her now, straddling her, panting and crying. They were both crying. Kate felt the blade sink into her lower back, then her side, then her back again.

'No,' she managed to say. 'Please.'

Hot urine spilled down Kate's leg and her bowels let go.

At the top of the hallway, the front door swung open, letting in a rush of cold air from outside. It momentarily sharpened Kate's senses, and she was able to crane her neck to look.

For a moment she thought, *Fisher?* Then she recognised Ed Gilpin's pale-grey work shirt. Ed stared back at Kate in dumb disbelief, then looked at the woman on her back.

'… Mum?'

'Shut the door, Ed,' she heard Abby say, before darkness engulfed her and she slipped away into unconsciousness. 'Shut the damn

door,' Abby said.

But Ed just stood staring at her from the top of

the hall, one hand resting on the doorknob, the other dangling slackly by his side.

Over his shoulder, Abby could see clear across Milt Street. It was empty, but all it would take was a single car driving past at the wrong moment, and for the driver to glance inside.

The widow had fallen still beneath her, but she was still breathing in a laboured, raspy tone.

'Ed, the door!' Abby shouted again.

Ed's hand fell loose from the knob and he went on standing there, staring.

Despite the fact his fight or flight response had apparently shut down, it was a good thing he was there, Abby thought. She wished he didn't have to see this and wished harder that he didn't have to see *her* like this, but she would need his help.

She had taken care of John Keddie quickly. He hadn't seen it coming, and years of reading true crime and performing taxidermy had made her surprisingly efficient at the job. It had been messy, but quick. All she'd had to do when she was done was lean over him, slip his Prius into neutral and let it roll into the sea.

This was different. John's widow coming over unannounced meant she had to improvise. When she was done – and please God let that be soon – she'd need help moving the body and scrubbing down the house.

But there was another reason she was glad Ed was

here, although she would never admit it out loud: a deep, slightly twisted part of her thought it was good for him to see this. This was the cost of keeping his secret. This was what sacrifice looked like.

'Ed,' Abby hissed, in the same tone she'd used on him as a boy when he was getting up to mischief. 'Shut the fucking door right now and come help your mother.'

He flinched, then finally did as he was told. He took three small and cautious steps forward, leaning forward to look at the widow. 'Is she …?

'Not yet,' Abby said. 'You don't need to be here for this part, but I'm going to need your help.'

The widow shuddered, spat up a mouthful of blood, then fell still again.

'It was you, wasn't it?' Ed said. 'You killed John.'

'Oh, come on, Ed, don't give me that. You must have figured that out.'

'I … I think I was afraid of the answer,' he said. 'I didn't want you to … I didn't want *this*.'

'Well maybe if you hadn't been lurking around his house like that she wouldn't have made it here.'

'But I didn't want *any* of this,' he said again.

'Jesus, okay, Eddie, neither did I. But he was going to undo everything. He was going to undo the sacrifice your father made. The sacrifice we all made, for you. This is all because of you.'

'No. Enough, Mum.'

'Your dad is coming home, Eddie. This is nearly over. This is all nearly over.'

He took out his phone. 'I'm calling Bobbi.'

'Stop.'

He was crying now, which got Abby started again. Hot tears streaked down her face. She had to end this now. She lifted Kate Keddie's head with her left hand and moved to drag the X-Acto knife over her throat.

One more time, she thought. *One more sacrifice.*

Big arms clasped around her, pulled her backwards, dragged her down the hall. She dropped the blade, struggling to break free of her son's grip.

'It's all over,' he said.

Abby, ragged and tired, fought once more against her son, then collapsed into his arms. Ed punched triple zero into his phone and made the call, but he didn't let her go. He just held her there, rocking her back and forth, the way she had rocked him when he was a baby.

A few minutes later, she heard police sirens in the distance, getting closer and closer.

Abby looked at the widow. The woman's fingers were twitching.

'I think she's

waking up.'

Consciousness drifted in around the edges of the black. Kate woke to sharp pain. Her lips were wet and tasted like blood. The air smelled like shit. She was lying in a shallow pool of her own blood in Abby Gilpin's house, but she wasn't dead.

'Help,' she managed to say.

'Help is here,' a voice said. It was Bobbi Eckman. She was kneeling over her.

'I ...'

'Try not to speak,' Eckman said. 'The ambos are on their way. You're going to be okay, Mrs Keddie. Kate. You're safe now.'

32

THE WIFE

Abby sat in the same windowless room at Belport Police Station where, twenty-three years earlier, Ray had confessed to the murder of David Stemple. Bobbi was on her way in to talk to her. She would have a lot of questions, but for the first time in many years, all Abby had to do was tell the truth.

She would be going away then, for a long time, she reckoned. Ray would be getting out just as she was going in. The thought stirred a smile on her face.

Like ships passing in the night, she thought.

Beneath the crushing grief of what she'd lived through and the horror of what she'd done, there was something else, brewing on the horizon. A strange and forgotten sensation.

Relief.

She hoped, at least, that Ed was feeling it too.

33

THE WIDOW

Seventy-two hours after her attack, Kate was discharged from the hospital. She was full of stitches, swollen and sore, punched up like a pin cushion and emptied out, but she was awake, she was there, she was present, and she could finally go home.

Fisher and Pam had come to pick her up. They were due to catch the four pm ferry from Belport back to the mainland, but they arrived at Elk Harbour early, so Kate and Mia walked down to the beach.

Watching her daughter, Kate thought about what Abby had asked her on the night of the attack. *Is there anything you wouldn't do for your daughter?*

There wasn't. It would take a long time for Kate to admit it to herself, and even then, it would hurt like hell, but she understood Abby. She even empathised with her. If it meant protecting Mia, she would have cut down as many men as it took. Even John.

'There but by the grace of God go I,' she said.

Mia turned to her and said, 'Huh?'

But Kate just took Mia's hand and kept walking.

Kate thought about fresh starts, and pictured the clean white wall in the living room of the holiday house. It was still unclear how much Ed Gilpin really knew about his mother's actions. If he truly had no idea about the murder, as he was claiming, then why had he covered over his name on the wall? He must have been scared when he heard about John's murder, scared enough to send him into the house with a brush and a bucket of paint. That was the most likely scenario – and the one that took into account the actual evidence – but it wasn't the most appealing one.

There was another option. Maybe John was the one who painted the wall, to make a clean slate for the future, for Mia, for Kate. Either way, if, in the end, Kate decided to keep the holiday house – and that was a big if – she decided she'd leave that wall blank.

Further up the beach, they came across a dead seagull on the shoreline. The tide was coming in, retrieving the bird for a sea burial. Further up the beach, live seagulls watched and waited.

Mia stood over the dead bird, studying it from a metre or so away. There was no apparent cause of death. As far as she could tell, it had suffered a mid-air heart attack and dropped out of the sky. Its beak was caked with dry sand.

Its eyes were wide and startled.

'It looks surprised,' Mia said. Then, in a mock-English accent, gave the bird a voice. '*I simply cannot believe I'm dead.*'

The tide drifted in and reached the seagull's wing. It lifted, then dropped, lifted, dropped, as if waving.

'Do seagulls have nests?' Mia asked.

'I don't know. I don't think so. I guess they just sort of hang around the sand dunes and huddle together for warmth at night.'

'Will another seagull be waiting for this one to come home?'

'I don't know, monkey.'

'Should we bury it?'

'I think we should let the sea take it instead. That feels right, don't you think?'

'I guess,' she said.

On their way back to Elk Harbour, Mia waded in the shallows with her shoes in her hands. Kate took off her sneakers and joined her. The water was icy, but the sky was blue.

AUTHOR'S NOTE

That old cliché about the difficult second album is absolutely true. While writing this book, I spent much of my time thinking it would expose me as the fraud I really am. What kept me going, again and again and again, was you. The reader.

Since publishing *The Nowhere Child*, I've met many of you in person and received emails from readers all over the world. I have been moved, warmed and inspired by your words. I even named Bobbi Eckman's cat after a reader's feline companion (thanks again, Mary Anne from Texas, please give Joe a scratch for me). So, this is a little note to say thank you, and to say, keep 'em coming.

While you're here, I thought I'd talk a little about what went into building *that* twist. There are some major spoilers ahead, so if you've skipped to the Author's Note before reading the book, turn back now.

Juggling multiple time lines in *The Nowhere Child* and making sure each twist and plot-point was revealed at the exact right moment was hard work. By design, I told a simple story in a complex way. So, with *The Wife and The*

Widow, I set out to tell a simple story in a simple way. I wanted the narrative to be clean and linear. Things did not turn out that way. You know what they say about the best-laid plans of mice and men, right?

Instead, I decided to build an elaborate time-jump twist into the narrative. Years ago, I was watching a particular episode of *Lost* in which a flashback is revealed to be a flash*forward*, and my mind was blown apart. I wanted to do something like that. I wanted to write something that would make the reader's eyes bulge and send them back through the book in search of all the clues they missed. The trouble was, I had no idea how to do that.

I drove my publisher crazy by going back and forth with ideas. In one version, the dead body being investigated in Abby's chapters turned out to be Kate (I have no idea how I would have pulled that off). In another version, Ray's mum and John's dad were swingers and half the book would take place in the '70s (again, NO idea how I would have done that). Just as I was beginning to think the time-jump idea was impossible and I'd wasted months of my life trying to put together an unsolvable jigsaw puzzle, I was hit with a stroke of genius. A guiding voice from within whispered: *if you want to solve this problem, you know what you have to do ... ask your wife, stupid.*

So, I asked my wife.

There's a beautiful lake near our house where Summer and I walk the dog in the afternoons. On one of these walks, I unpacked all the different options, all my hopes and fears, everything I wanted to achieve. Sum was quiet for a few steps, and then said, 'What if one of Abby's kids was the killer and Kate's husband used to be friends with them and years later Abby killed Kate's husband to protect the secret.'

'Hold on,' I told her. 'I need to write this down.'

With this key piece of information, the story flowed out. I belted out a draft. Martin Hughes (publisher) and Ruby Ashby-Orr (editor) helped me make it make sense, and then helped me make it good. The best ideas in this book came from them (and Summer). Come to think of it, I really didn't do that much.

That's it for me. If you enjoyed this book, reach out. If you have some constructive criticism, let me know. If you hated it, take that secret to your grave. You can contact me through my website (christian-white.com), find me on Twitter and Instagram, or email me direct at christian@christian-white.com.

From the bottom of my heart, thank you. I'll keep writing them as long as you keep reading them. Until next time ...

ACKNOWLEDGEMENTS

So many wonderful people helped create this book.

Martin Hughes and Ruby Ashby-Orr, the manuscript I delivered to you was a mere shadow of what it became thanks to your guidance, support and pure genius. Keiran Rogers, thank you for selling the shit out of my first book, and for letting me take pictures of you while you were sleeping. Grace Breen, you were stuck with me more than anyone else on *The Nowhere Child* book tour. Hanging out with you never felt like work. Emily Ashenden, you are the Radar O'Reilly of Affirm Press. You might be too young to get that reference. *I* might be too young to get that reference. Everyone else at Affirm Press, you continue to be amazing and amazingly supportive and, even better, you let me bring my dog into the office.

Daniela Rapp from St. Martin's Press, it's been an absolute pleasure working with you (twice!).

My agents, Jennifer Naughton and Candice Thom, you continue to have my back, both in business and in life.

My F.R.I.E.N.D.S, Jon Asquith (Ross), Sophie Asquith (Rachel) and Chris Dignum (Kramer), life is a highway and I'm blessed to be riding it with you.

My siblings and their partners (Niki and Brian, Peter and Deb, Jamie and Catherine), my second set of siblings (Monique, Tassy, Bree, Abra and Torre) and all the De-White nieces and nephews (there's too many of you to name but you know who you are).

My second mother, Chris DeRoche, I'm not sure if you noticed but the climax of this book took place in your kitchen.

My parents, Ivan and Keera White, your pride and support fills me up (if anyone has seen a bearded man lurking in the book section of their local Kmart, pushing copies of *The Nowhere Child* onto unsuspecting customers, then you've seen my dad).

My dog, Issy, you continue to be my favourite person in the world. I don't know if I'll ever have any human children, but if I do, I doubt I'll love them as much as you. I'll pretend to, but we'll both know the truth.

Then there's Summer. Best of wives, best of women. Sum, I couldn't do any of this without you. You're my best friend, my first reader, and the love of my life. More importantly, you told me who the killer should be.